THE HEART OF HIM
By Iris Bolling

Siri Enterprises
Publishing Division
Richmond, Virginia

ISBN-13: 978-0-9801066-1-9
ISBN-10:   0-9801066-1-3

The Heart of Him
Copyright ©2008 by Iris Bolling

Cover and book design by: Judith R.E. Wansley

Edited by: Battinto Batts, Batts Communications

Published by:
Siri Enterprises
Richmond, Virginia 23222

The Heart Series
By Iris Bolling

Book One – Once You've Touched The Heart

Book Two – The Heart of Him

Book Three – Look Into My Heart

www.irisbolling.com
www.sirient.com

Acknowledgements

Thank you my heavenly father.

Raymond, Chris and Champaine, thank you for your love and support.

Judith Wansley, thank you for the ability to
"draw a little bit."

Linda Gordon and Kathy Six thank you for your time and knowledge.

Roz Terry, LaFonde Harris, and Gemma Mejias: the roots to my tree,
thanks for always answering the telephone.

Valarie Johnson and Tanya Thompson, thank you for keeping it real.

Battinto Batts and Wiley "Devin" Franklin, thank you for sharing your
knowledge.

To the beautiful people, Monica Jackson, Sakeitha Horton and Stephen
Howell: three very special people in my life. May God's blessings always
be with you.

To my mom, Evelyn Lucas, my sister Helen McCant and brother Albert
"Turkey" Doles, family is the strength that binds us forever and always.

To all of my readers, your wait is over. Thank you for your patience.
Enjoy book two of the Heart Series as the saga of JD and Tracy's journey
towards the White House continues. James and Ashley's story will make
you laugh, cry and say "oh my."

This book is dedicated to my son, Chris. Stay focused on your dream.

THE HEART OF HIM
Book Two

Blank

Prologue

Ocho Rios, Jamaica was a beautiful seventy-six degrees in February. Ashley Harrison stood on the balcony in a shirt that belonged to the man lying in the bedroom. Naked as a jaybird under his shirt she was wearing, a gentle breeze tickled the lower part of her back. She looked around appreciating her surroundings and smiled at the way her life had turned out.

During her senior year of high school, her father, a police officer, was shot and killed by a fourteen-year-old gang member. At the end of that year, she entered Harmon University, where she met her business partner, best friend, and now sister-in-law Tracy Washington-Harrison. That marked the beginning of the changes in her life.

Ashley smiled as she sat on the lounge chair, crossed her legs and held her head back to allow the cool breeze to swim over her face. Here she was, Ashley Renee Harrison, a partner in a multi-million dollar consulting firm, the sister to the candidate for Attorney General of the State of Virginia and the woman James Avery Brooks allowed into his very guarded life.

Ashley turned to look at James, who was still asleep on the bed and chuckled to herself. *The best thing to ever happen to her was snoring loudly from the inside of the room.* She made a mental note to call Tracy, thank her for the trip to sunny Jamaica and to tease her about the weather. In Virginia, which was home, it was snowing with no signs of it letting up according to the weather report. She smiled, while drinking a glass of champagne and thinking of her brother Jeffrey, who everyone called JD and her best friend Tracy who are now happily married.

For a moment, Ashley found herself wondering if she would have a fairytale wedding like theirs. The two were married on New Year's Eve in a wedding ceremony reminiscent of Princess Diana's. Two months later the event continues to be the topic of conversation for many. Ashley didn't need all of that, a simple ceremony with family and friends would suit her just fine.

Ashley stood and leaned against the balcony railing with her back to the beautiful landscape and pool that was below. She set her eyes on the muscular body of James Brooks and a frown appeared on her face as a thought manifested, *James never talked about his family.* His friends appeared to be those acquired through JD. At different events they attended, she met several business associates who all seemed very impressed, if not in awe of him, but never anyone introduced as a friend.

There were women who let her know instantly, usually in a "checking a sister out from head to toe" sort of way, that there was more than a business relationship between them and James. However, James' actions sent a clear message that he was no longer available to anyone but her.

Her eyes traveled up the long muscular leg that lay half covered by the sheet from the bed, over the hump that was his impressively firm behind, up to his strong back and wide shoulders that were exposed. She inhaled and smiled. Hmm," she sighed, for just the sight of him turned her on.

"Ashley?" James called out lifting his head from the pillow. She blinked. It was amazing that the sound of her name coming through his lips could make her moist in hidden areas. Each time he called her name with his rich deep baritone voice, it reminded her of a song coming from the smooth sound of a saxophone. It was his voice and that ever so manly smile that captured her heart the first time they met.

The day Ashley set eyes on James, the words her mother spoke to her as a little girl came to mind. Martha Harrison would say, "Never settle for someone that is less of a man than your father." Of course, at the time there was no man that could compare to her father, or so she thought. Then one day, while standing at the receptionist desk in a state office building, there he stood, smiling as their eyes met. She estimated him to be at least six four. Standing five feet, eight inches tall with three-inch heels, she had to look up at him. It was evident the brother had a well-built body, because he was certainly wearing that suit as if it was tailored made. Returning his smile, she wondered *how funny is this.* She wasn't supposed to be there. On the other hand, maybe, as fate would have it, it was exactly where she needed to be.

Tracy, her business partner, prepared a bid for their company, Next Level Consulting, to be considered for an organizational efficiency project. The deadline for the submission was five o'clock that evening. This was a State contract and Tracy wanted to make sure the proposal was in the proper hands. Instead of using a carrier, Ashley volunteered to deliver the proposal in person to the name listed on the advertisement. As she entered the building, she noticed a small group of people standing near the receptionist desk in the midst of a conversation. It was impossible not to notice the handsome brother that stood out from the rest. He looked up as she walked by, smiled and continued with his conversation. Unfortunately, she did not have time to get her "mack" on. Tracy had entrusted her to deliver the package that could kick the company to another level. She was not going to let her down. Ashley politely returned the smile and approached the receptionist. She explained she was there to submit a proposal to a Mr. James Brooks and asked if she could deliver it personally. The receptionist began to respond when the man Ashley noticed a moment before stepped over and introduced himself. "Hello, I'm James Brooks. How may I help you?" Ashley thought she was going to die the moment she heard his deep baritone voice. From that moment on she began imagining waking up every morning to him calling her name.

Ashley's lips formed into a small smile as she remembered agonizing over that man for weeks.

"Are you going to join me or just stand there watching?" James asked, interrupting the memories flowing through Ashley's mind. He sat up on the edge of the bed with the sheet still partially covering his body.

She stepped inside the room and slowly walked over to the bed into his outstretched arms. "I think I'll join you." She smiled as she knelt between his legs and kissed his chest. "I can't believe we have been inside this room for two days."

"Since this is our last day here," he kissed the side of her neck and said, "let's go for three."

She moaned as his kisses moved from her neck to the opening of his shirt, she was wearing. Instinctively she held her neck back to allow him access to the center of her throat. His kisses journeyed lower until he was able to capture her nipple between his lips. Ashley held his head to her breast, increasing the pleasure of his lips. He removed the sheet that covered his nakedness. Stretching out as he pulled her onto the bed her legs widened and she straddled his body. She looked downward then back up to his face smiling at the arousal she had ignited in him. "Well hello Mr. Brooks. Hmm---," she moaned as the tip of his desire slid easily into her moist fold.

Slowly she began to move, allowing her body to embrace him inside her, inch by inch, by inch. She eased down his shaft, loving the way he filled her. The two moved in a rhythmic pattern, slow and easy. Entering a place, which no other person could take either of them.

James lay back on the bed, carrying Ashley with him. Ashley slowly rose bracing herself with her hands against his chest. Sitting straight up, she moved her body in a slow circular motion, allowing him to hit that spot, signaling he was fully embedded within her. The tension began to rise as her nails dug into his chest. Her passion began soaring closer to the fire that he had quenched so many times before. Feeling his hands tightening around her waist verified, he was at the same point. Her movement began to intensify.

The feel of her thighs pulsating against his, and the essence of her surrounding him, so completely, was sending indescribable pleasure through his entire body. James refused to surrender to it. Like every other time, he wanted to savor each moment of every mind-blowing stroke. The reward for his patience was the expression on her face as she climbed closer to her release. Feeling the end coming near, he rose to a sitting position, to close the space between them. One hand held her hips merged with his, while the other moved up her back to her shoulders pulling their bodies together so close it was as if they were one.

Ashley's arms circled his neck holding on. Her head fell backwards as their bodies moved together traveling towards the destination of ecstasy. There it was! The explosion so deep it reached the core of him causing a chain reaction. He lifted her body up and thrust into her one last time. His lips went to the base of her throat as they simultaneously screamed out each other's name.

They sat there holding each other, his arms wrapped around her body and her legs wrapped around his waist, both drenched. Ashley placed her head on his shoulders and he held her protectively as perspiration from their bodies dripped down his chest and the juices from their mating flowed between their legs.

Minutes ticked away on the clock before either of them could safely speak. Once her mind cleared and her heart stopped racing, Ashley exhaled, "I think we better leave this room before one of us dies of exhaustion."

James caressed her back, kissed the top of her shoulders, and sighed, "If it's my time to go, this is exactly the way I would want my life to end." He smiled still nestled inside of her.

Ashley's hand absent-mindedly traced the muscles of his arms. "I love the feel of your hands on my body," she said almost in a whisper. "I love the feel of you inside of me. And I love you James Brooks." When James did not respond, her hand stopped tracing his arm. She raised her head from his shoulder, looking away from him, and began to stand. "I'll go take a shower now," she said, trying to hide the hurt by his lack of a response.

James held her in place with one hand. He placed a finger under her chin and turned her face to him. He looked into her eyes and she could see the love there. He leaned his forehead against hers and gently kissed her. "Ashley," he whispered as he closed his eyes.

She waited for the words, but they never came. She cupped his face in her hands and kissed his forehead. He wasn't ready, she inwardly accepted. One day he will say the words she longed for from him. "Would you like to join me?" she smiled.

"I'll be there in a minute," he replied. He watched as Ashley walked into the bathroom and closed the door. Stretching back on the bed he closed his eyes. The disappointed look in her eyes tugged at the heart of him. There was nothing he could do. He had to protect his heart. He survived the damage his ex-wife caused, and swore he would never allow another woman to have that much power over his heart again.

James stood, and walked over to the bathroom door. He slowly pushed it open and watched Ashley as she showered. Exhaling he acknowledged, he could not imagine a day of his life without her in it. She crept in unexpectedly with her zest for true love and happiness. Reflecting on the last year, he began to feel alive the moment he met her.

Standing in the lobby of the Department of Special Service, an agency he was commissioned by the Governor to lead, he overheard his name from a woman with gorgeous legs that seemed to go on forever. He stepped over to the receptionist's desk and introduced himself. The woman was young, attractive and feisty as hell. Not at all the type of woman for James' conservative taste, but certainly one that was hard not to notice. He accepted the proposal she offered and took it home with him that night to review.

The proposal for change was nothing short of ingenious, and captured his attention immediately. He pulled up the web site listed on the document and reviewed the bio of the two owners. The first thing he noticed was both women were very attractive and very young. Ashley was clearly the most noticeable and the oldest at twenty-five. The other, Tracy Washington, was twenty-four and was the founder of the company that was started during their junior year in college. He looked at the proposal on his desk, then back at the computer screen. He concluded someone else had to have prepared the proposal. It was too in-depth to have come from either of the two young women on the screen.

The next morning he asked his secretary to set up a meeting with the representative from Next Level Consulting. The only time he was free was after business hours; therefore a dinner meeting was set.

When Ashley strolled into the restaurant wearing a black cocktail dress that revealed a very trim, shapely body and those beautifully shaped long legs, James immediately regretted the dinner meeting. His mind wandered to her body, rather than the business at hand. Experience had taught James that physical attraction fades. It was more prudent to concentrate on the mind.

They discussed the proposal and details of the contract. During which time James discovered Ashley was not the mastermind that designed the proposal. The presentation was quite polished and professional. She was more than capable of handling herself in the professional world. However, she was very attractive and that was distracting to him. Ashley certainly stimulated his body, but he needed someone who could stimulate his mind as well. He mentally ordered his body to ignore the attraction.

James later realized Ashley was not going to be ignored. Repeatedly they found themselves present at public functions. At which times, she never had a problem expressing her interest in him. Soon she began inviting herself along to events they would both be attending. "We are both going to be there, so we might as well be there together," she would say. The professional relationship turned into a personal one before he realized it was happening. He began to enjoy the attention from her and found he missed it once it stopped.

There was a lot more to Ashley Harrison than just her apparent beauty. She was sassy as hell, and had no problem speaking her mind. At times, he never knew what might come out of her mouth. Surprisingly, he found that trait enticing. Then there was the way she had with people. She made them feel like they were somebody special to her all the time. She made him smile inside and out. He looked forward to the next day and definitely nights. She had a zest for life and family that had him longing for the family he exiled himself from years ago. That was credited to his ex-wife James unconsciously frowned.

"Are you going to stand there gawking or are you going to join me?" Ashley asked from the shower door. James smiled as he closed out the memories and joined her in the shower. He conceded, he cared deeply for her, but that was as far as he would let it go.

Chapter 1

The evening of their return from Jamaica, James went to his home and Ashley to hers. During the flight home, he noticed she was unusually quiet. She was pleasant and responsive when they talked, but seemed a little withdrawn.

James called her as soon as he arrived home, knowing Ashley needed reassurances from him from time to time. It was his doing. Before they became a couple, he expressed an interest in Tracy, causing Ashley to pull away for a short period. He did not want that to happen again. Relieved when she answered the telephone he smiled. "Did I mention how much I enjoyed our trip?" James asked.

"Yes you did, several times if I remember correctly." Ashley smiled, too, but did not expand. Her feelings were hurt when she declared her love for him and he did not return the sentiment, but that's for her to handle. She loved James and was not going to give up on him that easily. "Is this my thank you for the ten-day booty call?" she joked.

"You are not and never have been a booty call, Ashley." The tone of his voice took a dip and she knew he had become serious. "I can get sex from any woman. That's not what I ever wanted from you."

"Hold up. Back down a little," she said, feeling the tension building. "I was only joking with you. JD always made it a point to call his female companions after a night of fornication. I figured it was something all you guys did." She hesitated then asked testily, "What do you mean you don't want sex from me? I certainly want sex from you Mr. Brooks, and lot's of it."

James sobered. "I believe I can accommodate you on that," he smiled, then continued. "You were a little quiet on the flight home, something on your mind?"

"Yes, but it's for me to deal with, not you. Now get off my phone and let me unpack, call my mom, JD, Tracy, Cynthia..."

"Okay, okay, I got the message," he laughed. "I'll call you later."

"Bye," Ashley said, and hung up the telephone. She would get through to that man one day. She looked around the room and decided unpacking could wait. Picking up her car keys and cell phone, she called her mother who filled her in on the happenings with the family. Then, she called JD, who was in a meeting, as usual. She left a message with Mrs. Langston, his secretary, for him to return her call. Heading out the door to her car, she called Tracy. "I'm home," she said to Tracy.

"How was the trip?" Tracy beamed with an air of excitement and hope. "Did you two get married? Or at the very least, is a wedding being planned?"

"Don't make plans to buy a maid of honor dress, just yet," Ashley replied. "But we did have a great time. I'm on my way to your house. I'll tell you all about it when I get there. What are you cooking?"

"We are doing seafood tonight, shrimp scampi, broiled shrimp, crab cakes, baked potatoes, tossed salad and hush puppies."

"Who's cooking?"

"I am," Tracy proudly replied.

"Oh my God, Tracy hold on, I have an emergency!"

"What is it?" Tracy questioned with a concerned cry.

"I have to call Rosaline before you murder the shrimp, or those crab cakes," Ashley laughed.

"That's not funny. I thought something was seriously wrong with you. I don't know what you are laughing at. I can cook."

"Tracy, be for real. You can put a steak on the grill and bake potatoes in the microwave. Shrimp is out of your league and don't even think about touching those crab cakes!"

"Jeffrey is not complaining," Tracy laughed.

"That's because he loves you and can always go to Mommy's house to eat. Now get off the phone and let me call Cynthia and Rosaline, before you kill the shrimp."

By the time Ashley reached Tracy's house, she had spoken to Cynthia, Rosaline and JD. JD thanked her for intervening on dinner. He told her Tracy had been experimenting with different things in the kitchen. Some were not half-bad, but the last time she tried the seafood, things didn't sit well on his stomach or hers.

The four friends; Ashley, Tracy, Cynthia and Rosaline, sat in Tracy's kitchen and talked the same as they had in college. Ashley and Cynthia led the conversation, while Rosaline and Tracy chimed in when they could. It was funny how things stayed the same between the friends, although they had each grown in different ways.

Rosaline was always self-confident. She knew from day one what she wanted to do with her life. She loved cooking, but even more, she loved people enjoying her cooking. Her goal was to open a restaurant in several cities across the east coast. When she graduated from college, her parents sent her to the islands to study Caribbean cuisine. It did not surprise anyone when Rosaline came home married to one of the chefs from the islands. The two complimented each other with their personalities and cooking skills. Michael "Marco" Marable opened a restaurant and Rosaline started the catering business, TNT, with Cynthia.

Cynthia, easily the most beautiful of the friends, and the most outspoken, knew she wanted to get married to a man who could afford to give her the lifestyle she believed she deserved. On the outside, she seemed to be the most secure of the friends. Now her confidence was taking a dip with Tracy and Rosaline married, and Ashley on the verge. She wasn't so sure of the direction of her life. None of that affected her confidence. Cynthia had a way of making everything she touched beautiful. She could walk into a room and decorate it in her mind within a matter of minutes. Her attention to detail made her selection of items for a room stand out. Cynthia, unfortunately, always looked for love through a person's status or bank account, and not what was in their heart. That led her into a relationship with a married man. Slowly, the realization hit: She wanted what Rosaline, Tracy and Ashley had. She wanted someone to love only her.

Tracy, well she surprised everyone. The very shy, introverted young woman, with no real family, started her own business during college. With Ashley's help in public relations, Next Level was now one of the most sought after consulting firms on the East Coast. She fell in love with JD, when she was nineteen, and although he seemed unattainable, she never wavered. Now the two were happily married and JD was running for Virginia attorney general.

Ashley accepted everyone for who they were. She handled life the way she always thought her parents wanted her to. She went to college and majored in public relations, which was only natural, Ashley had a way with people. She could convince anyone to do just about anything, without trying. When her father was killed during her last year in high school, Ashley turned to her brother, JD to help her through the rough spots in her life. The two were always close, but their father's death brought them closer. JD became more than a brother--he was her confidant, her mentor and her friend. When Tracy became her roommate in college, Ashley thought she would be a good fit for JD. However, when the two finally got it together, Ashley found she had lost both of her best friends in one day. During the same time, she met James. The man had an immediate impact on her. He was a combination of her father and JD all wrapped up in one. The attraction was so strong it frightened her. At one time, she tried to pull away, but Tracy convinced her to open the line of communication with the very *Alpha male* and Ashley never looked back.

Within the hour, the four friends had filled Tracy's kitchen with a plethora of seafood delights, with Rosaline at the stove, Tracy and Ashley preparing side dishes and Cynthia sitting at the counter with a glass of wine. Ashley was glad to be with her girls. There was always drama in their lives that would take her mind off her issues. "Okay Cynthia, who is the target this week or is Gavin still, lurking around?" Ashley asked jokingly.

"Oh just put my business all in the street," Cynthia snidely replied.

Ashley looked around. "Somebody in here don't know you been sleeping with the Governor, wanna-be?"

Tracy raised her hand. "I didn't know she was sleeping with him."

"What the hell did you think they were doing Tracy?" Ashley laughed. "You saw them at the man's own engagement party, locking lips."

"Tracy is just saying they could have been playing tongue twister or something," Rosaline teasingly laughed.

Tracy put her hands on her hips. "Um, before you all get too carried away with your sarcasm, it would be wise to remember, you are in my house about to eat my food. I have no issue putting your asses out the door. Well, except you Rosaline, you have to finish cooking first." They all laughed.

"That's right girl, don't mess with the cook," Cynthia laughed.

"Alright whoreletta, what's the deal?" Ashley smiled at Cynthia.

"I had to let that go. After JD and Tracy's wedding it appeared Gavin and Carolyn were getting closer. So I'm on the prowl again."

"Oh hell. Sisters grab your man and hold on tight," Ashley laughed and the others joined in.

"You come after Marco and I will have to cut you, okay," Roz said, half joking.

"You come after Jeffrey and he will cut you," Tracy laughed.

"Okay, enough about me," Cynthia replied, not finding humor in either statement. "I want to know about Jamaica and James. Did you rock his world or what?" All the women stopped what they were doing and looked at Ashley.

"You know I don't kiss and tell," Ashley said faking shyness.

"Oh please. That's exactly why you called us all together." Cynthia smirked.

"Well," Ashley paused. "All I can say ladies, is when we got there it was only one island." Ashley stood and shook her head then ran her fingers through her hair. "I rocked that man's world so hard; I now believe there are two; the original and the one where the hotel is located. I felt the earth move," Ashley laughed and her friends joined in.

James was in his home office sorting through telephone messages. His attorney called, he closed on the purchase of the building James wanted and the renovations had begun to build JD Harrison's campaign headquarters on the first level. He indicated the keys would be sent by messenger. James looked around the office and noticed the mail neatly stacked on the table next to the door. There was a package at the bottom of the stack. He smiled thinking of his housekeeper Clair. With her around nothing was ever out of place. He knew just where to find the package. Continuing through his messages, he found one from Karen Holt. She was his right hand person at the Department of Special Services. When JD decided to run for state office, James resigned his position to manage the campaign. His full concentration needed to be on developing JD as a politician. In his mind, he was not only preparing JD for the attorney general position, but for the governor's position sometime in the future. Thinking Karen's message could wait, he sat it aside.

The next message was from Stanley Covington, head of the Democratic National Committee. Realizing JD would need to announce his candidacy soon, James immediately returned the call. "Stanley, this is James Brooks. How are you this evening?"

"James, thank you for returning my call. I wanted to confer with you to assure we are on one accord regarding Harrison's future. As we discussed, the attorney general spot is just a catalyst. We want him primed for the governor's seat in the next election. Your guidance is needed to steer him in that direction. As his campaign manager, he respects you. It is up to you to develop him for that position."

"Stanley, I know JD well enough to say he is not going to commit to anything at this time. He wants to succeed in this campaign before venturing or thinking about another. The best we can do this early in the game is to make sure there are no major mishaps and keep him close to Gavin. In addition, we need to make sure Gavin and Daniel have successful campaigns."

"I agree. The more JD learns from Gavin, the better prepared he will be to take over that office. Let's take this time, while JD is settling into his new role, to align him with some people we know he will need in his corner."

"Do you have any specifics in mind?

"As a matter of fact I do. I will be meeting with a few people of interest this week. I want people who will be committed to preparing JD and Tracy for the next level. Anyone I believe can advance that agenda, I will send to you for your approval. I want the best and brightest on this team."

"Let's make sure we keep the youthfulness on the team we put together. The biggest part of JD's charm is his energy level and the maturity he demonstrates with it."

"James, its imperative we keep him focused. The attorney general and governor's race is not the last stop for him. Keep that in mind."

"JD's political career has my full attention, Stanley. Let me know who you come up with for his team of advisors."

"Thank you, James. I appreciate your help with this."

"Anytime Stanley." James hung up the telephone and sat back in his chair. This was his first time committing fully to politics. It took meeting JD to get him into the political arena. That was something his father always wanted for him. Of course, he thought James would be the one running for president some day. James smiled, picked up the telephone and dialed. "Hey Pop, how's it going?" He spoke when his father's voice answered.

"Your mother is driving me crazy. I have to find something for her to concentrate on. You think you could get someone pregnant and give her another grandchild or something?"

James laughed robustly. "I would like to accommodate you there Pop, but um, no."

It was good to hear his son laugh. He noticed the last few times they spoke James tended to laugh quite often. With all that happened with the family Avery Brooks was glad to hear the sound easily escaping from his son. "Alright, I'll just have to get Nick to do it. What do you need son, it's not Sunday?" he asked.

"Pop, I want to tell you about a decision I made and then I need your guidance on it."

"I think you call for guidance before making the decision. But then, you always had your own way of thinking."

"I believe I got that independence from you," James replied. He continued, "Pop, I resigned my position with the state. I've decided to become the campaign manager for JD Harrison. He's a young district attorney here in Richmond who's running for attorney general."

Thrilled with the idea of James entering into the political world Avery eagerly responded. "I know who he is. I've followed his career for a while now. He has a very promising future ahead of him. It was my understanding he had no interest in politics."

"Well, he has decided to try his hand at it and I will be steering his career. That's where I need you." James sat forward and spoke sincerely to his father. "This is not an ordinary man, Pop. He's young, with the maturity and sense of responsibility of a man twice his age. He has the charisma to pull in everyone who is in his presence, man, woman or child. He is intelligent, articulate and has a heart that truly belongs to the people. Then there's a touch of arrogance that makes him believe he can accomplish anything and everything he sets out to do. He has no inhibitions."

"What about his background son? Before you put your all into a man, you have to know his background and the stock he comes from."

"I had a background check done on him and I did one on his wife. There are issues with the wife, but nothing that cannot be handled early on. Pop, have your people run a check on him. I'm sure you will come to the same conclusion. For the next twelve years, I'm committing myself to his success."

"Son, it sounds like you are developing a presidential candidate rather than an attorney general."

"I am Pop, and Stanley Covington is in agreement with me."

"Alright son, I'll look into him for you. In the meantime, why don't you invite him and his wife up for dinner? That will give your mother something to do. You know, she loves social events for the high and mighty." Avery heard the enthusiasm drop from James voice. He still wasn't ready to come back into the full fold of the family.

"I don't know about that just yet, Pop. Let's see what happens."

"Alright son, whenever you are ready." Avery smiled inwardly, at least he did not say no.

After talking to his father, James thought about going home again. It would be good to see Nicky and Nicole. He had only spoken to his brother and sister over the last five years by telephone. The twins were ten years younger than him, putting them at Ashley's age. He could see all three of them getting along just fine.

James stood at the window of his office looking over the grounds of the home he built. At five acres and forty-two hundred square feet, it was a small replica of his childhood home. He loved and missed his parents' home. However, the rift between him and his older brother, Vernon, was not a simple one to repair. James put his hands into his pockets and smiled. A year ago, he would have said it was beyond repair. What made him think it was repairable now? The telephone rang. He glanced at the Caller ID and answered it. "Hello." He smiled recognizing the number.

"After ten nights of having your hard body next to mine, I couldn't sleep holding a soft pillow. I know it's late, but would you mind opening your door for me?"

James smiled, "I never locked it." He heard the door open and Ashley walk in. He looked up as she entered the office and closed her cell phone.

"Is Clair here?" she asked standing in the doorway.

"No, she'll be in tomorrow."

"Good," Ashley exclaimed. She untied the belt to her coat and allowed it to drop to the floor. She walked towards James with nothing on but a very sheer black lace teddy with a matching thong and a pair of three-inch stilettos.

As he stood, James could not take his eyes off the dream that was walking towards him. Nor could he ignore the bulge growing against his zipper. "You are going to catch pneumonia walking around like that." He joked sounding calmer than he felt.

"Then I suggest you find a way to warm me up real quick," Ashley replied as she rounded the end of the desk. James reached out and eagerly pulled her into his arms. His lips tasted her earlobe, sampled her neck and then devoured her lips. Their tongues entwined with each other sending delicious surges through their bodies. He leaned forward, easing her on top of his desk. She kicked off her heels and wrapped her legs around his waist.

James ended the kiss. His smoldering brown eyes looked into hers. The woman never ceased to amaze him. With her, he could face anything. He used his thumb to move her hair from her face and asked, "How would you like to meet my family?"

The question surprised James more than it did Ashley and it shocked the hell out of her. He never discussed his family. She started to ask why, but at the moment did not really care. "Are they here?"

James saw the different emotions going through Ashley's mind and knew the moment she went into the protection mode of devilishness. Her nervous moods usually led to very satisfying events for James. "No" he replied enjoying the feel of her soft body.

Ashley smiled and rubbed her foot against the bulge in his pants. "I would love to meet your family, but right now my cookies are wet. Your family is going to have to wait." She replied as she brought her other foot around his waist to join in the arousal of him.

James pulled his silk T-shirt over his head, removed her thong and dropped the sexy material to the floor. Massaging the inside of her thighs, he lowered his head to feast on what he referred to as his "sugar cookies." He placed a feather kiss there, then stood to unbuckled his pants. He dropped them to the floor, placed her legs over his shoulder and leaned over her. "I'll take those wet cookies now," he smiled, as he thrust into her.

The next morning, James noticed the papers to the building he purchased were laying on the desk in the very spot he and Ashley made love the night before. The memory and her scent still lingered in his mind. He picked up the mortgage papers, smiled and promptly named the building, *The Ashley*.

After speaking with James, Stanley Covington met with David Holt, a young advisor who did the preliminary work on Gavin Roberts' campaign for governor. He discussed the possibility of David working on Harrison's team as a political advisor. David was an impressive young man and politically savvy. Since Gavin's campaign was on solid ground, Stanley decided to pull David in as a part of JD's team. He was young, energetic and intelligent. Just the type of person to fit right in with what James wanted. Stanley advised David of the change, pending approval from the Harrison camp. When Stanley asked if there was any reason he would not be able to serve on the team, David indicated there was none, knowing full well that James Brooks wouldn't let him within ten feet of JD's campaign or Ashley.

David was thrilled with the chance of working on JD's campaign for two reasons: One it would be a professional coup d'état to work on the campaign of the man some considered the front-runner to becoming the first African-American president. Second, the most interesting prospect for David was being near Ashley regularly. He made a few mistakes when they were together in college. But with time, he was certain he would win her heart back, if he could get James Brooks out of the way.

After his meeting with Stanley Covington, David was excited with the news. He went to the hospital to visit his wife, Karen, James's protégée from the Department of Special Services. According to police accounts, an unknown assailant attacked Karen in their home. At least that was the story the police got.

Before going into her room, David stopped by the florist to pick up roses for her. He walked into the room anxious to give her the good news. "Hello sweetheart. These are for you." He handed the flowers to Karen and kissed her. When he brought his hands up to caress her cheeks she jumped. He ignored the movement and rubbed the spot where the bruise was on her face, "I hope that did not hurt."

Karen's heart began to settle down when she realized he was in a good mood. "Thank you," she replied meekly.

"They are no comparison to your beauty, by any means." David smiled as he looked lovingly into her eyes. "Honey I met with Stanley Covington today," he said excitedly as he pulled the chair up and sat closer to her bed. "He asked me to be a personal advisor to JD Harrison for this campaign; the next campaign and possibly," he paused. "Are you ready for this honey, for the presidential race twelve years from now." He sat back in his seat and chuckled. "After the attorney general's race this year, they want Harrison to run for the governor's office in four years and then for the White House after that term. You do realize what that means? They recognize my talent. They know I'm the man who can get the job done. I'm the one who can get Harrison on the road to the White House. It's about time they recognized. I will be working for the next twelve years non-stop. Isn't that wonderful honey?"

Karen sat there and listened to David ramble on. Did he forget he tried to rape JD Harrison's sister, Ashley, in college? Had he forgotten JD Harrison's wife, Tracy, can't stand the sight of him? Had he forgotten James Brooks, her ex-boss and JD Harrison's campaign manager hates him? She wondered what world David was living in. But, Karen knew bringing those things up would set his temper off. Therefore, she decided to sit there, smile and be happy in the moment.

"Now, I realize I will need your help with James Brooks. I need you to convince him to allow me to be a part of this team. Do you think you could help me with him honey?"

Karen did not know if she could convince James to let David be a dogcatcher in JD Harrison's camp, much less an advisor. James was a fair man, but not even a saint could ignore or forget the things David had attempted with Ashley. Karen may not have believed the rumors when they were in college, but now, she wasn't so sure. Even if the events with Ashley were not true, it was difficult to keep the abuse from James.

There were many days she had to miss work due to bruises left on her by David. James was a very perceptive man. She never told him what was taking place in her home, but he knew.

Seeing the excitement in David's eyes filled her with a little hope. Maybe this is the break he needs, she thought.

Political jobs come and go with the candidate. Something stable might keep him calm, which in turn, might keep his hands off her. That thought made her want to try. "David you know I would do anything for you. But, James is going to be a hard sell, especially after this. You know he suspected you were hitting me before."

"Honey," David shook his head, "you know I didn't mean to hurt you. I love you, Karen. I was frustrated and upset about the job, you know that. But, honey, with this job it will be a permanent gig. Karen, you have to help me. I promise, baby, I will never, never raise my hand to you again." He kissed her, "please sweetheart, help me with this."

Karen smiled and thought, *maybe he means it this time; the job seems to be important to him.* "Okay honey, I will do all I can to help you."

"Here sweetheart, call James over here now. Let's start working on this tonight," he said, handing the telephone to Karen.

"Honey, why don't you let me speak to him alone first? I will set up a meeting for just the two of you so you can sell yourself to him. You are so good at that."

David frowned for a moment. "Why do you need to meet with him alone?"

Karen saw the look in his eyes and withdrew a little. Then she quickly explained, "Well... I...I want to set the stage for you. Let him know it's coming from me, not you. I don't want him to think you asked me to talk to him."

It took a moment before his frown dissolve, then a moment later he agreed. "Okay. I could work with that," he smiled. "Sweetheart this could be a whole new start for us," David beamed. "If this goes well, we can start working on having a family. Would you like that?" David asked as he hugged Karen.

"Yes, David, that would be wonderful."

Karen waited until David left before calling James. When she reached him, he was at campaign headquarters and was surprised to know she was in the hospital. She advised him she would be released the next day and asked him to come by the hospital to see her.

James was her mentor and always proved to be a brilliant and caring administrator. Karen knew he suspected things in her home life were not quite right, but he never interfered or questioned her and she appreciated that. Now David was asking her to cross the professional line and ask James for a personal favor. David had no idea what type of man James Brooks was, but Karen did. If she crossed this line he would begin to ask questions and would not take just any response.

When James arrived at the hospital, the first thing he did was look around for David. He had a low level of tolerance for the man. He was certain David was the reason Karen was there. As much as it disgusted him, it was not his place to interfere in her marriage. When it was apparent he wasn't around, James went into the room. One look at Karen made him wonder if she was ready to admit her husband was abusive. "Hello Karen. How are you?" James asked, taking her hand and kissing her on the bruised cheek.

"I'm doing better," Karen replied. "Thank you for coming," she smiled as she sat up.

"Well, I would have come sooner had I known. Would you like to tell me what happened?" James asked as he took a seat. He hoped her response would be an honest one.

"Someone attacked me in my home a few days ago." She replied looking away.

He looked at Karen, *so much for hope*, he thought. He leaned forward. "What is it going to take for you to realize your life is not as it should be?" She started to say something but he stopped her with a wave of his hand. "Karen, you don't have to tell me what happened, but you should tell the police."

"They were called this time. My neighbor noticed the back door was opened and came in looking for me." Tears began to fall as she continued. "I honestly don't know what would have happened if she hadn't come by."

James saw the despair in her eyes. "Did you tell the police what actually happened?"

Karen hung her head, "No," she said sadly. "I can't do that to David." She wiped a tear from her face. "James, sometimes I can be very irritating. I don't mean too, but it happens. I think the fact that I'm successful in my career and his success comes and goes with each campaign, puts him on edge sometimes. He doesn't handle defeat very well; he never did."

"That's no reason for him to hit you, Karen. It may be the excuse you want to put on it."

"I have to put that excuse on it because the alternative is not acceptable to me."

"What alternative?" James hunched his shoulders

Karen smiled. "The alternative would be David doesn't love me. And I'm sorry I can't accept that." He started to speak but she continued. "James, David is the only man I have ever loved. I was seventeen when I met him. I am twenty-nine years old. David is all I have known for my adult life. I love him. I understand him and his needs," she exhaled. "Besides, husbands and wives fight. Don't you and Ashley fight?"

"Yes, Ashley and I fight, but I don't hit, Karen. Men don't hit!" He stopped when he noticed the despair in her eyes. "Karen," he sighed. "I understand your position, but there is a life out there without violence, especially from the person who is supposed to love and protect you."

"I know there is James and I want that life. But I want it with David. That's why I called you here tonight. You can help me get that life with him."

James frowned, "The only way I know to help you with that is to kill David and resurrect him. I don't think that is happening anymore."

Karen snickered. "No, I don't think so either."

James was glad to see she could still smile with all that happened. "So how can I help you?"

She exhaled. "You have it within your power to give David the success he so desperately desires. I know what I am about to ask of you will put you in a difficult position with Ashley. But before you answer please look at the total picture. What I'm asking you to do will possibly save my life and my marriage."

James sat up curiously. "What are you asking me to do Karen?"

"Give David a chance to work on Harrison's campaign." Before James could reject, Karen continued with her selling points for David. "You know he is an excellent political advisor, he's brilliant in that area. JD could benefit from his experience."

James had a stunned look on his face and as hard as he tried, he could not keep the angry tone from his voice. "Have you lost your mind? Do you know that's a mine field you are asking me to step into?"

"James I know what position it puts you in with Ashley---"

"Hell, Ashley isn't the one I'm concerned with," James said as he stood. "Do you know what JD will do if he found out about David and Ashley?" James paused. "Do you?" He shook his head, "I don't think you do." He paced the floor. "Let's say the story never gets to JD. How do you propose I convince Tracy to have David working with her? She will be a major part of this campaign." Then his voice began to rise, "and since you mentioned it. How in the hell do I explain any of this to Ashley? Have you thought about that? Do you realize I love that woman? How will she feel if all of a sudden she has to endure being around David if I do this for you?"

"James," Karen interjected desperate to get him to see things her way, "you could tell Ashley and Tracy, the assignment came from the DNC, which would be the truth."

James stopped pacing. "What are you talking about?"

"Stanley Covington asked David to begin working as Harrison's political advisor effective immediately and throughout not only this campaign, but the one for governor also. James, this could give me the chance I need to get my life together, hopefully, to a point where I can at least confront David about counseling. With his life in turmoil, he would never go. If he is doing well, he would not do anything to jeopardize the job. I can at least begin putting my well being first. James," she shook her head in despair, "this may be the chance I need. I honestly did not think I was going to survive this one. Please, just tell me you will at least meet with him before you completely close the door."

James shook his head. "Karen, you are asking a lot. I don't like David. I don't like anything about him. It would be difficult for me to look past what he did to Ashley or what he continues to do to you."

"James if you can't do this because I asked, do it because he is the best and the brightest at what he does. Do it because he can be a vital part of the campaign. Just take a meeting with him before you make your decision. Please!" she begged.

James shook his head. "I have to think about this Karen. I can't promise you anything."

"That's all I ask James. Just, just think about it."

"All right Karen. I'll think about it." He kissed her cheek and said good night.

James was grateful for his attached garage. It was lightly snowing again and he silently wished he was back in Jamaica. He was late getting home and Ashley was not going to be in a good mood, but neither was he. However, he conceded this bad moment was strictly on him. He had called her earlier in the day and asked her to meet him at his house that evening. Most of his day was spent inspecting the new office space for the campaign headquarters, before he went to see Karen. Her request kept his mind reeling and he never called Ashley to let her know he would be late.

Ashley was sitting at the kitchen table in one of his dress shirts eating a cup of pudding when he entered. She looked up as he came in but did not say anything. James placed his briefcase on the island and walked over to her. He took the spoon of pudding she was about to put into her mouth and put it in his. "Hello," he said

"Hello," Ashley replied taking her spoon back from him.

James sat in the chair next to her, "I'm sorry. I got caught up on something with Karen and was not able to leave."

Ashley continued to eat her pudding. "There's this invention called a telephone. It was invented by a black man, you know. They give Bell the credit for it but I know better."

"Yes, I know about that communication device well," he smiled. "But I was not in a position to make a call until I was already late."

James could see the anger in her eyes. She was not one to hide her feelings about anything. As he looked at her, he realized what he said to Karen. He told her he loved this woman, and he does. Last week in Jamaica, love was a distant thought to him. Sitting in his kitchen looking at Ashley with chocolate pudding on her lips and a shirt that barely covered her thighs; it was foremost in his mind.

James smiled and pulled the chair she was sitting in closer to him. He placed her legs across his and ran his hands under the tail of the shirt, up her thighs. Please forgive me for not calling." James said as he ran the tip of his tongue over the corner of her lips.

"No." Ashley replied curtly with his mouth a breath away from hers.

He pulled her completely into his lap and then kissed the front of her throat. "Pleaseeeeee?" He asked again.

She put her arms around his neck. "Are you begging?" Ashley teased.

"With my tail wagging," he replied as he smiled into her eyes.

"You beg so well." She smiled then kissed him.

"Hmm, you taste like chocolate pudding," he moaned.

"Wait until you taste the rest of me."

"Really," James said in a low growling voice as he kissed the spot between her breasts.

"James," Ashley laid her head on his shoulders and smiled, "Why were you with Karen?"

He sat up as his mind went back to his conversation with Karen. "Ash, can I ask you a question?"

The tone of James voice changed and he did not answer the question. She looked at him, "You can ask, it doesn't mean I will answer."

Smiling for a moment he looked directly into her eyes and asked, "When you went out with David Holt, did he ever hit you?" Ashley tried to push away from him but he held her still. "You know I'm not going to let you go until I'm ready."

"Why are you asking me about David?"

"I need to know, did he?"

"Sometimes," Ashley replied turning her head as if she was ashamed.

James held in his anger at her admission, he did not want her to stop telling him things, "Did you ever tell JD?"

"No."

James exhaled as he rubbed her back. "You did not tell JD about the attempted rape or the fact that Holt hit you. Why not?"

Ashley was still looking away as she shrugged her shoulders. "I was young, I don't know."

James turned her face back towards him with his finger. "Why didn't you tell someone; anyone?"

"It's not something to be proud of, you know."

James lovingly smiled at her. "You know I would never touch you in that way, right?"

Ashley frowned but then changed her expression. "Well, at the moment you are not touching me in anyway. Do you think you could do something about that?" She asked while kissing his neck and adjusting her position on his lap.

The thought of David putting his hands on Ashley angered James. As he looked at her, he knew if David came anywhere near her, he would kill him. He cleared his mind and concentrated on the woman in his arms. "Hmm, I may be able to do a little something," he said as he captured her lips with his in an attempt to kiss away the pain David inflicted.

Chapter 2

Tracy's deepest wish was to stay under the comforter in her husband's arms and sleep for the next few hours, but it was not to be. The churning taking place in her stomach indicated she'd better move. She gently moved the covers back and slid out of bed. The chill in the air hit her immediately. *Thank goodness some things never changed,* Tracy thought as she picked up Jeffrey's top to his pajamas off the floor and put it on her naked body.

As she reached the bathroom, she pulled a washcloth off the shelf and ran cold water onto it. She felt as if she was breaking into a sweat. Tracy placed the cold cloth on her face then around her neck. The cloth felt so nice and had a soothing effect for a minute. Unfortunately, that was all it lasted, a minute. She ran over to the commode, pulled the

seat cover up and began to deposit her entire dinner from
the night before. The action left her a little weak, so she sat
on the floor next to the sink and wiped her face with the
washcloth. After a moment things seemed to calm down with
her stomach so she attempted to get up off the floor. The
movement sent her stomach in motion again and she found
herself hugging the commode again. "Okay, it can't be
anything else in there," Tracy said aloud. She needed to
rinse her mouth out, so she tried to get up a third time and
her stomach was not cooperating, again. This time Tracy just
sat there with her head on the commode. "The hell with it,"
she reached up, flushed the commode, pulled the seat cover
down and placed her head on it. While dozing back to
sleep, she made a mental note not to eat seafood before
going to bed.

JD stretched and reached out for Tracy, but she wasn't
there. He looked at the clock, it wasn't quite six. The alarm
had not gone off. He got out of bed, put on the bottom to
his pajamas and preceded to her office to put her back in
bed. When he stepped into the hallway, there was no light
on in the office. He wondered for a moment where could
she be. Standing in the hallway he listened for anything that
would give him a clue as to what direction he should
venture; there was no sound. Stepping back into the
bedroom, he looked around. The bathroom door was
closed and a shimmer of light was coming from below. He
smiled, walked over to the door and slowly opened it. The
vision made him smile and frown at the same time. Tracy
was sitting on the floor with her head on top of the toilet,
sound asleep.

"Trace," he called out as he bent down beside her. "Did
you fall asleep cleaning the toilet?" he laughed.

Tracy moved her head a little as she tried to wake up,
"No," she said.

He tried to pick her up off the floor, but she cried out,
"No, just let me sit here and die."

JD laughed, "I don't think I will." He proceeded to pick her up. The motion started her stomach action again. She pulled the seat cover up and emptied the remaining contents of her stomach inside. JD frowned as he ran water over another washcloth, held her hair back and wiped her face. "Babe, how long have you been in here like this?" He asked while handing her a cup of water. "Rinse and spit out," he said and she obeyed.

"I don't know, a while."

"Do you want to try to get up now?" He asked after a few minutes of wiping her forehead.

"No, I'll just stay here."

"Babe you can't stay here forever.

"Yes, I really can."

JD stood, "I'll be right back." He left the room. When he returned to the bedroom with a cup of hot tea, Tracy was back in bed, under the covers sound asleep. He stood there in the middle of the floor for a moment wondering if he just dreamt all that happened this morning. Sitting the tea on the nightstand he looked down at her. It was as if he was seeing her for the first time. She was simply beautiful. The alarm sounded and he quickly reached over to cut it off. He bent over to kiss her cheek. JD did not know how long she had been in the bathroom sick, so he let her sleep.

Tracy woke up to the sound of the telephone ringing. She looked at the clock; it was after eight a.m. She was late. She jumped up and got into the shower. Normally, she and JD would have breakfast together before leaving for the office. She wondered why he did not wake her before he left. She dressed quickly and went downstairs. JD was sitting at the kitchen table drinking a cup of coffee. He looked up as she walked into the room. "Good morning, are you feeling better?" he asked

"Yes, you're still here. Why did you let me over sleep?" Tracy smiled as she kissed him and began to walk away. He grabbed her hand and pulled her down into his lap. What was supposed to be a good morning peck turned into a long tongue twister of a kiss.

As the kiss ended Tracy looked into JD's dark brown eyes and smiled. "Good morning to you Mr. Harrison."

He smiled. "Do you want some eggs?"

Tracy stood up. "No," she frowned. "I'll just have some toast."

"Ashley called. She was wondering why you were not in the office. I told her you weren't feeling well and would be late."

"Hmm, thank you for that." She said as she pulled the toast from the toaster. "I must have eaten something bad last night."

"You look better now." JD finished his coffee, "Well, babe, I have to go. I told Mrs. Langston I would be in around nine. But I didn't want to leave until I was sure you were okay."

"That's sweet, thank you, but I'm fine"

"That you are." He pulled her to him and kissed her good bye.

Ashley was sitting in her office when Tracy arrived, which was unusual in itself. Everyone in the office knew Tracy was an early bird and Ashley was the one to rarely make it to work before noon. Walking directly to her office Tracy closed the door behind her. Ashley waited a moment, thinking she was taking off her coat and would come in to say hello.

Ten minutes passed, no Tracy. Ashley decided to go into her office. She knocked on the door before she entered. "Tracy, you in here?" She called out as she entered the room. Tracy was not at her desk. Looking around the office she noticed the bathroom door was slightly opened. "Tracy?" she called out again.

"Yes." Tracy replied, not able to get up.

Ashley walked over to the bathroom that was between the two offices. Tracy was sitting on the floor near the commode empting the little contents from the morning out of her stomach.

"Tracy, what's going on? Are you okay?" Ashley asked as she ran into the bathroom.

"Yeah, I'm wonderful. Don't I look wonderful?" She asked laughing at herself.

"You look like crap if you want me to be honest. My question is why?"

"Thank you so much Ash. You always have a way of making me feel better." Tracy smiled sarcastically.

Ashley handed her a cup of water and Tracy rinsed her mouth. "Well, anything I can do to help the cause along." Ashley smiled. She then looked at her friend and became concerned, "How long have you been sick?"

"A few days." Tracy replied right before she stuck her head back over the commode again and threw up.

"I'm calling momma," Ashley said with a little panic in her tone. She picked up the telephone and dialed a number. She explained to her mom what was happening. She wrote down her mom's instructions. "I'll be right back." Ashley said, and then left the office.

When Ashley returned she had a six-pack of ginger ale, saltine crackers and several pregnancy tests. Tracy looked at her as if she had lost her mind. "Don't look at me like that, it is conceivable." Ashley handed a test to Tracy. "Do you want me to read the instructions?"

"No, I think I can read." Tracy replied as she took the test from Ashley.

Tracy went into the bathroom to take the test. She came out and sat on the sofa next to her friend. Ashley handed her a can of ginger ale and opened a pack of crackers. Tracy drank some ale and bit into a cracker. Ashley bit into a cracker with her as the two sat there together waiting. Tracy continued to drink the ginger ale. Ashley started laughing. Tracy began laughing too. "How long do we have to wait?" Ashley asked.

"It was done five minutes ago," Tracy replied.

"Are you going to check it?" Ashley asked.

"No," She turned to Ashley, "You going to check it?"

Ashley stood up, "Okay, chicken."

Tracy sat still and waited with her heart pounding until Ashley reappeared. Standing in the doorway with the plastic tube in her hand she asked, "Well, what do you think; a boy or girl?"

Tracy stared at her, slowly smiled, and then frowned, "Let's do it again."

Ashley knew her friend just that well. When they were in college, Tracy was the one who was never satisfied with the first results. She always wanted to redo things just to make sure it was accurate, hence the Magna Cum Laude ranking. Ashley went over to the bag and pulled out another test. Tracy took the test and sat back on the sofa with Ashley. They ate crackers together, each into their own thoughts until the second test was complete. Same routine, Ashley went into the bathroom and checked the results. She leaned against the door jam. "I'm sure JD would prefer a boy. You know how men are about preserving the family name."

When the third test was complete Ashley stated, "It doesn't matter how many times you take the damned test. It's going to say the same thing: she picked up the first test and looked at it—"pregnant." Then she picked up the second—"pregnant." Then she picked up the last test— "pregnant." She blew out air. "Okay now. Will you give your baby the same initials as daddy and JD? You know you could mix the two; Jeffrey David or James Daniel. Well, maybe not. I think I may want to use the name James. Then again, I really couldn't since James already has a son name James Jr."

Tracy smiled, not listening to Ashley ramble on, "We are going to have a baby," she sighed breathlessly and stood.

Ashley began nodding her head and walked over to Tracy. She hugged her and said, "I'm going to be an aunt." They both hugged as tears of joy sprung to their eyes.

"I have to tell Jeffrey," Tracy pulled away. "I have to tell him," she said with enthusiasm.

"He is going to be so excited. GOD, I am not going to be able to live with him for the next nine months. Call him," Ashley suggested.

"No, I have to go see him. I need to see his face when I tell him. Oh GOD, Oh GOD, Oh GOD," Tracy laughed.

Ashley hugged her and they both started laughing. "Okay, go, go. Call me as soon as you tell him." Ashley smiled as Tracy left the office. She was so excited about the baby she ran into her office to call James. She wanted to share the news with him. But before she could tell him about the baby, James began answering her question from the night before concerning Karen Holt and his visit with her. He mentioned she was in the hospital and told her what he suspected happened, but he did not tell her the reason Karen called him to the hospital. Ashley listened as he expressed his outrage to David's actions and Karen's lack of action. That explained why he was late getting home the night before. But Ashley wondered why Karen would call James. Why not call a family member or a friend? She dismissed the question in her mind and continued to listen.

On Friday nights, the group of friends would meet at JD and Tracy's house to enjoy each other's company. The men, with the exception of James all grew up together and were more like brothers than friends. Their professional relationship was an extension of their friendship. James was accepted into the fold with no questions asked and became one of the brothers.

Before JD and Tracy were married, the men, JD, Calvin, JD's best friend who also worked at the DA's office, Brian, another childhood friend who was a FBI agent and James would all meet at Maxi's, a local jazz club for drinks after work. However, once JD met Tracy, the men migrated to where JD was, which was wherever Tracy was.

The women, Tracy, Ashley, Cynthia and Rosaline, who always found time for each other at least once a week, would hang out in the sunroom, while the guys, were at the kitchen table playing bid whisk.

The rivalry between JD and Calvin versus James and Brian became more competitive each week. It was not just a game with them it was a meeting of the minds, you might say. Once James and Brian adjusted to each other as partners, the victories were not as easy for JD and Calvin. Now, there was a balance around the table and from Friday to Friday the winners would change. The group used to include Tracy and Ashley, but to make the game fair, Tracy was banned from the table. Whoever partnered with her, usually won because of her gift with numbers. Before the group of friends realized what was happening JD and Tracy would never leave the table; losers rotate. Once they figured out Tracy's skill, she was put out of the game completely. But for tonight, the game was an even match.

JD sat at the head of the table. To his right was Brian, James to his left and Calvin across the table from him. Brian was about to make his books for this hand and was talking boastfully. To be honest, all the men were bantering with the exception of JD. He just sat there as if he was in another world with this real satisfied grin on his face. Every now and then he would look over at Tracy and smirk. She would return the look with a smile as if they were sharing a secret.

"Come to daddy!" Brian yelled as he pulled in the last book for that hand.

"I believe that puts us on a dead heat. You need five books to win, we need four," James laughed as he turned to JD.

"Put us down for seven, before you deal the cards," Calvin ordered. James looked at JD.

"Put it down. Somebody's getting up on this hand," he laughed and looked at Calvin. "You better play man."

James handed the cards to Brian. "Your deal; give them nothing, man, nothing!"

Tracy watched as Jeffrey collected his cards. She could tell he was more than comfortable with what was coming his way. He looked up at her, but never changed his facial expression. They held each other's glance; a lot was spoken between them. So much, that Tracy wanted to be close to Jeffrey at that moment. She sat there debating what to do. She chewed on her bottom lip and thought, *hell, that's my husband and this is my house, I can kiss my husband anytime I want.*

JD read her mind before she put her foot on the floor. He slid his chair back and folded the cards in his hand. Tracy stood, walked over to the table, put her leg across his lap to straddle him, placed her arms around his neck and proceeded to kiss her husband, thoroughly. JD put his arms around her body and ran his hands up her blouse, pulled her so close it seemed they had become one in front of their friend's eyes.

The guys sat back and watched as Brian pulled a note pad from his jacket and began to take notes. James shook his head, smiled, then looked at Ashley. The display of emotion between JD and Tracy was something the friends had become accustomed to. It actually was rewarding to see, with all the two had gone through to be together.

The kiss became more intense. JD stood and laid Tracy on the table where the game was taking place. She wrapped her legs around his waist as he stood, carried her back into the sunroom, sat her back into her seat and then ended the kiss. "Thank you," he whispered in her ear. He went back to the table and took his seat "You ready?" he asked the men.

"Wait a minute." Brian said as he continued to write in his note pad. "Right hand behind head—left hand around waist. He put a period behind his sentence then looked up, "Okay I got it, let's play." Calvin and James laughed as Brian smiled, "Man ain't no shame in my game. I have to take notes on this love thing."

JD winked at Tracy, "Don't worry about it, man, you'll know what to do when the time comes. But for right now," he spread his cards on the table, "read them and weep my people; read them and weep. I believe that's called a B-town boys; Boston."

Calvin gave JD a high five over the table. "Now, that's what I'm talking about," he laughed.

"I'll be damned," Brian, yelled as he slammed the cards on the table. "She must have changed the cards or something when she came over here."

"Oh man, just accept it, love conquers all; even in cards," James laughed.

"You keep doing that you going to get pregnant before you want to," Cynthia said with a snort.

JD smiled and Tracy began to giggle, "Too late to tell us now."

Everyone stopped except for Ashley and Calvin, "You're pregnant?" Cynthia screamed.

"Very much so," Tracy beamed. The women screamed and began hugging her.

"Man, get out." Brian said as he hit JD in the chest, "You're keeping secrets," he smiled.

"No, we just found out," JD boasted

James shook JD's hand. "This campaign is getting better every day," he hugged Tracy, "Congratulations little momma."

"I'm the godfather." Calvin bragged knowing it would tick Brian off.

"Man, what's up with that?" Brian said to JD. "I was polite when you made him your best man, but now he's the godfather too. I'm beginning to get offended."

"Believe me, we are going to have others, you will be a godfather several times over." JD said consoling Brian. Calvin sat there grinning like a Cheshire cat.

"Oh come on Brian." James said as he put his arm over his shoulder. "You can be the godfather to Ashley's and my first child. Come take a walk with me I need to talk to you anyway." Ashley looked up shocked at the statement James made. She looked at Tracy who was laughing at the expression on her face.

The evening continued with the friends celebrating the news as James took the opportunity to speak with Brian alone. He was the only person other than Tracy and Ashley who knew the issues involving David. James wanted to help Karen, but he could not get over his dislike for David. Nor could he ignore the history between David and Ashley. They took their drinks into JD's study and sat. "I need some professional advice," James started.

Brian was a FBI agent and a childhood friend of JD's. The night James met Brian, David had approached Tracy at a function. Brian witnessed the incident and confronted him. When he determined it was Ashley, David was hounding, Brian asked what the situation was. Ashley did not answer Brian's question. She played it off and ended up going home with James. In a tearful confession she told James, David was a boyfriend during college who attempted to rape her. Tracy walked in and called security. The incident was never reported because at the time, David was a football star. The coach and the college administration covered up the incident. Ashley was too ashamed to tell her brother and swore Tracy to silence. Once the information was revealed to James, Ashley also swore him to secrecy. That was the first day they kissed. He remembered how shocked he was at the reaction she generated in him. To this day, James has not been able to stay away from Ashley's sassy mouth or her sexy body.

"You sound serious man, you going to ask Ashley to marry you or something," Brian asked bringing James from his memory.

"No man," James laughed.

"And why the hell not?" Brian asked curiously raising an eyebrow. "You realize Ashley is like a little sister to me."

"Depending on the outcome of this conversation Ashley may not want to marry me."

"What's going on?" Brian asked interested.

"You remember David Holt?"

"Yeah, the ass from the wedding."

"Yeah that's the one," James smiled. "His wife works for me. I believe he is abusive to her. In fact she was just released from the hospital the other day. I suspected it for a while, but was not able to confirm it until this time."

"Did she tell you he did this?"

"Not directly, but yes. This is my issue. Holt is a political advisor and damn good at what he does. The chairperson from the DNC wants him on JD's campaign. Ordinarily, I wouldn't have him anywhere near Ashley. However, Karen has asked me to consider him for the position. She feels it will give him the success he craves and in turn keep him off her. She believes if he is working the abuse will stop." James sat in the chair across from Brian. "You and I both know that will not happen."

"I guess my first question to you would be: Why you are considering it at all? Is there anything between you and his wife?"

James shook his head, "No, nothing like that. She's a good person—young, bright with a good future ahead of her. I just hate to see someone with all that going for them pulled down by the likes of Holt."

"Okay, will he be an asset to JD?"

"There is no question about his ability. If we don't pick him up, someone will. And that someone may be one of our opponents."

"Is there someone else out there who can do the job just as well?"

James hesitated, "To be honest I don't know." He sipped his drink. "My problem is I don't like him."

"Yeah, but you don't like him because he dated Ashley. That's personal, not business. You have to separate the two. At least talk to the man. See what he can do before you make a decision you might end up regretting."

James knew Brian did not know the full story about David and Ashley. And James did not intend to break his promise to her. Part of what Brian was saying was true. He did not like the idea of David being around Ashley. Actually, James was a little insecure about her love for him. He was ten years her senior. She was young, beautiful, energetic and sexy as hell. David had her love at one time. Was it possible for him to get it back? He sat his drink on the table, "You might be right."

Brian only knew James for a short period, but he could read people fairly well. He felt something wasn't on the up and up. "Everything okay with you and Ashley?" he asked.

James turned and looked at Ashley in the kitchen. "Yeah, we're good."

"I'm glad to hear it, but you know if it's not, I'll be more than happy to take her off your hands."

"I appreciate that especially coming from you, being her big brother and all. If it's alright with you I think I'll keep her for now."

"All right man, I don't put that offer out there too often," they both laughed.

James picked his drink up and sat forward on his seat. "Tracy mentioned you may be interested in leaving the agency and starting your own business. Are you still considering that?"

Brian looked at James. The frustration of the red tape connected with the agency was getting to him. The incident with Tracy's attack left a bad taste in his mouth. He knew there was a strong possibility the gang JD was prosecuting was planning an attack on Tracy and he shared that information with the agency. They refused to allow him to provide protection for her. The decision almost cost Tracy her life. "I could be persuaded. What did you have in mind?"

"Would you be available to meet with me?" He gave Brian a business card with an address on it. "I have a business proposition for you."

Brian raised an eyebrow. "You sure you can afford me?" he laughed. "I mean you did just quit your job and Ashley is your woman. We are all aware of her spending habits."

James smiled, "I'm pretty sure I could handle you and Ashley."

JD knocked on the opened door, "Private conversation?" he asked.

"We were just talking about Ashley and shopping," James smiled.

"Two words that are consistent with each other, always has been," JD laughed.

"James wants to talk about a business venture with me," Brian offered. "I wasn't sure if his pockets ran deep enough to cover me and Ashley. He just assured me it does."

James smiled. "I want to convince Brian to take on your protection detail as a full time gig. The last incidents occurred because his hands were tied with red tape from the agency. I want to eliminate that issue."

JD sat in the chair behind his desk. He remembered both incidents all too well, he exhaled. "The last time Tracy was pregnant we never had the opportunity to celebrate. This time we know. I don't want to take any chances with her life or the life of our child." The room that had a casual feel at the beginning of the conversation turned serious as JD hesitated. Each man was dealing with their individual feelings surrounding the attack on Tracy. "Brian, you have been the big brother I never had. I realize asking you to consider leaving the agency is a lot. With all we have been through and all we are about to embark on, I need to know my family is safe. I can handle anything if I know you are watching over Tracy. With all the crazy ideas you have about women, I know you love Tracy as much as I do." JD hesitated as he watched for Brian's reaction. As hard as he tried to conceal it, JD knew Brian had a soft spot when it came to his wife. Brian did not respond, but the stare shared between the two friends established the unspoken fact. JD moved on. "I don't know how deep James' pockets run, but I will give all I have to make it worth your while financially, if you decide to take this job."

James watched the exchange between the two. JD made a heart-filled request of his friend and from Brian's reaction, he was sure the request would be honored. James knew the bond between JD and Brian was tight. He believed Brian would never act on his feelings for Tracy because of that bond. Those two facts would make it easy to persuade Brian to leave the agency.

"Anything you need that's within my power is yours," Brian replied with a sincerity James never knew existed in him. James watched as a stronger bond developed between the two friends. It was at that moment, he knew, whether it was the attorney general's office, the governor's office or the presidential office, Brian would be there to protect JD.

"That's settled," James smiled as he stood. He turned to JD, "Now, I will leave you two and try to find that beautiful sister of yours."

"Make sure you hold on to your wallet," Brian laughed.

Ashley and Tracy were sitting in the sunroom talking when James approached. "You ready to leave?" he smiled at Ashley.

"Sure," she returned the smile.

"I'll pull the car around and meet you out front. Good night Tracy and congratulations."

"Good night James," Tracy smiled.

Tracy looked at Ashley. "So, what are you not telling me?"

Ashley stood and put her glass on the table. "I told James I love him, but he did not reciprocate. Then the other night out of the blue he asked if I would like to meet his family. I'm so confused." Ashley exhaled, "Tracy, everything in me tells me that man loves me. The way he talks to me, the way he laughs with me, the way he makes love to me, everything, but he can't seem to bring himself to say it." Ashley hesitated and looked around. She picked up her purse as Tracy waited. She knew Ashley had not finished her thought. "Did you hear him tell Brian he would be godfather to our first child?"

"Yeah, I was wondering why you didn't step in and say I would be the godmother."

"I was too damn shocked at the statement." Ashley bit her lip. "He asked me about David again. He wanted to know if David ever hit me."

"What did you tell him?" Tracy asked curiously.

"I told him the truth. I can't lie to him. But I'm not sure I did the right thing. When I told him, there was a look of hatred in his eyes I have never seen on anyone. He tried to conceal it, but I'm telling you if David had been in that room with us," Ashley shook her head, "James would have put him six feet under."

Tracy stood and hugged her friend, "Don't give up on James. I don't know what's holding him back, but that man loves you, that I do know. As for David Holt, well, I don't want to see anyone get hurt, but if James happens to punch him out, I would not shed a tear."

Ashley smiled, "I would probably kick him once or twice myself." Ashley took Tracy's hand as they walked to the door. "Thanks, Tracy and don't worry, I'm not letting that man go anywhere."

Chapter 3

Brian walked through the door of ***The Ashley*** at ten Sunday morning. He looked up at the building, "Well I'll be damned. He named the building after the woman." Brian shook his head and walked inside the building. He could see parts of the building were still being renovated, but the lobby was very stylish and large enough to hold a small convention. As he looked around, there were several offices with glass window fronts. The office to his left was furnished with desks, computers and telephones. The office to the right, which is the one James told him to enter, had a receptionist's desk. Brian pulled the gold plated handle door and walked in. Behind the receptionist's desk was an open space with several desks in the middle and offices with closed doors along the walls. The door furthest back was open with music playing. Brian called out, but did not receive a response. He was walking towards the open door when the door behind him opened. "I see you found your way." James smiled with two cups of coffee in his hands. He pushed one towards Brian. "I thought a cup of coffee would come in handy for our discussion."

"Black?" Brian inquired.

"The only way to go," James motion towards his office.

"You know we are both going to hell working on a Sunday," Brian joked.

James laughed, "Ashley informed me of that very same notion before she left for church this morning. Have a seat." James replied as they reached his office.

"James, why hasn't anyone told JD about Holt and Ashley?"

James froze at his desk. "You don't mince words do you?" He smiled and pointed to a chair for Brian to take a seat.

"Not when it comes to something like this. You left a number of things unsaid Friday night regarding Holt. I remembered Douglas mentioning an incident at Harmon involving a Harrison. I took the liberty to do a little research and the incident appeared on my radar. Ashley should have told JD about this when it happened."

"I agree. However, it was her decision not to and I have to respect that."

"Tracy was a witness she hasn't told JD either?" Brian asked.

James looked at Brian and smirked, "Do you seriously think Tracy or Ashley would tell anyone anything about the other? Those two are thick as thieves."

Brian laughed. "Thicker, thieves will eventually give you away. So what are you going to do? There is no way in hell you can hire this man to work on JD's campaign."

"I have no plans to. I spoke with Karen, that's Holt's wife. I explained to her my first responsibility is to JD. My second priority is Ashley. I can't bring myself to do anything that would put her in harm's way. Holt being anywhere near her does that. With that said, I do plan on meeting with him. Once that's done, he will be furious. After he beats the hell out of Karen, which I'm sure will happen. I think he'll come after Ashley. Brian, our conversation centered on protecting JD and Tracy. With what I see in their future, you will be needed. However, that would not be the only task. At the moment I need you to make sure Ashley is protected without her knowing."

"How far do you think Holt will go?"

"Look at his history. He approached Tracy at a public function. Then he approached Ashley at Gavin's fundraiser, with JD and me present. Let's not forget he showed up at the wedding." He pulled an envelope from his briefcase. "These are notes he was leaving on Ashley's car last year. I don't know how far he will go, that's what concerns me."

"All right, we know I can't handle the assignment. Ashley will spot me in a minute. Legally I can't put anyone on her. I can get someone to handle it as a private issue, but that is going to cost you."

"I don't care what it costs. I don't want anything to happen to Ashley."

"When do you plan on meeting with Holt?"

"I'll set it up for tonight, six thirty at the Renaissance."

"Since it appears Holt is a threat to his wife and Ashley, I will put the man on Holt. At least we will know where he is at all times."

James sat back in his chair and exhaled. He was relieved to know Brian would handle the situation. "Brian I don't want to spend the rest of my life in prison. Make sure you put someone good on Holt. If he does anything to Ashley, I will kill him."

Brian raised his eyebrow. "What makes men willing to go to jail for women. JD said the same thing about Tracy."

James smiled, "Not just any woman, Brian, just the one who makes your life worth living." James hesitated; surprised he spoke the sentiment aloud. He cleared his throat, "Let's talk about your future. You mentioned earlier, that legally you could not put anyone on Ashley. That was the same issue for Tracy last year. If you had your own protection agency that would no longer be an issue. I know you are loyal to the agency." James said as he turned to face Brian, "If you had the financial backing, are you ready to step out?"

Brian sat forward, "Head my own agency, not having to answer to anyone?"

"Except the law, of course," James said.

"Of course," Brian smirked.

"I would be a silent partner. Once the upfront loan is repaid, no interest, I'm out completely. It's your company," James replied.

Brian frowned. It never dawned on him to do an investigation on James. Now, he wondered, "What do you get out of this?" Brian asked.

James stood and walked over to the window, he turned back to Brian. "I believe ten to twelve years from now, JD may very well be running for President of the United States. I want to be a part of that history. You and I know, any African American who comes that close to that office will become a target. I need him to have unfaltering protection. You can give him that, because of your love for him and Tracy." James hesitated and continued, "In the years preceding that time you can develop the staffing and connections you will need to keep them safe. You are well liked in the agency and your path was heading to detail at the White House in a few years anyway." James sat back at his desk. "You will need to have a working relationship with all agencies, FBI, Secret Service, CIA, Homeland Security and any other agency that may be in existence. Your reputation is already established with two." James looked at Brian and it did not seem any of his statements surprised him. He chuckled, "Tracy has prepared a business plan. It's on your desk upstairs in your office."

"Office?" Brian questioned.

James pulled a set of keys out of his desk drawer and handed them to Brian, "Follow me. I'll show you, your office suite."

"You were that sure I would accept?" Brian asked as he took the keys. He noticed the gold plated keychain in his hands was engraved, The *Ashley - Suite 201*. Brian smiled inwardly and thought, *this man is either in love with Ashley, or he just likes the name a whole lot.*

James smiled and walked out of the office as he followed. When they reached the elevator James stepped inside and pushed the button to the second floor. "I saw the look shared between you and JD last night. You pledged your life to him. He accepted it and so did I." The elevator doors opened and they stepped off. "These offices go around the building. I started you here, but if you prefer one of the other offices, feel free to move into it. Everything on this floor will be available to you."

"Damn James, what did you do, lease the whole building?" Brian joked.

James unlocked the door with the sign that read, "*The Thompson Agency*" and stepped in, "No, I purchased it."

Brian froze and looked up at James, who at six-four stood above his six-two frame. "How damn deep do your pockets go?"

James smiled, "You're the investigator, you tell me." He walked over to one office, "I thought this space would work well for you. Brian walked into the space where James stood by the window. As they looked out James pointed. "That's the entrance to the Governor's Mansion. If all goes according to plan, JD and his family will be using that in four years."

Brian had a newfound respect for James. This man was a mover. He did not wait for directions from anyone. Brian wondered why JD did not make Calvin his campaign manager and instead turned to a virtual stranger. Now he clearly understood the move. "What is this?" Brian asked referring to a folder on the desk of his new office.

James laughed, "Tracy set up an interview for your first investigator. I believe you know her."

"Her?" Brian questioned.

James started walking towards the exit, "Yes, Magna Rivera," he smiled. "I'll leave you here to get used to your new surroundings. Your business plan is in the top drawer of your desk. A budget is included. The funds required to start you off will be placed in your account as soon as you open one." James hesitated. "I realize a lot was thrown at you this morning. I have a meeting with a few other people downstairs that will be a part of this journey. Join us when you get ready. If you accept my offer a simple handshake will seal the deal."

James turned to walk out of the office. "When did you start working on all of this James?" Brian asked.

"Christmas Eve, at JD's dining room table."

Brian smiled, "I remember the conversation well." He looked around then placed his coffee cup on the desk, "I'll turn in my resignation, effective immediately."

As James closed the door, Brian took a seat at his desk. He surveyed the office, smiled, then opened the folder and began reading.

James received a call from Brian around five thirty that evening, letting him know things were in place. The man he assigned will pick up Holt's movements once he leaves the club. James was in his kitchen listening to Ashley and Clair talk. He loved the way Ashley was around people. Their background, social or financial standing did not faze her one way or another. Everyone was someone to Ashley.

According to her, "Everyone had something unique and interesting about them."

Ashley was certainly the complete opposite of his ex-wife. His ex-wife was above all—that was the bottom line. She would never set foot in the kitchen or hold a conversation with Clair, his housekeeper. Oh, she would give her orders, but never a conversation. Ashley never missed an opportunity to talk with Clair about her family or other issues.

James smiled watching the two women expressing themselves. Clair with her Puerto Rican background was just as feisty as Ashley. Listening to the two was exhausting and when they began speaking in Spanish; James knew it was time for him to leave the kitchen. "Ashley, I have to leave for a meeting. Are you going to hang around until I get back?" He asked with a smile that let her know it really wasn't so much a question as a demand.

She smiled. "I think I could hang around for a day or two."

He gave her a wicked smile. "I think I would like that. Walk me to the car."

Ashley got up, "I'll be back Clair."

"What's on your mind Mr. Brooks?" She asked once they were in the garage.

He leaned against the car, put his hands around her waist and pulled her to him. "You are, Ms. Harrison."

"Is that a fact?"

"Yes it is."

"Then why are you leaving?"

"I have to put some things in place, tonight. But it shouldn't take me long."

Ashley loved James, especially when he looked at her like he was at that moment. She smiled. "Take care of whatever you need to, then hurry back home to take care of me."

He gently kissed her lips. "I can do that," he whispered against them.

"You can?" She asked as she put her arms around his neck.

"Yes," James murmured as he wrapped his arms completely around her, pulling her so close he could feel her breathing against his chest. He continued to kiss her deeply as she leaned into him, both of them silently promising a night of passion upon his return. James pulled away and exhaled, "There's something on the nightstand beside the bed for you. I'll be back soon."

"Okay," Ashley smiled, "I'll be here."

James entered the Renaissance Private Club around five fifteen p.m. He spotted Douglas, the owner of the club and another childhood friend of JD's, behind the bar. Douglas and James had become friends. He invited James to become a member of the exclusive club and he accepted. Whenever James could, he would have a drink with Douglas, just to talk about whatever the topic of the day may have been. "Hey Doug, it's good to see you, man."

"James, what brings you by tonight?" Douglas asked as they shook hands.

"I'm meeting someone here. Are you working the bar tonight?"

"Yeah, I like to keep in touch with the small jobs around here. Do you need something?"

"Possibly," James sighed. "I'm meeting with someone I don't particularly care for. But it's about the campaign. Do you think you could hang around, keep me in check?"

Douglas laughed, "James, man I have never seen you lose your cool, except for the night of the wedding, when that ass said something to Ashley." Douglas looked up, "Speaking of the ass, he just walked through the door."

Without turning James replied, "That's who I'm meeting."

Douglas glanced at him with a questioning look on his face. James just shook his head, "Campaign business."

"Courvoisier, Hennessey or Jack?" Douglas asked.

"Paul, straight," James replied.

Douglas turned his back as David approached. "Brooks," David said as he extended his hand.

Douglas put the drink in front of James. James picked it up and swallowed the shot then looked at David without extending his hand. He hated the man standing before him. This man had attempted to rape Ashley. She trusted him, and he betrayed that trust. In addition, this man abuses his wife. This man had an affair with Carolyn Roth, Gavin's fiancée, while working for the man. James stared intently at David. He was the typical athletic type, not bad to look at, but he could not understand why women fell for him. By all indications, the man was a good political operative—just not good enough for James.

"You have fifteen minutes to speak, and then I'm out," James said.

"That is not a lot of time to tell you how I can help your candidate win the AG's seat."

James looked at his watch. "You now have fourteen minutes. You may want to use that time to tell me why I should even consider you being in the same room with my candidate."

David took a seat at the bar just as Douglas put another drink in front of James. "What are you having?" he asked David.

"Hennessey," David replied.

"Brooks you know I'm good at what I do. The governor's race is going smooth because I had a hand in it. I can do the same with the attorney general's race. When Harrison goes after the governor's seat, things are going to get dirty. The higher you go, the dirtier the game gets. Harrison is about as straight laced as they come. He is going to need someone like me who knows how to play the game at that level.

Currently, he is carrying out someone else's vision of what public policies should be in place. At the next level, he will be developing those policies. I have a proven record on being very effective in that area and you know it."

James looked at his watch, "You have five minutes left."

David exhaled, frustrated. "Brooks, I can't believe you would let what happened between Ashley and I back in college affect Harrison's future. I was young she was young. Shit happened, but that was the past. We are talking about now."

"Since you brought it up, let's talk about now." As hard as he tried, James could not reign in his temper. "How's Karen? Is she bruise-free at the moment? How do you anticipate keeping your temper in check if you become a part of this campaign? How much harm do you think you would cause this campaign if it became public knowledge that a member of a candidate staff was a wife beater? Or how much damage do you think it would cause if that candidate killed a campaign staffer because he attempted to rape his sister in college. These things don't go away Holt. So you see, even if I did not hate your guts, you would be a liability to JD and that I will not allow!"

David shook his head, "You had no intention of considering me for this position. Why in the hell did you waste my time?"

"Because your wife asked me to meet with you and I told her I would."

Something snapped in David. He despised men like James Brooks who thought they owned the world. Most of all, he hated the fact that he had Ashley. The woman he believed should have been by his side always. The woman he planned to leave Karen for during college. The woman, he taught to make love to him, just how he liked it. "Did you tell Ashley you were granting this wish for my wife? And speaking of Ashley, how long do you think it will be before she gets tired of your old ass?"

James calmly set his drink down and looked at Douglas. Douglas moved to the end of the bar just in case James was not able to keep in check the anger that appeared in his eyes. James turned back to David. "I have no idea, Holt, but whatever time it takes, will be just enough time for me to kick your ass!"

"Gentlemen!" Douglas interjected, "I believe it's time for this interview to come to an end."

David stood, swallowed the last of his drink and placed the glass on the bar. "Brooks, what are you, hitting about forty, now? What makes you think you can keep a young, vibrant woman like Ashley satisfied? I taught her to be very passionate. Hell, I used to call her my little wildcat. Don't you think she would be better off with someone young and vigorous, like me?"

James stood ready for battle in David's face. "It appears not, since I have her and you don't. Ashley's taste has improved. She now prefers a man whom she chooses to give herself. Not to a little boy who could only handle her by force." He stepped closer to David with his nostrils flaring. "Don't be foolish and think that this old man can't teach your ass a lesson!"

Douglas made it around the bar and stepped between the two just as James grabbed David's throat. "I think it's time for you to leave, my friend," Douglas said facing David. David stepped back then looked at James. "It's a good thing you don't have the final say on this, Brooks. Expect a call from Covington. Like I said before, I know how to play the dirty game. I'm good at it. Ask Ashley."

As David made his way out of the club, Douglas walked back behind the bar and poured James another drink. He placed it on the bar. "You can't lose your cool like that in public over a punk. You are above that crap. You are an intellectual; beat him with your mind."

James took the drink in one swallow, held his head down and said. "You're right. I shouldn't let him get to me."

"I don't know his connection to Ashley, but I'll say this. It is not about where Ashley has been; it is about where she is now. She's with you; keep her there. In the meantime, if you need his ass kicked, you call me."

James looked at Douglass and realized he was very serious. "Thanks man," James laughed. "But I've wasted enough energy on Holt. I'm going home to Ashley."

When James arrived home the house was dark downstairs. Clair was gone and the food was put away. As he walked up the stairs, he came across several pieces of Ashley's clothing. First there was her silk blouse, he picked it up. Next was her red lace bra, he smiled as he gathered it. Next was her skirt, then her lace top stockings, and last but not least, her red lace panties. James entered the bedroom to the sound of Teddy Pendergrass, *And If I Had.* He walked into the candle lit bathroom. Ashley lay in the marble tub with her hair pinned up and her body surrounded with bubbles. Her arms and those beautiful long legs of hers were stretched out in the tub. The sight caused a rise in James. The thought of Holt having his hands on her entered his mind.

He walked back into the bedroom and placed Ashley's clothes on the chair in the sitting area. He removed his suit jacket and placed it on the hanger, along with his tie. He sat on the chaise while unbuttoning his shirt and Holt's words made him think. Ashley was twenty-six, young, beautiful and yes, very passionate. The music changed to *Love TKO.* James laughed, as Teddy sung. He lay back, kicked off his shoes and deeper thoughts of Ashley invaded his mind. He was ten years older than she, a difference that was eventually going to be an issue, even if Ashley didn't see it. She's in the prime of her life, now is the time she should be settling down and having babies. Maybe he should let her go; but how could he? Like it or not, he was in love with, every inch of her.

Sitting up, he continued sorting through his feelings. He and Ashley had been together for about a year, and had come to this crossroads. The last thing he wanted was for Ashley to wake up ten years from now married to him and then realize age did matter. The other option would be to let her go; she would meet someone in no time who would love to have her as his wife and mother of his children. He could live with that, as long as it was not David Holt.

The music changed again. *"Turn off the Lights..."* also by Teddy P. began to play.

James smiled, that woman knows him to damn well.

Ashley stood in the doorway of the bathroom with a towel wrapped around her, looking at James on the chaise. She could tell he was struggling with something; something that had changed his romantic mood. Knowing the depth of his pride, Ashley realized James never wanted to share his worries or concerns with her. But that was what she was there for; to love and comfort him—the two came together. Why did James have such a hard time understanding that? Ashley never asked any questions about his first marriage, but she got the impression that his wife was a manipulator. James did not trust or love easily because of it. Ashley accepted that and knew she had an uphill battle from the beginning. But tonight, when she opened the box on the nightstand, there was a set of keys to his home. The small step on his part indicated he was ready to move forward.

Now, as she stood there watching him brewing over whatever was going through his mind, she wondered if it had anything to do with her.

James saw Ashley walking toward him. He swore her legs were long enough to pull a dying man from the depths of hell to heaven. Right now, he would settle for her wrapping them around him. She straddled his lap and put her arms around his neck. "I believe this was where we left off earlier this evening," she said.

James ran his hands down her thighs, and then pulled her legs up around him. As he looked into her eyes, in his heart he knew, he could never let her go, not now, not ever.

"Ashley," he whispered as he kissed her throat.

"Yes," she replied as his hands moved up her hips to her waist. She began to unbutton the rest of his shirt to expose his chest. She loved that chest and began demonstrating just how much by placing kisses down to his navel then back up to his throat. As she reached his lips, he engulfed her lips within his.

Ashley heard the moan escape his throat as his tongue went deeper, dancing with hers. She pushed the shirt from his shoulders as he released her waist long enough for it to slide down his arms. He cupped her face in his hands and planted kisses over it. Something about his embrace tonight made her feel safe, secure and, yes, loved. She grabbed the outside of his hands that was holding her face, and looked into his eyes. Ashley was breathing heavily, but she had to stop and say this before she lost her nerves, as she had so many times since Jamaica. "I love you James," she whispered. "Now, I know you may not want to hear that, but I'm going to tell you that every day until you tell me to stop." James remained silent as she talked. "I know with everything in me, I have loved you from the day I first saw you in your lobby," she continued looking into his eyes. "I love the way you say my name. I love the way you look at me when you think I'm not looking. I love the way your hands explore my body. I love the way you are holding my face, right at this moment." A tear rolled down her face. "I love you James Brooks."

James wiped the tear from her face and smiled. "I've been sitting here contemplating how I was going to let you go. I thought it was time for you to find someone your age to settle down with and have babies." He laughed at himself.

Ashley pulled back as her heart stopped. James saw the hurt in her eyes and pulled her back to him. He softly kissed her lips, "Please understand, letting down my guard is not easy for me. I don't like feeling vulnerable to anyone." He looked into her eyes. "GOD, help me here," he said as he closed his eyes. He could feel Ashley's heart beating as if it was about to come out of her chest. "I love you Ashley. I should have told you that long ago, but I couldn't."

Ashley kissed him gently on his forehead, then his cheek, then his nose, then his lips. She held his face in her hands. "Would you say that to me again, please?"

James smiled, then pulled the pin out of her hair and fanned it down her back with his hands. "I love you," he kissed her again.

Tears flowed down Ashley's face. "Say it again," she cried with her lips still on his.

James smiled and whispered, "I love you Ashley Renee Harrison."

"Again and every day for the rest of my life would do just fine," she giggled.

"That's not asking for too much." He sat there for a moment looking into the chestnut colored eyes that twinkled up at him. He never saw that look in his ex-wife's eyes. Never felt her heartbeat as he felt Ashley's, never felt as if someone else was breathing for him.

Ashley saw the intensity of thought going through his mind. She wondered if he wanted to recant. "You don't have to say it every day. Once a week would be okay," she smiled.

James stood with Ashley's legs and arms wrapped around him. He carried her over to the bed as her head rested on his shoulders. He gently placed her on his bed and lay on top of her. He rubbed his thumb across her forehead trying to ease away the worry crease that was there. He ran his tongue over her lips, "I love you Ashley and I don't mind saying it to you every day for the rest of my life. But it will cost you," he said while kissing her left cheek and then her right.

Ashley tried to ease her breathing that was raging out of control from the feather light kisses he was strategically placing on her face. "Whatever the price, I will pay it willingly, just name it," she managed to whisper.

"Marry me."

"What?" Ashley asked pulling away. "What did you just say?" Ashley asked sitting up in the bed with the towel falling around her.

James grinned as the towel fell exposing her naked body. He kissed her calf, and then pulled her leg causing her to fall backwards on the bed. He kissed her kneecap, then the inside of her thigh. When he reached the core of her, she placed the palm of her hand on his forehead to stop his progression. "Repeat yourself Mr. Brooks, looking up here," she said breathlessly.

James looked up into her eyes. "The price of me saying those words to you, everyday is you marrying me and never leaving me no matter ...." before James could finish the statement Ashley threw her body on top of his kissing him with everything in her. "Yes," she said, then kissed him again. "Yes, yes, yes and yes again!"

James began laughing as he hugged her tightly. "Yes to which part?"

"All of it," she said smiling down into his face and pushing her hair back. "I couldn't leave you anyway. No one can leave their heart behind; they wouldn't be able to survive."

"I need to hear you say it."

Ashley looked into James' eyes. "Yes, I will marry you. And no, I will never leave you, no matter what."

James smiled and at that moment it seemed years of tension and hatred dissolved. "I think it's time for you to meet your future in-laws. I want you to remember your words," he said as he flipped her over and kissed her, again and again and again.

Chapter 4

James had made a decision—now he had to make it work. On his drive to the office, he thought about the night before and his declaration to Ashley. Smiling he thought, *it was time.* For the last month, since the trip to Jamaica, something was tugging at his heart. Not any longer, his heart was now free and his path was clear. He knew what he had to do. It was not going to be easy. There were family issues he chose not to deal with that had to be reconciled before he married Ashley. "Whew, marriage!" James laughed aloud. He never thought that would be on his mind ever again. However, unlike before, the thought was not repulsive to him. Neither was the idea of having a family, children and a wife.

However, at the moment, James had a more pressing issue to handle, David Holt. During the meeting, Holt mentioned a call would be coming from Stanley Covington regarding his employment on JD's campaign. That was a bomb waiting to explode and James knew he had to keep it from happening. David Holt was good. Nevertheless, the people he worked for did not know his true nature. James did.

James was sure David had given Covington some type of convincing story regarding the situation between the two of them. Probably claiming James was jealous of his past relationship with Ashley. If it were just James' reputation that was on the line, the situation would not concern him. But there was more at stake. JD Harrison could possibly be a future presidential candidate. It was James' responsibility and duty to ensure nothing interfered with that possibility. Since it seemed Holt wanted to play dirty, James would have to refer to a higher power who knew the players and the game; hell he developed it. "Hey Pop, how are you this morning?" James smiled as his father answered the telephone.

"James, it's good to hear from you son," Avery Brooks replied. "What do you need?"

"Why, can't I just call my old man to hear his voice?"

"Now, son, we had this conversation earlier. This is your second call in a week's time. Give you old man some credit."

"You're right, Pop, as always. I need to talk to you about the campaign."

"Do you think we could have a one on one tonight? I'll drive up this evening around seven. We could meet at the club."

"How about your home—at the dinner table, at six thirty, as usual? Afterwards, we can talk in the study. I know your mother would be happy to see you, it has been a while, you know." Avery held his breath waiting for his son's reply. Although the two of them spoke every Sunday, James had not spoken with his mother in years. It was time for the family to reconnect.

James thought about it, there was no need delaying the inevitable. "Does everyone still sit in on dinner?"

"Yes," his father replied hesitantly.

"Okay, Pop, but I will be bringing someone with me."

Avery sat straight up in his chair. "You're coming?" he asked just to clarify.

"Yes Pop, I'll be there before six p.m."

Avery stood at his desk, franticly pressing the button for his secretary. "Get my wife on the phone!" He anxiously said to his secretary. "James, I'll see you tonight."

James disconnected the call and smiled at the chaos his visit was going to cause. He then placed a call to JD. It was time to reveal his identity. Since JD was on his way to his mother's house, James decided to meet him there; might as well knock out two stones at once. He then called Ashley and asked her to join him for a road trip. She replied by saying she would go to the end of the Earth with him. That had him smiling as he hung up the telephone. He wondered if Ashley had told Tracy, yet.

As James pulled up to Martha Harrison's house he noticed JD's car was already there. He knocked on the front door and walked in, "Hello!" he called out.

"We're in the kitchen," JD yelled back.

James walked into the kitchen and kissed Martha on the cheek. "Good morning Mrs. Harrison, how are you?"

"Good morning James, I'm just fine. Sit down. I fixed a plate for you, when JD said you were stopping by. Where's Ashley?" she asked looking behind him.

"She's at her place getting dressed for work or talking to Tracy on the phone."

JD and Martha looked at each other. "Talking to Tracy on the phone," they both laughed.

James sat at the table.

"Brian came by the house last night," JD said. "That's an amazing offer you made, James. There is no one more deserving."

"I agree." James replied as Martha placed a platter of pancakes, sausages, apples and a cup of coffee in front of him. "Thank you." He said grace and began eating with a smile on his face.

Noticing James' unusual smiling disposition, JD looked at his mother and his mother returned the questioning look. James looked up at them. "Would either of you have any problem with me marrying Ashley?" He asked smiling as he continued to eat...

That same morning David placed a call to Covington to discuss the meeting with James Brooks. He explained his past relationship with the woman James was currently seeing. David made sure to express his dismay that this issue may prevent him from being able to accept the position on JD's campaign. Covington, in turn, assured David that James was not the type of man to let a trivial issue such as this interfere with the election of Harrison into office. When David completed his call with Covington, he was convinced steps would be taken to ensure him a spot on the campaign. However, a price had to be paid for the way in which Brooks treated him. He picked up his car keys and left the house.

Ashley parked her car in her normal parking space at the office. She was hurrying to get into the office to share her news with Tracy. The tears were still lodged in the corner of her eyes from James repeating the words he spoke last night.

She shook her head, stepped out of the car and opened the back door to retrieve her laptop and blazer. As she turned towards the back door of the office she saw David leaning against the entrance. Immediately she looked around, no one was in sight. Her heart began to race. She inhaled to try to calm herself. Then her mind began to take over. *Okay, he weighs about a hundred pounds more than I do., Don't be afraid of this man, and if you are, don't let him see it.* "This is private property, David, and you are not welcome," Ashley said with more strength than she felt.

David leaned against the building with his arms crossed over his chest. As he stared at Ashley, he reflected on their past. She was beautiful, innocent then, but even more beautiful, now. She was the one who got away. He was still in love with Ashley. If David had to, back then, he would have left Karen to be with her. He was shocked last year when he ran into Ashley at Karen's job, of all places. The attraction was still physically powerful for him. All he needed was a chance to talk to her, to tell her his feelings. If she knew how he felt about her, they would have another chance. But Brooks was interfering with that possibility and Ashley wasn't helping by avoiding him. She never gave him a chance to explain things during college and she was not giving him a chance now. She gave him no other choice, but to approach her this way. He had to make her understand, she belongs to him; she was his property. "There was a time when you liked me to show up unannounced," he smiled.

"There was a time I liked eating Fruity Pebbles on my peanut butter sandwiches too, but, just like you, I've moved past that."

David chuckled, reluctantly. "Fruity Pebbles and peanut butter! Only you Ashley," he shook his head.

"What do you want David?" She asked impatiently

"You, Ashley. I want you!"

Ashley laughed, "It's a good thing you are old enough for your wants not to hurt you. Besides David, you have a wife.

Or have you forgotten, the same way you forgot you had a girlfriend eight years ago."

"Eight years ago I would have left Karen if you asked."

"I couldn't ask about something I didn't know about. You never told me about Karen. It was all about you getting with the new girl on campus. Well, you got me. You got the bragging rights, David. If I remember correctly, you were so proud of it. You told the entire football team. Did it feel good, when you told them, not only did you get me, but I was a virgin at the time? Did it David? I hope it did. I hope the feeling was worth hurting me the way you did. However, that was the past. You will never have a chance to hurt me again. Now, would you mind moving out of my way; I have work to do?"

David had a cynical smile and stepped closer to Ashley, "You know I never let go of anything that belongs to me, Ashley. And you were mine, heart, body and soul."

"I didn't belong to you or anyone else back then," Ashley snapped back.

"Do you now Ashley?" David asked as he walked towards her, "Do you belong to someone now?"

Ashley backed up until she was leaning against the car. The closer he came to her the more she remembered how angry he could get. She cowered from him during college, and she swore he, nor any other man, would have that kind of power over her again. Ashley stood her ground. "Yes David, as a matter of fact, I do," she smiled with firmness.

David reached her. He could see the fear in her eyes. He smiled. "You should fear me Ashley, especially if you believe you now belong to Brooks." David tilted his head to the side and looked at her. "Is that what you are about to tell me, Ashley?" He said as he ran a finger down the side of her face.

If there was ever a time Ashley believed she was about to piss in her pants, it was now. She was truly afraid of this man. Still, she stood her ground. She jerked her face back away from him, "Yes," she said unequivocally. "James asked me to marry him, and I said yes. I am willingly giving myself to him." she smiled. "Oh and just so you know. I'm not the same as I was in college; anything you try with me will come back to you. I may not whip your ass, but you will damn sure know I was there." She stood straight up, no longer cowering against the car. "Now would you mind moving? As I said, I have work to do."

Ashley stepped around David, but he reached out grabbing her around the throat and slammed her against the car. "Don't walk away from me Ashley! Don't you remember how irritating that was to me?" he snapped.

The laptop case fell from Ashley's shoulder onto the ground as she tried to release herself from the hold David had on her. She raised her knee and hit David square in the balls, which caused him to buckle, but he did not release her. All of a sudden, a hand pulled David away from her. Ashley bent over gasping and holding her throat as David's body was propelled backwards. When he began to refocus, David recognized the man standing above him with his foot in his chest. The same man threatened him at JD Harrison's function, when he approached Tracy. The man stood there with a .357 Magnum pointing at him. "Now, we can end this and no one would ever find his body Ashley. The call is yours," Brian said smiling. "Of course if you ask my opinion, I would suggest we call James and let him handle this. I'm sure he would be thrilled to see those marks on your neck."

Ashley appeared next to Brian, her hand still rubbing her throat and David wisely lying still on the ground beneath her. "James would kill him and I don't want to say "I do" with bars between us. Just let him go."

David made a motion to push Brian's foot off his chest. Brian moved his foot up to David's throat applying more pressure, and then frowned at him. "Go inside Ashley," he demanded.

"No," Ashley said, grabbing Brian's arm that was holding the gun. "You come with me," she said pulling at him.

Brian slowly slid the gun into the back of his jeans, and then removed his foot from David's throat. "Man, you must have nine lives or something," he said as he stepped back. "But you only have one left with me. If I ever see you near either one of my women again, I will kill you on the spot." Brian walked Ashley into the building.

David got off the ground and limped over to his car. Once inside, he cursed himself, knowing he had made a stupid move. He had looked around, there was no way anyone could see that parking lot from the street. How did Brian know they were behind the building? David looked around at the scene. Only those business owners with access to the back entrance to their offices would use that parking lot. David started his car and pulled off with the question still nagging him.

Ashley walked into the building and fell into the first chair she reached. She was visibly upset. "You okay?" Brian asked as he kneeled in front of her, taking her hands inside his. She didn't speak as tears rolled down her face. That pissed off Brian. He has known Ashley since she was a little girl and the only time he'd seen her cry was at her father's funeral. Ashley was afraid of David, deeply afraid, Brian realized. James was right to want her to have protection.

Tracy stepped out of her office to get a ginger ale from the kitchen and saw Brian and Ashley. "What's wrong?" She asked while consoling her shaking friend.

After she calmed a bit, Ashley told Tracy about the incident. Brian stepped away as he watched the two friends. People would look at them and always assume Ashley was the strongest. The truth was, Tracy was the one talking and Ashley was listening. Whatever Tracy was saying to her, was calming her down. The Ashley he knew was re-emerging. Within a few minutes, the two were smiling and Ashley was being a smart mouth, again. The ladies looked up at Brian with a look so intense that it caused him to look over his shoulder.

"What?" Brian asked as he leaned against the desk.

"Brian," Tracy began with a smile.

He knew immediately she wanted something. The friends walked over and flanked him on each side. Ashley took his arm and put it around her shoulder as Tracy laid her head on his other shoulder. He knew what they were about to ask. Brian kissed Ashley on the forehead and rubbed the back of Tracy's head. "Yes, I am going to tell JD and James what happened here. If you two had told them what happened when you were at Harmon, this would not be an issue now."

Ashley hit Brian on the back of his head with her opened palm, "It's not your business to tell."

"So much for the loving feeling," Brian smirked. He then looked down at Tracy. "What do you have to say?"

Tracy smiled at him, "Nothing," she said as she took a step away and held his hand. "You have always been a man of reason to me. Whenever I need someone to confide in or feel I need protection, I come to you." She then hugged him, "I know you always have my back, no matter what. And I know you will always have Jeffery's best interest at heart, too." Tracy started to walk away, but stopped and frowned.

"What?" Brian asked a little concerned.

"Well, do you think Jeffery will try to hurt David when you tell him about Harmon and what happened this morning?"

"Probably," Brian chuckled.

"Hmm," Tracy said and shook her head. "I hope no one from the media is around or gets wind of it. That could really cause an issue for someone running for attorney general." Tracy walked over and picked up the telephone. She began dialing a number, and then stopped. She looked at Brian, "Is David the type to file a charge against Jeffrey if he hurts him?"

"Probably," Brian replied without smiling.

Tracy exhaled, and then continued dialing the telephone, "Isn't James' father an attorney?"

"Yes, so are his brothers," Ashley replied.

"Hello James, this is Tracy. Please give me a call when you receive this message." She hung up the telephone. "Brian would you do me a favor?"

Brian smirked. He could see Tracy was going to get her way. "What's that?" he asked, out of curiosity.

"Would you give me a chance to tell Jeffrey about Harmon? He is going to feel I should have told him about this in the past. And I know he is going to be upset with me. I would like to explain my reasons for keeping this from him."

Brian thought for a moment, that's not where he thought Tracy was going. He thought she would try to convince him it was in JD's best interest not to tell him about David for legal and publicity reasons. It never dawned on him JD would be upset with her about the incident at Harmon. The last thing he wanted to do was be the cause of an issue between JD and Tracy. "I won't tell JD," Brian said.

"Are you sure that's best, Brian?" Tracy asked almost smiling.

"Hell no!" Brian exclaimed, "But, I see your point. And I'm still telling James. It's time to put an end to the David Holt bull."

"Oh, you're going to protect Tracy, but throw me out to the dogs?"

"No, I'm going to keep that ass from putting his hands on you again. "

"You don't think James is going to try to hurt David when you tell him what happened this morning?"

"Yeah, I know he will. But James is not running for a public office. Unlike JD, James doesn't let his emotions run amok when it comes to family. He has a certain amount of control, which you are testing his limits on. This issue with

Holt has bothered you and James for too long. This needs to end before you get married."

"You and James are getting married?" Tracy asked, surprised.

Ashley smiled brightly, "He asked me last night." The two friends looked at each other and screamed. As they ran across the room to embrace, Brian rolled his eyes upward, picked up the telephone, and called James.

When James left Martha's house he noticed there was a message from Tracy and one from Brian. He was about to return the call to Brian when JD hit him on the shoulder. "James, it's going to be nice to have you officially in the family. I don't know how you are going to be able to afford Ashley's shopping sprees. But I am more than happy to turn that problem over to you." He laughed. "My credit cards are now safe."

James smiled, "I think there's something you should know about me now that we are going to be family."

"What's that?" JD asked as he leaned against James's car.

James exhaled, "I know you've noticed I rarely talk about my family, and there is a reason." He hesitated for a moment. In the past, once people found out about his family they acted differently towards him. He didn't foresee that happening with JD, but it was still difficult for James to share the information. James leaned against the car and stared at JD. "My full name is James Avery Brooks. My father is Avery Anthony Brooks."

JD frowned for a minute, "I know that name." The look of recognition replaced the frown, "The civil rights attorney, Avery Brooks?"

"Yes," James replied.

"The multi-millionaire Avery Brooks, with three sons who are attorneys and a daughter who heads up the real estate corporation--that Avery Brooks.?"

"Two sons practicing law, one chose public service. I never told you I had a law degree and I'm able to practice in Virginia, New York and the District of Columbia, did I?"

"No James, I don't believe you ever shared that information with me." JD snickered, "I always wondered about your depth of knowledge with legal issues." JD smiled "I guess you can afford Ashley's shopping sprees." They laughed. "Does she know?" JD asked.

"No," James replied. "I'm taking her to meet my parents tonight." James chuckled. "She'll definitely know then."

JD shook his head, "She is going to be mad as hell at you for keeping this from her."

James looked away, "I know." He hesitated, "JD, I've gone through most of my life around people getting close to me because of my status, including my first wife. That's the reason I stay low key on my family. Ashley loves me, for me. Damn if I know why," he smiled, "but she does."

"She loves you because you are a good man, James, and Ashley knows it." JD began laughing as it truly began to dawn on him, who James actually is. "Man, if I had known who you were last year, I might not have gone up against you for Tracy."

"Yes, you would have." James laughed.

JD thought for a minute, "Yeah, you are right," he said as he shook his head. "I would have fought you to the wire for her and still will."

"No need." James laughed, "Now if you try to step in between Ashley and me, we are going to have issues."

"Man, I wouldn't dream of it. You are the perfect person for my little sister," JD said, as he began to walk away. Looking back at James, he added, "Your problem is going to be holding on to her once you tell her the truth."

"I have a get out of jail, free ticket on that one." James smiled as he opened his car door.

"Really, what's that?" JD asked.

James smiled. "I made her give me her word not to ever leave me when she accepted my proposal."

"Ah, use her own words against her," JD said smiling.

James nodded his head and smiled. "You got it."

Chapter 5

James steered his car through the midday traffic of Interstate 95 towards Northern Virginia. He silently cursed. He wanted to get into Mclean before the horrendous Northern Virginia traffic the interstate was famous for began to pile up. If he could make it to Dale City in Prince William County before three p.m., there was a possibility he could bypass the afternoon build up. James looked over at Ashley. She was unusually quiet. Earlier she mentioned her laptop was damaged during a fall that morning and a lot of information for one of their clients was unattainable. Before they left Richmond, he left her laptop with a friend who could retrieve the information from the hard drive. Unfortunately, the system itself would have to be replaced. He arranged for another laptop to be built and ready for her upon their return. "You know you will be able to recover your client's information when you get home?"

Ashley looked over at his smiling face, "I'm not worried about that. I could always redo the work. It's just," she hesitated. Ashley did not like keeping things from James. However, she did not want to ruin the day talking about David. She was on her way to meet his parents. That was enough stress to deal with, without adding the morning events to it. She decided to tell James on their way home.

"It's just what Ashley?" James asked bringing her thoughts back to him.

She looked out of the window, "I guess I may be a little nervous about meeting your family," she replied.

"Ashley Renee' Harrison nervous?" James took her hand and kissed the back of it. "I refuse to believe you are afraid of anyone, especially, my family. My dad is a sucker for beautiful women. You will have him wrapped around your little finger in no time. My mom, well, that's another story, but definitely not one for you to be concerned with."

Ashley sat up excited, "James look, that's the exit for Dale City. You know what's over there?"

James began to laugh. He knew exactly what was over there and why it excited her. "No, Ash, what's over there?"

"You know very well, Potomac Mills is over there. There are a lot stores in that mall, and surrounding it. Can we stop there?"

"I'm afraid we are on a time schedule. I'll take you to a mall closer to my parent's home. After you shop at Tyson's Corner or Tyson's Galleria, you may not want to go to Potomac Mills."

"Do they have discount shopping at Tyson's Corner or the Galleria? You know I'm a working girl on a budget. Of course if you just happen to have your credit cards with you, it's not a problem."

James laughed, "I always carry my credit cards when I'm with you."

"I don't want you to spend all of your money on me, James. I don't mind going to Potomac Mills. I can bargain shop at Nordstrom there.

"There is a real Nordstrom at Tyson's Corner, a Neiman Marcus and a Saks at the Galleria, and you will not have to bargain shop."

"I can't afford Neiman Marcus or Saks on my salary. I mean, I do okay and I'm not complaining, but I would go broke shopping at those stores." Ashley laughed as she looked out the window. "It's beginning to snow," she said, "maybe we should turn around and go back before the roads get bad."

James looked out the window as he drove further down the highway. "It's a light dusting; and no, we are not turning back." Ashley smiled. "That was a good try," James said. "If we get snowed in, we have a place to stay."

"You can't blame a girl for trying."

James merged onto Interstate 495. They rode another ten minutes before James pulled off the highway onto a single-lane road which led up to a beautiful gated archway. He slowed as the gates automatically opened. Ashley was looking at the landscape, which seemed to go as far as her eyes could see. She could see the outline of what appeared to be a small castle. It must be a resort they are staying at, she thought. As they drove further, they crossed a bridge over a pond that was lined in rust colored stones. The stones seemed to follow the same trail as the wrought iron fence that went on forever. Ashley could imagine someone skipping stones over the lake and smiled. James pulled the car over and stopped.

He took Ashley's hand and kissed it, "I want to show you something."

Ashley put on her jacket as she got out of the car. The snow was falling slightly harder than before. Ashley smiled as she saw a number of horses surrounded by a white fence on the opposite side of the road. James took her hand and led her to the fence. The horses migrated towards them and Ashley hesitated. She loved animals, but had never been around horses. She pulled back for a minute. James smiled at her. "They won't hurt you," he said. "Horses are very sensitive, they know if you are afraid of them. But they are so loyal and caring animals. They will treat you as well as you treat them. He moved closer to one of the horses. There was one horse in particular that seemed anxious to get to him. The horse was a beautiful silver color with a black and silver tail. He came right up to them and began prancing. Ashley smiled, "That is so cute." The horse nudged James with his nose and made a sound Ashley never heard. She stepped back.

James held her hand, "Hello, Snowball," he said as he rubbed the horse's nose. "It's been a while, hasn't it?" The horse seemed to nod as if answering him, and then began to move his hoof across the ground. James released Ashley's hand and jumped over the fence. He reached back to her, "Come on, let's ride him."

Ashley looked at James as if he had lost his mind. "I am not riding that big thing."

"You ride big things all the time," James smiled.

"Well, yeah," Ashley smiled, getting his drift. "But I tend to get pleasure out of that ride."

Ashley saw the excitement in James eyes and she couldn't deny him. But there was no way in hell she was going to get horse manure on her Antonio Melani shoes. James stepped over to help her across the fence. "You know, I must really love you. Here I am in the snow, taking off my shoes to ride a damn monster of a horse." She removed her shoes, tiptoed to him, and pouted, "My feet are cold and wet."

James laughed as he mounted Snowball then reached down to help Ashley up. One of the other horses decided to nudge Ashley's butt just as James was pulling her up. Ashley let out a little scream and Snowball moved slightly. James settled Ashley in front of him and wrapped his arms around her. "Why did you take off your shoes?" he asked.

"I didn't want to mess them up." Ashley replied as she held on dearly to her shoes.

James laughed, "Take it slow Snowball, we have a city girl on board," he said as he gently rubbed the animal's neck. Snowball apparently understood. He walked slowly, close to the fence, then turned in a circular motion and began to trot. Ashley never experienced anything so wonderful. The snow was falling, a magnificent animal was moving beneath her and the man she loved had his arms wrapped securely around her. "This is wonderful," she whispered.

James kissed the side of her face, "Not as wonderful as you feel to me." He hesitated then decided this was as good a time as any to talk to her. The one thing he knew for sure was the woman in his arms loved him for him, Not for his money or family name; just him. He pulled her a little tighter. There was no way he was going to give her a chance to get away. At the very least she would not be able to smack him in this position.

James guided Snowball around with his leg until they were facing the house. "See the house over there?" He pointed to the mini castle Ashley saw when they entered the estate. She nodded, as she leaned back into James chest. "That's my parents' home. The first four windows on the second level coming from the left side of the house are my quarters. The next four belong to my youngest brother Nicolas. The center, with the archway and the white columns are my parents' rooms. The next four windows belong to my sister, Nicole and the last four belong to my brother Vernon and his wife, Constance. My parents are rather wealthy. I'm moderately wealthy."

Not fazed by what James had said, Ashley asked. "When you say wealthy, you mean they work and make a living like the rest of us do just at a higher income, right?"

"Not exactly," James replied. "My father is Avery Brooks. He is the third generation of the Brooks and Brooks Law firm located in DC, Atlanta, Chicago and Los Angeles. We own Brooks Global investments, specializing in high-end real estate throughout the world."

"What do you mean, we?" Ashley asked as James held her tightly in place when she tried to face him. "You mean it's a family thing? Like a whole lot of you own a share of it."

"Not, exactly."

"Then what exactly do you mean?"

James exhaled and cleared his throat. "At the age of twenty-one, each child received twenty-five percent of the real estate company, in addition to access to a ten million trust fund."

Ashley sat quietly for a moment, "Would you ask Snowball to take us back to the car?" she asked softly.

Before James could say anything, Snowball began walking towards the car. He smiled for two reasons. Snowball actually liked Ashley, if he didn't they would have been thrown off by now. Secondly, Ashley was letting all of what he said soak in before she reacts. It's a good sign when she thinks before she yells.

When Snowball reached the fence, he was close enough for James to sat Ashley down on the road near the car, and then he stepped down. Ashley walked over to the car and wiped her feet off before she put her shoes back on. James smiled at Snowball and rubbed his nose. "What do you think boy? If I buy her a shoe company will she stay?" Snowball nodded his head up and down. James smiled; if he didn't know better he would think Snowball really did understand what he was saying. He prayed Ashley would.

James drove up to the house, just as the front doors were opening. A gentleman dressed in what appeared to be a tuxedo came to the car and opened the door for Ashley. "Good afternoon, Mr. James. It is wonderful to see you home, sir."

"Hello, Charles," James smiled warmly as he shook the man's hand. "It's good to see you, too. How is everyone?"

"They are fine, sir, and thank you for asking."

"Charles this is Ashley Harrison, my fiancée. Ashley, this is Charles Gooding, the butler for our quarters. When we purchase our home, I hope to persuade him to head up our household."

"Hello Mr. Gooding. It's a pleasure to meet you, sir," Ashley smiled, wondering why they would need to buy a new house.

Charles smiled, "The pleasure is all mine."

James noticed Ashley's smile did not reach her eyes. He extended his hand to her. She hesitated, then stepped forward and took his hand. James stopped right outside of the entrance and turned to Ashley. "Before we go in, I need to apologize for not telling you about all of this. It was important for me to know you loved me, for me." He looked into her eyes and saw there were many questions and for a moment James was concerned.

"I love you, James, but you have a lot of explaining to do before this night is over." Ashley gently kissed his lips, but that wasn't enough for him. He pulled her closer and parted her lips with his tongue. He needed to feel the depth of her love for him, and Ashley conceded. She wrapped her arms around his waist, leaned into him and she felt his tension begin to subside. Their tongues danced in rhythm, closing out the rest of the world.

Someone cleared their throat, but they chose to ignore the sound. "Excuse me," someone from the entrance said, but neither of them noticed. "Butchie, release that woman that minute!" A loud male voice that resembled James' exclaimed.

Ashley opened her eyes, "Butchie?" she said into his lips.

James ended the kiss, but continued to hold her, "Pretend you never heard that."

She began to laugh, "Not on your life."

James turned, still holding Ashley's hand. "Pop, you look well," he smiled as they stepped inside the mini castle. James and his father hugged for a minute then he pulled Ashley front and center, "Pop, this is Ashley Harrison, my fiancé'. Ashley, my father, Avery Brooks."

Ashley extended her hand, "It's nice to meet you," she said in a voice James never heard from her before.

His father took her hand and pulled her to him for a surprising hug. "We are about to be family, there's no hand shaking around here. It's wonderful to meet you." He smiled as he examined her. "My goodness, you are a beautiful young woman."

"Thank you," Ashley replied.

Avery held her hands outstretched between them as he continued to smile at the woman who brought his son home. Charles cleared his throat, "Mr. James, Mr. Jerome Pittman is requesting your presence. Shall I place him in your study?"

"Thank you Charles. Please tell him I will be there shortly."

Charles nodded and proceeded to take the gentleman up the flight of stairs to the left of the room. Ashley's eyes scanned the room as James and his father talked. They stood in a foyer, which was larger than her condominium. There was a curving staircase to the left, one in the center of the room and one to the right, all meeting at the landing directly above where they were standing. The center staircase curved in both directions at the foyer. Between the staircases were huge white columns that seemed to be twelve feet tall. There were double doorways around the room, and an archway that led into what seemed like a grand ballroom with a black baby grand piano in the center.

"Ashley," James called out. Ashley looked at James as if she was a lost child in a big city. "I want you to meet someone." James said as he took her hand and led her up the staircase. "Pop, we will be down shortly." James yelled back as they ran up the stairs.

When they reached the top of the stairs, they turned left and walked past several rooms before entering the double doorway at the end of the hall. They walked through the doors and Charles was there. "Mr. Pittman is in the study. Would you care for some refreshments before dinner?"

"That would be great Charles. Something light."

"Ms. Harrison, may I take your jacket?" Charles smiled.

"Sure," Ashley smiled as she removed her jacket. "Thank you, Mr. Gooding."

"Charles, will do fine madam," he replied.

"Ashley will do fine for me."

James smiled as he opened the door to his quarters. The room was almost an exact replica of the bedroom suite at his house, with a few exceptions. Windows covered the room's three walls, with drapes strategically placed above them. The view was breathtaking with the snow falling over the landscape. Ashley stood at the doorway frozen at the sight of the room. James walked in as if it was normal. Ashley slowly stepped down the three marble steps and looked to her right. There was a sitting room with a fireplace encased in stone with a burgundy leather sofa, in front of it and two chairs on either side. Closer to the window, off from that room, was a large, cherry wood dining table. Charles came through a swing door with dinnerware and placed it on the table. Directly in front of Ashley was a bar with four stools and a rack of glassware hanging above. To her left were two rooms. One with the door closed and James standing at the double doors of the other watching Ashley adjust to her surroundings. He walked over to her. "Let me show you around," he smiled. He walked her straight into the bedroom and closed the door behind them. "This is my bedroom." Ashley stepped inside to find a large room with a king size bed, another fireplace, with a sitting area to the right. On the left was an archway with columns similar to the ones downstairs in the foyer. She walked through the doors and found a dressing room and closet to the left and a door that stepped down into a marble bathroom. The floor was marble, the whirlpool tub was sitting in a marble setting, the shower, with four heads, similar to James's house was encased in marble with glass doors. The commode was in a room by itself. Ashley walked through the bathroom and stepped up into what had to be his dressing room. She walked back into the bedroom and found him waiting for her on the bed. She stood in the doorway speechless. The reality of what he told her was slowly beginning to sink in. She shook her head, and parted her lips, but nothing came out. "Let's go see Mr. Pitman and then we will talk," James said as he took her hand and walked toward his study. He inhaled. He knew the enormity of what Ashley was experiencing. Nevertheless, it was snowing a little harder outside and Jerome was waiting on them. "Jerome," James smiled as he walked into the room, which looked a lot like JD's office, and shook the very slim gentleman's hand. "Please accept my apology for the delay." James pulled Ashley close to him and placed his hands around her waist. "This beautiful woman, Ashley Harrison, has agreed to become my wife."

"Congratulations Ms. Harrison. Mr. Brooks is a very fortunate man."

"Thank you," was all Ashley could say.

"Shall we get started?"

Ashley looked at James, "Started on what?"

"Jerome was kind enough to bring a few samples of engagement rings for you to select from."

Ashley smiled, "You came out in the snow to bring pictures of rings?"

Jerome smiled, "Oh my no" he stepped back and on the table behind him was a black velvet case with at least ten different rings sparkling at her.

"Ha, ha, ha," escaped Ashley's mouth as she looked at James stunned. "They are not real, right. Tell me they are glass replicas or zirconium or something."

James led Ashley to the sofa and sat beside her. "They are very real and I need you to select one that you like. Or just tell Jerome what you would like to have; he will make it for you."

Ashley looked at James, hoping to see if he was joking, but he wasn't. She looked from James to the rings. Ashley swallowed and began to study the rings. Like always, Ashley never had a problem determining what she liked when it came to shopping. One ring stood out for her. She picked it up and studied it closely. The ring was a pear shaped diamond that was so clear Ashley believed she could see James' face in it. She looked up at him and smiled, "I like this one."

James smiled at her with pride, "I would have selected that for you." He took the ring from her, placed it on the third finger of her left hand, and kissed her gently, "I love you Ashley."

Ashley smiled and lowered her head, "I love you James."

"I'll be happy to take the ring and have it sized for you," Jerome smiled at the commission he was about to receive.

Ashley looked at Jerome as if she was about to cry, "Why?"

"Well, it's a little large for your finger. You may lose it."

Ashley pulled her hand close to her chest. "Oh, no I won't."

"We'll have it sized later, Jerome," James said.

"At least allow me to put a guard on it until you can have it sized." Ashley hesitated, but gave the ring to Jerome. He put a guard on it, placed it back into its box, and gave the box to James. "Mr. Brooks, we will take care of the insurance in-house." Jerome said as he packed up his cases and locked them inside a briefcase. He looked at his watch.

"Oh my, it's after four. I must make my way back. You know traffic can be a bear this time of day."

"Thank you Jerome, as always, you have worked your magic."

"An exquisite ring for an exquisite woman. The best to both of you," Jerome exclaimed as he exited the room.

Ashley stood there as James walked Jerome out. She didn't move; she didn't sit; she just stood there wondering how things had changed in a matter of a few hours. James walked back into the room and knew the moment had arrived for him to answer a few questions. He closed the door behind him, leaned back against it, and waited.

"Why did you keep this part of your life from me?" Ashley asked. James took a step towards her. She put her hand up, "No, stay over there. I want an answer James, not a distraction."

"Alright," James said as he sat in the chair behind his desk. Ashley followed his lead and sat in front of the desk. "Someone in my position never knows if a person is involved with them because of the material or financial benefits, or because they truly care for them." He cleared his throat and then continued. "Unfortunately, I learned that lesson the hard way. What people don't seem to understand is, regardless of how much money or power one may have, we are all still human. We hurt and bleed just like everyone else. I did not intend to be hurt in that way again. I wanted to be around people who did not know who I was, so I left this life behind and never allowed anyone to get close. One thing that attracted me to Tracy was her intelligence and her loyalty. I knew if we connected we would be good together and she would never leave. I was never in love with Tracy and wasn't looking for anyone to fall in love with. You slipped under the radar. It seemed the more I tried to keep you at a distance the more you pushed to get closer. The other night, when I met with Holt, he said something that made me think about you and our future. As I told you, I did consider letting you go. But the thought of you not being in my life wasn't something I could handle." He looked up at Ashley, "You've become the heart of me and I can't live my life without you." James stood and walked around the desk. He got down on one knee, and took her hand in his. "I have never lied to you about anything. I did intentionally keep this from you. I'm asking you to understand my reasons and forgive me."

A tear dropped from Ashley's eyes. She wiped it away and cleared her throat, "I like the way you beg." James leaned in to her, but she put her hand on his shoulder to stop him. "I will forgive you, but you will pay a price for this. And I do mean a big price."

"I think I can afford it."

Ashley shook her head. "Your price will not be money that would be too easy."

James smiled. "Name it and it's yours," he said while kissing her neck, then her cheek and when he reached her lips, the doors burst open.

"Butchie!" The young woman screamed and jumped on his back causing him to fall backwards. "I can't believe you're home. I missed you."

James laughed and wrestled the woman to the floor holding her in a headlock. "Hello, Nicki, I thought you were in New York."

"When Pop told me you were coming home, I had the jet fueled and came right in before the weather got bad," she replied as she wiggled out of his hold and jumped on his back. "How long are you staying?" Ashley moved her feet into the chair giving the two room to wrestle. She looked up and saw a young more attractive version of James coming into the room. *Damn, is every man in this family tall dark handsome, and oh yeah rich,* she laughed to herself. The man put his finger up to his lips for her not to give his presence away.

The man grabbed the girl around the neck from the back, "Don't worry Butchie, I got your back," he yelled. Nicki released James' neck, grabbed the other man around his neck, and flipped him over. James grabbed Nicki's feet and the man grabbed her arms.

Ashley stood, "Wait a minute, that doesn't seem fair." She grabbed James neck from behind, wrestled him to the floor, and sat on his back. The Nicki tripped the other man. When he fell to the floor, she sat on his back. "Okay, this is better. Girl, I like your moves," Nicki said as she gave Ashley a high five.

"Woman!" the man said smiling at James.

"Ashley," James said, "You are supposed to have my back."

"I do, babe. Right under me, where it is supposed to be."

James reached behind him and pulled her under him. "I think you had that a little backwards," he smiled then kissed her much longer than he intended. He ended the kiss and saw the twins looking at him in amazement. "Hmm," he said as he looked down at Ashley, "that's my little sister Nicole and her twin brother Nicolas. He stood and helped Ashley up.

"It's good to have a real female joining the family and not another mannequin."

"Nicki..." James said. Nicki put her hands on her hips and smirked at him.

"I'm Nick, it's nice to meet you and I agree with Nicki. It's nice to have someone alive around this house again." He punched James. "My big brother here left us to deal with the deadbeats around here."

"You two know I had to go."

"We know, but you didn't have to stay away so long, I missed you." Nick replied.

James punched Nick in the chest. "I missed you too."

"Excuse me, Mr. James," Charles entered. "Mrs. Brooks is downstairs and has requested the presence of you and Ms. Ashley."

"Thank you, Charles, tell her we will be down as soon as we are dressed."

Charles looked at James and smiled, "Dinner is at precisely six-thirty."

James looked at his watch, "Tell her Ashley is holding me up, we may be a few minutes late."

Ashley smacked James on the back of his head, "Don't you tell her that, Mr. Gooding. We will be down at six-thirty, as requested." The twins looked at each other with eyebrows raised and smirks on their faces.

"Very well, Ms. Ashley." Charles left the room smiling.

"You have been summoned, and you know you better not keep Gwendolyn waiting," Nicki said with a smile.

"Give us a few minutes to get dressed, we will meet you downstairs," James said.

"We'll see you downstairs," Nick replied as they walked out the door.

"I like them." Ashley smiled as they walked into the bedroom.

"Yeah, it's good to be around them." He forgot how much fun it was to be around the twins. In many ways Ashley reminded him of them, especially Nicki. He looked up. "We can take a shower together that will save time."

"Not the kind of showers we take." Ashley smiled as she stepped out of her clothes and walked away naked.

An hour later, James and Ashley emerged down the staircase as if it was their natural habitat. James dressed in a black mock turtleneck and slacks with black loafers and Ashley was radiant in a black dress that hung off her shoulders with long sleeves and tastefully showed her curves. The dress fell a few inches above her knees and revealed a perfect outline of her tall frame. The two were a couple that would turn heads in any room.

The family was gathered in the sitting room, all waiting for the couple to appear. The conversation came to an abrupt end when the two entered the room. "Good evening," James smiled as he held Ashley's hand in the crook of his arm.

Gwendolyn Brooks rose from her seat and walked over to her son. The sight of James literally brought tears to her eyes. It had been more than five years since she last saw him and the circumstances were not good. She would not change the steps she took during their conflict, but she certainly would not have allowed the bad blood to flow as long as it had. Gwendolyn loved all her children, but of all of them James was the one she believed would always be on solid ground, like his father. Standing five feet four in heels, she reached up, brought her son down to her shoulders, and hugged him gently, not certain what his reaction would be. James released Ashley's hand and hugged his mother tightly almost lifting her from the floor. Everyone seemed to release a sigh of relief at the sight of mother and son embracing. "Hello, mother." James said brightly as he looked into her eyes.

Gwendolyn held his face in her hands and kissed his cheek. "Hello son," she said smiling. They gazed at each other a moment longer, acknowledging the hurt and the forgiveness silently, one to the other. As Gwendolyn looked into her son's eyes she saw happiness. The kind she once saw in his eyes when he was a child. She smiled. Her child was happy as a man. She looked to the woman standing next to him. She took Ashley's hand and held them in front of her. "I don't know what you have done to bring a smile into his eyes. But I thank you from the bottom of my heart."

Ashley smiled and looked at James. "Mother," James started as his hand encircled Ashley's waist. "This is Ashley Harrison—Ashley my mother Gwendolyn Brooks."

"It is a pleasure to meet you," Ashley smiled.

"The pleasure is mine," Gwendolyn smiled and then turned to her family. "Everyone this is James' fiancée, Ashley. Ashley this is everyone. I believe you have met my rambunctious twins, Nicole and Nicholas. My husband, Avery, who you can see, James took his looks directly from. The couple in the back is my oldest son Vernon and his wife, Constance. We have a few minutes before dinner will be served. Would you like a glass of wine or whatever?"

"A glass of wine would help my nerves," Ashley admitted.

"I'll get it," James offered.

"Thank you," Gwendolyn replied. "You have no reason to be nervous around us. We are family, or at least we will be very soon. Speaking of which, come have a seat and tell us about your family." Gwendolyn led Ashley to the sofa and sat next to her.

Ashley looked around. Nicki and Nick were already seated, as was Avery. Vernon was standing behind the chair Constance sat in, scrutinizing Ashley's and James' every move, it seemed. She looked away from the forbidding man and smiled at Gwendolyn. "There's not a lot to tell." Ashley smiled as James handed her a glass of red wine. He sat in the chair furthest away from them, but directly facing Ashley. "My immediate family is my mom and my brother. However, my extended family goes on forever. My mother is Martha Harrison; she's retired from the Richmond School System. My brother, JD is a district attorney in the area."

"Okay enough about that. How did you meet Butchie?" Nicki interrupted.

"Yes, do tell," Vernon, remarked with a bit of harshness. Ashley noticed the look of irritation directed at Vernon from Avery, and then dismissed it.

She smiled at James, "I met Butchie," she giggled, as James frowned at her, "at his office. I was putting in a bid for a project for my company."

"And you are part owner of that company?" Vernon asked.

"Equal partner," Ashley replied.

Shaking her head and waving Vernon off, "That's not important," Nicki waved his question off. "How did you two get together, I want dirt."

"Yeah, I want to know if Butchie got game," Nick joined in.

Ashley smiled and looked at James, "I don't know if Butchie has any game, but James owns the court." James smiled as he watched Ashley interacting with his family. She was holding her own. The conversation went on for a few minutes longer before they were all called in for dinner.

Avery sat at the head of the table with Gwendolyn at the opposite end. James sat to his right with Ashley next to him. Nicki sat next to Ashley and at her mother's left. Vernon sat to his mother's right with his wife Constance next to him, and then Nick.

The dinner conversation was pleasant with most of the questions directed to Ashley at the beginning and then to James as the conversation turned towards politics. Ashley noticed, not a word had passed between James and Vernon. Everyone, including Constance had spoken with James and hugged him, but not Vernon. Actually, other than irritating questions directed at her, Vernon did not say much to anyone.

"So, Ashley, tell me. How did you get my son's attention?" Gwendolyn smiled.

"Yes, I would like to know the answer to that," Vernon said in a questioning tone.

James looked away from his father and smiled at Ashley.

Ashley sipped her wine, "Well, I had to redirect his attraction."

"You mean, there was someone else, James was seeing?" Nick said, and then laughed at James, "You've been busy, playa?"

James smiled and listened to Ashley.

"In the beginning, James was interested in my best friend, Tracy."

"Then you must have been his second choice, the runner up," Vernon said in a derogatory manner.

The table became quiet as the expression on James's face changed. Ashley felt the tension, "No," Ashley smiled. "I'm not second to anyone. But if I had to be, Tracy would certainly fit the bill."

"What tactics did you pull to beat Tracy out?" Vernon asked.

Ashley was trying hard to keep a pleasant demeanor about her. After all, this was the first time she has met James' family and she wanted to make a good impression. However this brother was really getting under her skin with his questions. Each one seemed to have an underlying meaning. Ashley looked at James, and he could see she was losing the little tact she managed to keep all evening. "I don't use tactics. Never have and never will." Ashley began speaking directly to Vernon. "I have no reason to. I'm a very straightforward person. I say what I want; do what I want and ask for what I want. This is apparently something new to you. If you have a question for me, simply ask it. If I choose to, I will answer you. And if I don't choose to, I won't."

No one said anything, and all eyes went to Vernon.

Nick cleared his throat and smiled. "Well, big brother, I believe the lady has put the ball in your court."

If looks could kill, Ashley would have doubled over where she sat. But she did not waiver from her position or the stare she directed at Vernon. "I have no problem speaking my mind. I wonder why someone so young, with your apparent attributes would be seeing a man considerably older. Could it be the financial benefits he possesses?" Vernon asked.

James began to rise, but Ashley placed her hands on his leg.

"Vernon! You will not insult a guest in this home. I believe you owe Ashley an apology," Gwendolyn ordered.

"No," Ashley said never taking her eyes off Vernon, "No apology is needed. I'm sure Vernon has not said anything that had not crossed each of your minds at some point this evening. So, please, allow me to address the issue." Ashley hesitated, and then continued. "I was attracted to James the moment I saw him." She shook her head and smiled. "I fell in love with him the first time he spoke my name." She smiled, "I felt chills go down my spine. Unfortunately for him, I set my sights on him, long before he did on me. And I will admit, I literally pushed myself on him. Once I got to know him, I just couldn't imagine my life without him. I was informed this afternoon about all of this," she said, pointing around the room. "As angry as I am with him, for keeping this part of his life from me, it was, and is, too late for me to walk away, for I am hopelessly in love with the man. As for our age difference, we are ten years apart. I believe one day I will catch up with James sense of understanding and sexuality. Until that time, I pray he has the patience of Job. Because frankly, that's what it is going to take for him to deal with me." She looked around the table, then directly at Vernon, "Do you have any further questions?"

Neither Vernon, nor anyone else said anything as Ashley looked around the room. She pushed her chair away from the table and stood, "I'll take that as a no." Ashley turned to Gwendolyn. "Thank you for your hospitality, but, now, I would like to be excused." She turned to James, "Would you mind taking me home, now?" she then began to walk away.

James grabbed her hand to stop her. He put her in this position with his family. He knew they may feel Ashley was after his money. But he knew better. James stood and put his napkin on the table.

A sense of panic grew in Gwendolyn as she looked to her husband. Avery stood, "James, don't leave, not like this again. Ashley, please forgive us, for the inquisition. I don't care how or why you and James are together. I only care about his happiness."

"Mr. Brooks, I don't know anything about your family. But, it seems to me, there are a lot of undercurrents happening in this room, which has nothing to do with me. I am not offended by the questions."

"You should be," James said. He turned to his family, and then looked at Vernon. "I took the first step to reunite the family. I am happy with my life the way it is, however, if we decided to have a family, I did not want any of our children not to know my side of the family. There will be no further steps on my part." James put his arm around Ashley's waist as the two walked towards the stairs.

"Ashley!" Gwendolyn called out. She ran and stood in front of them. "Please, don't leave now. Stay the night. Give us a chance to spend some time with James." She took Ashley's hand and held it, begging. "I have not seen James in more than five years. It was my doing, I accept that. But, now he's home," she said as a tear rolled down her cheek. "Please don't take him away, again."

Ashley's heart went out to the woman standing in front of her. Whatever went wrong between her and James, cut deep, for both of them. James stepped forward and hugged his mother, then kissed her cheek and smiled. Avery walked up behind them, with the twins in tow. Nicki looked at Ashley, "They have some wonderful shoes at Tyson's Galleria. We can shop till we drop."

"James, we haven't had a chance to talk about the campaign. Let Ashley and your mother talk while we have a brandy," Avery smiled.

James looked to Ashley. She was now home for him. Whatever made her happy was now his life's mission. Ashley saw the look in James's eyes. She knew, whatever she said would determine where this family went from now on. Since this was going to be her family, it was partially her responsibility to help reunite them. She turned to James and released Gwendolyn's hand. She looked him in the eyes, "I love you James Brooks, but you have taken me through more in this one day, than I have taken you through in the last year. This is going to cost you. I want the unlimited platinum and uninterrupted shoe shopping," she said as he held her hands out.

James smiled then cupped her face with his hands and kissed her. Gwendolyn sighed with relief as Nicki laughed. Nick stepped over and closely examined James and Ashley.

"What are you doing?" Nicki asked.

"I'm taking notes, just in case I run into an Ashley along the way," Nick laughed. Gwendolyn turned and frowned at her son. Nicki grabbed Ashley's hand and pulled her away from James.

"You two have all night for that. Come on Ashley, we have things to talk about," Nicki smiled.

That night as they lay in bed wrapped in each other's arms, James chuckled. "I never thought I would be back in this bed."

Ashley wedged her leg between his, arousing him with just a touch. "James?" she whispered.

"Yes?" he replied while massaging the back of her head.

"Just out of curiosity, how rich are you?"

"I told you this afternoon."

"You told me in Tracy terms, with numbers. You have to give me examples."

James shifted his body on top of hers. He stretched her arms above her head and entwined his fingers through hers. "Let's see," he kissed her eyelid. "I could purchase enough shoe factories that would allow you to wear a new pair of shoes every day for the rest of your life without a repeat." He kissed her other eyelid, "with a matching purse without a repeat." He kissed the top of her nose, "with matching outfits without a repeat. He then kissed her lips, claiming them completely.

"Wow," she gasped "What an aphrodisiac," she smiled looking into his eyes.

James looked down into her eyes and saw nothing but love looking back at him. "I would give it up in a heartbeat just to have your love." He kissed her tenderly. Ashley wrapped her arms around his neck and smiled, "If you give it all up, can we keep the shoe factory?"

Chapter 6

It was now early April, and James could not be happier. He had indulged in the warmth of knowing Ashley was going to be his wife and now it was time to get to work. It was time for them to develop their campaign strategy for the election. James met with JD at campaign headquarters to begin the journey that he believed would lead to the White House.

Some financial assistance was provided by the DNC, but as with most state campaigns, the attorney general's race was not given the same priority as the governor's position. James believed open communication on strategy was important with the other two camps. Today's meeting was to foster a united front. Gavin Roberts, who began his campaign for governor six months earlier, was having a difficult race.

Daniel Graham, who was seeking the lieutenant governor's spot, was experiencing some positive feedback and JD, who just began campaigning, was unofficially the top seed for the attorney general's office.

Following in his father's footsteps, James was about to embark on a journey, that would lead his candidate towards the White House, or at least that was his intention. However, unlike Gavin and Daniel, JD was not a politician. He has the potential to be a great leader, but there were apparent weaknesses that concerned individuals in the political realm. It was now James' responsibility to strengthen those areas to prepare JD for his intended future. All the weaknesses did not have to be addressed for this campaign, but a plan needed to be in place to begin tweaking his image.

JD entered the office precisely at nine, as James had asked. They smiled as they greeted each other. "Your sister put a serious dent in one of my bank accounts," James stated as they each took a seat.

JD laughed, "You knew there was going to be a price to pay for keeping your background from her. What did it, shoes?"

"Actually, I believe I purchased the entire mall."

"From what Ashley was telling Tracy, you can afford it. Be careful what you keep from her in the future. You may end up owning Lexington Avenue in New York soon."

James looked at JD, a little bewildered, "Don't tell me, Nicki."

"Is that your sister?" James nodded and JD smiled. "I believe I heard something about a jet and a shopping spree in New York."

"I should have never introduced those two," James shook his head. "The damage is done."

JD glanced at James and said, "I don't think I have ever seen Ashley this happy. I owe you."

James detected the seriousness of JD's statement and realized just how responsible he felt about his sister. "Ashley is in good hands. Her happiness is my number one priority. You can put your full concentration on Tracy and that baby you are expecting."

The expression on JD's face immediately turned from one of seriousness, to pride. "It doesn't seem real yet, she's not showing. I can't wait to see her stomach expand."

"How far along is she now?"

"Four months," JD replied with the vote-winning smile. "In September we will have a baby in the house."

"You better enjoy the quiet moments, while you can. It will change."

"Tell the truth. If you could, wouldn't you have JJ with you all the time, noise and all."

James looked at JD, there was no way he could deny how much he missed his son. "He would be sitting right here beside me every day, if I had my way." They were both quiet for a moment. "Well, let's talk about the campaign." James began. "We have a meeting scheduled with Gavin at ten a.m. Daniel will be joining us. Before they come, tell me what issues you want emphasized?"

"The priority is safety, reducing gang violence across the state. I believe that will involve improving our educational system. We have to find a way to get and keep our children interested in attending college. The thing is we can't afford to wait until they are in high school to encourage them. Most of the gangs are targeting children in middle school or the last year of elementary school. The other component will be giving children other options. We can shut down gang after gang, but if we don't give the kids alternatives they will simply develop another gang. An option could be reopening recreation facilities, or summer camps that provide entertainment as well as educational needs. I believe eliminating gangs will reduce the number of murders, robberies and other violent crimes." JD stopped and looked at James. "Am I expecting too much?"

James smiled. "No. And I have the distinct impression, you are not finished."

"You're right. I also want to find a way to stop or at least deter domestic violence. I don't know what it will take to get women to step forward, but we have to find a way. Too many families are losing the father and mother, one because the other was tired of the abuse and decided to kill the other, with the other being placed behind bars for the rest of their life." JD stood and looked out the window. He put his hands in his pockets, as he always did when trying to find an answer. "Another pressing issue will be Internet crimes. The crimes against our privacy, but most importantly the way the Internet is used against our young children. And it's not just the young who are being taken in. Some way, we have to protect our elderly citizens from being taken advantage of. You know I can't leave out terrorism. Virginia is a target state, due to our proximity to the White House. Not to mention the Pentagon and the naval ports and other military installations." JD stopped. He felt he was going on a rampage of things he did not have in his power to correct. He looked out the window and remembered Tracy telling him, "Your shoulders are only so big. You can't carry the whole world on them." JD sat back in the seat he previously occupied. "Well, what do you want to start with?"

James began to chuckle, "I think we start with the gang issues plaguing the state, with a touch of the Internet issues. Let's get some research on those two issues and work from there. I think your kick-off should be held here, at the end of next month. Do you have any objections to TNT handling the event?" JD shook his head. "Good, do you have any one in mind as a speech writer or press secretary?"

"No," JD replied. "I never used one before. Besides, I hate talking to the press. But Ashley could do it. She certainly knows my position on issues."

James frowned. "I hope she will be busy planning a wedding, but I'll run it by her."

"You realize she is my sister, she's not your wife yet."

"I do," James replied. "You remember the words from The Bible, Forsaken, thy mother, father and brother; cling to thy husband," James smiled.

"I don't recall that wording," JD answered laughing. "Nevertheless, she's not your wife yet. I am the one who has to give her away, you know. Besides my baby sister loves me."

"But she loves me more."

JD hesitated, "Alright, you got me on that one." They both laughed.

"Private joke or can anyone sit in?" Daniel asked from the doorway.

JD stood, "Dan, it's been a while." Daniel worked for the attorney general's office, during which time he assisted with a number of cases JD prosecuted. The two formed a successful business relationship as well as a nice friendship. In fact, Daniel decided to enter the lieutenant governor's race, because JD threw his hat in the ring for attorney general.

"Daniel," James spoke. "Have a seat. How's the campaign going?"

"Hectic as hell, but that's how we want it." He turned to JD, "Are you ready to come on the road with me?"

"I believe it's time." JD replied.

"Hey, Gavin told me about the baby, congratulations man."

"Thanks Dan. What about you, any prospects? You know Ashley is off the market now."

Daniel looked surprised, "Who took my queen?"

"I did," James said in a commanding voice, "and I'm not giving her back."

"O...Kay," Daniel replied as JD laughed.

"I hear laughter, our numbers must be improving," Gavin said as he entered the room.

James stood and shook Gavin's hand, as did Daniel. Gavin shook JD's hand and hit him on the shoulder, "It's been a while JD. How's Tracy?"

"Beautiful as ever," JD smiled as Gavin took a seat.

"Good. I look forward to seeing you two at the wedding." Gavin turned to James, "I understand congratulations are in order James. Have you set a date?"

"Not yet, but the sooner, the better for me," James replied.

"Daniel?" Gavin thought for a moment. "No need to ask." They all laughed.

"Now wait. I believe someone will eventually come into my life who will understand my need to continue to explore other opportunities." Daniel replied feigning offense.

The other three men looked at him and laughed. "In your dreams," JD commented.

"A man can dream a little, right," Daniel replied jokingly.

"Any chance you could make that person appear before the election?" James asked. "It would certainly take away the concern for maturity on our ticket."

"What do you mean?" Daniel asked.

"A number of our opponents are strategically planning on using our youth against us." Gavin replied.

"The issue will be moot with Gavin once he marries Carolyn. Age will always be an issue for JD, which cannot be helped. But the fact that he is married with a child on the way will carry a long way and may actually balance out the age issue. The voters still see you as a young bachelor, loose and fancy free," James explained. "That makes them nervous."

Daniel sat forward, "My camp indicates the numbers are favoring me at this time. It may not be that much of an issue,"

"To-date we have only dealt with the primary," James stated. "When we have to put you up against the Republican candidate, his age and family stability will play well against you. But, we will leave that issue up to your camp to handle. What we need to discuss today is how our camp can assist you two. We are not in full campaign mode, since JD is unopposed. Beginning with Memorial Day weekend, JD will be free to campaign with either of you or we can begin setting up our own campaign calendar."

"JD, I could certainly use your help on the trail. If you are clear on the holiday, why don't you and Tracy join Carolyn and me?" Gavin asked.

"Why not do a joint appearance during that weekend. Let's give the full ticket's first appearance?" James suggested. He did not want JD to appear to be in Gavin's pocket at this point. "Where are you scheduled to be?" James asked Gavin.

"I believe we are in Northern Virginia on Saturday, Richmond, that night and Hampton Roads that Sunday, then back in Richmond on Monday."

"Dan, could you set up an appearance for Roanoke? That will give us a clear appearance across the state for that weekend."

"I'll get my people on it right away." Dan replied. "It may be good to do the same sweep after the primary, just hit different localities."

"We can certainly put it in our calendar. What about you Gavin?"

"I'm sure it can be worked out."

"Now, that dates have been established, what issues do you two want paramount during the appearances?" JD asked.

"Crime, for me," Gavin replied.

"Education here," Daniel added.

"We can handle those issues." JD smiled. "James set up a meeting with Gavin and Dan's managers to ensure the message is concise." JD stood and walked towards the window, "Gavin, there's something I need from you and now is just as good of a time as any to address it."

"Name it JD, what do you need?" Gavin sat forward.

"Carolyn has put out a few bad vibes with some of the wives of vital supporters. I need her to back off. Tracy hasn't said anything to me about this, but I know she has been shunned at your soon to be wife's request. Carolyn pulls a lot of weight with these people, even more so with her about to become the first lady. Tracy is not comfortable at certain events we have to attend because of this situation and although it may not be an issue at this moment, fundraising for my camp could become a challenge if this continues."

"JD, you know Carolyn. I will ask her to stop. In case that doesn't work, I'll speak with the husband's of the wives in question." Gavin hesitated. "You should know Tracy isn't the only person on her list. James, Ashley is also a target because of her friendship with Cynthia. Of course, you know Carolyn has put the word out that Cynthia's company TNT is not to be used by anyone she considers a friend. Now, I realize my past relationship with Cynthia may have created this issue and I offer my apology. If it's any consolation, at the moment, my home life consists of how to make Tracy and her friends miserable and the wedding."

The men laughed at Gavin and looked at each other.

"How do you put up with that?" Dan asked.

"What can I say, I love the woman."

"That's says it all." James smiled.

"Well maybe this will help," Gavin sighed, "I know Tracy will be asked to speak at a luncheon for the "Women of Business Association." As you all know, those women carry large checkbooks. I believe the plan is to ensure no one of considerable importance attends the event. This will show the public Tracy is a political nobody, and demonstrate," he looked at JD, "you selected the wrong woman to have at your side."

JD frowned, but before he could respond, James interjected. "Gentlemen, let's kill two stones at once. Gavin, if you don't mind taking a chance at being placed in the dog house for a while, I may be able to stop Carolyn's attack against Tracy without you having to speak with her or the husbands of her friends."

JD shook his head. "No. No games. Gavin I want Carolyn stopped. Tracy did not do anything to her, you know that. Her anger should be directed at me. I'm the one who broke things off with her."

"JD," Gavin responded, "the best way to get at you is Tracy, and Carolyn knows it. "

Dan looked from Gavin to JD, "You know, gentlemen, we have to have a united front going into the main campaign. This issue with Carolyn and Tracy could have a negative impact if our opponents get wind of it. James, if you have a way to squash this before it gets out of hand, do it now, and do it quietly."

James smirked. "I believe, now that we know the plan, it can be handled effectively."

"JD, Tracy is stronger than you give her credit for. She can handle Carolyn. You've seen her do it and so have I. Don't let the petty issues creep into the campaign," Gavin said as he stood.

"My wife is not a petty issue, Gavin. I have to go home to that woman for the rest of my life. Her happiness is the most important thing in the world to me." JD stood angrily.

"I know, you have made it very clear to everyone involved in this campaign and I did not mean to imply Tracy was a petty issue. I believe you know that. I know what the issue is with Carolyn and I will do all in my power to keep her under control." Gavin extended his hand to JD. "Acceptable?"

JD hesitated for a moment, and then shook Gavin's hand, "Acceptable."

"Good!" Gavin pointed a finger at JD "You need to work on that temper, I've told you that in the past. Take this bit of advice. When this campaign starts rolling, our opponents will use your temperament regarding Tracy against you. Find a way to get it under control. You are a good man, JD, and you are destined to go a lot further than I ever will. Don't allow minor issues to stop your progression. Let the women handle their issues. We could never really understand them anyway."

JD nodded in agreement, "You definitely have a point there. I don't understand it."

The tension in the room began to subside as the men continued to discuss campaign issues. James was relieved with the manner Gavin handled JD's weakest point, his love for Tracy, which also happens to be his strongest point. But just as Gavin said, people know that attacking Tracy was the best way to get at JD. It was now James' job to keep the attacks to a minimum. Unfortunately, that also meant keeping Carolyn under control. First, he had to put JD in check.

"JD, hang around for a few minutes," James said as he shook Gavin's and Daniel's hands before they left the room. He waited until the others left before turning to JD. "Once this campaign is over, I want you to order a magnum of champagne and send it to Gavin with a thank you note."

JD stared at James bewildered by his request, "I can do that, but would you clue me in as to, why?"

"Glad you asked. Gavin just exposed your greatest weakness and gave you some sound advice. Now, I'm going to add to it and before we go any further into this political game I want you to be receptive. Are you with me?" JD folded his arms across his chest and nodded. "Okay," James continued. "Go home and talk to Tracy. Make sure you have her support. When she assures you that you do, and I know she will, I want you to assure her, she has your support. Then I want you to stop treating her with kid gloves. Let her take punches and allow her to learn how to punch back." JD started to speak and James stopped him. "I realize you believe you are protecting her, but you are causing her more harm, by not believing in her ability to

protect herself. If you continue on this road, Tracy will never
learn to deal with the Carolyns and Lenas of this world. Stop
treating her like she is a weak woman, because she is not.
Your wife pulled herself through a very difficult childhood,
started her own business and deals with you on a daily basis.
She is anything but weak."

JD listened and was ready to explode. Nevertheless, as
James continued, JD realized some of what was being said
was true. "Tracy has been through so much with her family
and me. She almost lost her life, because she loves me. The
idea of my decision to get into politics causing her pain is
hard to handle. These issues with Carolyn, they're because
of me. When I stopped seeing Carolyn, she blamed Tracy.
The women that are snubbing Tracy don't even know her,
never met her. They are only following Carolyn. With this
little episode Gavin told us about, Tracy was about to be
blind-sided. She has a fear of speaking in public, but she is
not going to turn down the request, because she will feel it's
a way to help me. When she appears and no one shows up,
she will be devastated. I'm her husband. It's my job to
protect her. How do you think I feel knowing I caused her
that kind of pain?"

"I remember some of what happened with you and
Carolyn. But I also remember Tracy putting Carolyn in her
place on several occasions," James said. "But you are right,
she was about to be blind-sided. The good thing is, we know
about it and have an opportunity to counteract. As for the
public speaking, Tracy is going to be speaking in public for
the next twelve years. She might as well get started now. I still
want you to have that conversation with her. Don't tell her
about the Carolyn situation. I will handle that. However, talk
with her about everything else. Afterwards, I want you to
allow Tracy to fight her own battles. If she receives public
attacks, we will handle them tactfully, not emotionally.
Understood?"

Brian stopped in James' office on the way out that evening. It was the first opportunity he had to speak to James about the Holt incident. He had not received a call to bail James out of jail. Therefore he was certain Ashley had not mentioned the incident. He shook his head thinking about the confrontation he walked up on with Ashley and Holt. One way or the other, his friends' wives were going to be the death of him. He knew it as sure as his name was Brian Elliott Thompson. He was beginning to think working for the FBI was actually safer than trying to protect these women. He knocked on James' door. "Hey, you have a minute?" Brian asked as he entered the office.

"Sure," James replied as he looked up. "Come on in have a seat. I'm wrapping up the team for JD. If I can get this last person on board, I believe we are going to have a good group of people behind him."

"Who's the last person?" Brian asked.

"Pearl Lassiter, she's in public relations with the mayor's office. She is young, energetic and not afraid to speak her mind. But the best part is she is used to dealing with the elites and their sentiments. I'm looking at the press secretary position for her."

"Don't you think you would need someone with a little more experience for that position?"

James shook his head, "No, I think it would be a good fit for her. She can cut her teeth on this campaign and be ready for the next."

"Fresh blood?" Brian said as he took a seat.

"Exactly," James replied. "What's going on? Is our boy up to no good?"

Brian cleared his throat. "Funny you should ask. That's exactly what I want to talk to you about. Brian proceeded to tell James about the incident with Ashley. As he told the story he could see the blood rushing through the vein in

James' neck. Before he completed the events of that morning he made sure to mention Ashley's and Tracy's attempt to keep the information from both him and JD. There was no need in James being mad at all of them, Brian decided. "Ashley assured me she would tell you about this. Since I had not heard from you, I assumed she forgot to mention it."

James could hardly contain the anger that was building inside of him. Holt actually put his hands on Ashley. He stood and began to pace. He wanted to hit something, but there was nothing in sight. He looked at Brian who quickly informed him, "I hit back."

James looked at Brian and then looked passed him to the doorway. "So do I!" Pearl Lassiter said, seeing the look on James Brook's face.

James exhaled as he attempted a smile at the young woman. "Ms. Lassiter, please excuse us for a moment," he said as he closed the door. James turned to Brian, "I saw the marks on her neck. Damn it!" He exclaimed as he walked over to the window. "I'm going to have to kill this bastard to keep him away from Ashley. And why in the hell did she not tell me about this?"

Brian stood, "In her defense, a lot has happened in the last few days. It may have slipped her mind."

James looked at Brian, "Good try, but that won't fly. Where is Holt now?"

"In Arlington, meeting with Stanley Covington."

"The minute he is back in Richmond, I want to know."

"You got it," Brian said. "Umm James, what do you know about Ms. Lassiter?"

James looked out the doorway at the object of Brian's attention. "She's not married, gay nor has any other mitigating circumstances that I'm aware of. She does have several overly protective brothers who love nothing more than persuading interested parties away from her."

"Really?" Brian smiled. "Seems like the type of challenge I need."

"Brian, I want to know every step Holt makes."

"You asked me to handle this, now let me. The moment Holt stepped out of line, I was there. I will not allow anything to happen to Ashley, James, believe that."

James exhaled, "I do believe you Brian and thank you for being there. But the thought of Holt's hands on her is hard for me to accept."

"I understand, but you can't afford to get into any scuffles with Holt, not with what we are about to embark on."

"You're right. I'll let you handle Holt." James composed himself, "Would you like to ask Ms. Lassiter in?"

Brian smiled. "It would be my pleasure." He stepped outside the office, "Ms. Lassiter, good evening. My name is Brian Thompson," he said as he extended his hand. "Mr. Brooks will see you now. He was in a foul mood, but I've softened him up for you."

"Thank you Mr. Thompson, but I'm fully capable of softening a few moods myself."

"I'm sure you are, for your smile has certainly softened my mood."

Pearl reluctantly pulled her hand from Brian's and walked into James' office. Brian watched the fluid motion of her hips and it brought a smile to his lips. He stood in that spot for a moment, then he shook his head, what in the hell is wrong with me. He turned and walked out of the office.

James entered his home through the kitchen and found Clair there finishing dinner. His mood had not changed since Brian conveyed the information regarding David and Ashley. The mood could only be explained as beyond pissed and Clair recognized it immediately. "Good evening Mr. Brooks," she said. When she did not get a response, it wasn't taken personally. As pissed as he was, Clair was sure it could only have something to do with Ms. Ashley. She shook her head and turned to complete dinner.

"Ashley!" James called out from the bottom of the staircase, trying to determine which room she was in. "Ashley!" he called out again.

"Yes," she answered with a smile from behind him. In her hand was a glass of wine extended to him. James turned startled at her presence so close behind him, then distracted by the smile and outfit she was wearing. Her hair was up in a ponytail and she had on a two-piece bathing suit with a sheer scarf tied at the waist that flowed down her legs exposing one completely and covering the other, with heel sandals finishing the package. He smiled inwardly at the sight of her and the sensuous smile she was wearing that reflected in her eyes. She stepped over and kissed him gently on the lips. "I was hoping we could take a swim before dinner."

James smiled momentarily, relishing in the thought that this woman would soon be his wife. Every day for the rest of his life he would come home to that smile—she was his. Then he remembered the reason for his foul mood. Another man had his hands on what was his. Not just any man, David Holt.

"Tell me what happened to your laptop, Ashley." James said coolly.

Ashley wasn't too pleased with the tone of his voice and was about to say so when she remembered, she had not told him about that morning. "It broke during a small; let me say this again, a small altercation with David Holt."

"A small altercation, Ashley! Is that what you call a man's hands around your throat?" James yelled as she took a step backwards. "Why would you keep that from me?"

"Well, it could have something to do with your possible reaction," Ashley replied very calmly as she turned and walked back through the terrace doors she had entered.

"Do you feel I'm overreacting?" James descended upon her not bothering to hide his anger. "This is not any man, we are talking about. This is David Holt or have you forgotten what he is capable of! What did he say to you Ashley? And don't withhold anything from me. Do you understand? Nothing!"

Ashley was certain not only did she understand, but any neighbors who lived within fifty miles of them heard and understood. She thought to say that, but the look in his eyes, that were only inches from hers, did not indicate he would take it in the good natured manner she would be saying it. Ashley cleared her throat and backed up against the banister on the terrace. "He said he wanted me and that he will never let go of anything that belonged to him."

"What else?" James asked. He was certain there was something Ashley wasn't saying. Before she looked down he saw the fear in her eyes, Holt frightened her. No matter how hard she tried to cover up that fact, James could see it. He put his finger under her chin and turned her face up to him. "What else did he say?"

Ashley looked into his eyes. She prayed she was able to hide the fear she truly felt inside. "He said I should fear him, if I was about to tell him I belonged to you."

James wanted to reassure her. He wanted her to understand, she had no reason to fear Holt or any other person. He will always protect her. He placed his hands on the banister enclosing her between them and looked into her eyes. "I will go into the depths of hell to protect you, Ashley. I will not allow anyone to hurt you."

Ashley knew James meant what he said. He would never allow David to hurt her. But she also knew James did not have a dirty bone in his body. He may not know how to protect her from someone cold and calculating like David. James was straight up and honest. Oh she believed James would do all he could to keep David at bay, but eventually he would strike again. She looked at him and said in the most innocent voice she could, "He hurt me right here." She pointed to the right side of her neck pouting.

James could not describe the feelings that were stirring inside of him. He wanted to wipe any doubts from her mind that he would protect her. But he also wanted to take away the hurt that Holt had inflicted. He leaned in and kissed the spot on her neck she pointed too. His lips massaged the area until he felt the remnants of Holt's touch were gone.

The intimacy of James touch was missed the moment he pulled away. Ashley turned her face back to his, stared at him, and softly said, "He hurt this side, too," pointing to the other side of her neck.

James smiled and proceeded to cleanse Holt's touch from the other side of Ashley's neck. When he heard a low moan escape her throat, he began to lose focus on the purpose of his anger. He raised his head back to her face and touched his forehead to hers.

Ashley released the banister she was clutching and held out her arms to him. "I had to hit him with this hand," she said as she swallowed the intensity of her emotions back.

"Did you?" He smiled softly as he kissed the inside of her palm, then her arm, then her shoulder and finally her lips. He pulled her body to him and wrapped her securely against him. Before she left his embrace she will know the depth of his love. He parted her lips and deepened his kiss. His intentions were to reach the very core of her to soothe all her worries and doubts.

The need to protect her surged through him like hot liquid flowed over a volcano. There was no way he could keep the few defenses he had up against her any longer. Nor could he deny his love for her. He would not allow any man to come between them without a fight to the end.

Ashley put her arms around his neck to pull him closer, but that did not subdue the desire building inside. He was still not close enough. They had made love many times, each having its own meaning and fulfillment. This moment was different. James was showing how deeply he loved her and Ashley wanted to hold on to the feeling. Everything around them became nonexistent. Nothing or no one mattered, just him and her. She felt loved, safe and protected.

James moved his hand to cradle the back of her head holding her lips to his, demanding more and she complied, giving all the passion she had. His kiss penetrated her sense to a depth of release she had never experienced. She pressed her body closer to him, feeling his hardness; she thought she would have an orgasm at that moment. She inhaled at the touch and knew if the kiss did not end soon one of them would surely die of over exhaustion, or explode, whichever came first.

The last thing James wanted to do was end this kiss, but if he didn't they would be making love where they stood. Not sure where the strength came from he pulled back. Picking her up he carried her up the stairs with her legs wrapped around him and completely ignoring Clair as they passed her. Clair smiled. It was good to know Ms. Ashley could handle Mr. Brooks' moods. She went back into the kitchen and covered the food. It would be a while before they'd eat dinner. Clair picked up her purse and locked the door behind her as she left.

Before they made it to the bedroom James had removed the scarf from around Ashley's waist and dropped it to the floor. They kicked off their shoes as he placed her on the bed. He quickly dispensed of his trousers and briefs, only his shirt remained. While he stood unbuttoning his shirt Ashley released the buttons on the side of the bottom to her bikini, throwing the material aside and stretching her arms out to him. That was it; he could not finish removing his shirt. He placed his hands under her hips and entered her with a thrust so forceful he was certain he had reached the very core of her. He stilled himself, not wanting to move for fear he had hurt her. But Ashley was not cooperating with him. She raised her hips to pull the essence of him further inside her. The heat illuminating around him was the most sensuous feeling he had ever experienced. He pulled out and entered her again, and again and again. The feeling did not dissipate; it intensified. His need to fill her was driving him to the brink of no return; it was unyielding even with the increase of his pace.

Unable to control the ecstasy building inside, Ashley wrapped her legs around him and drew him deeper and deeper within. His thrusts were intoxicating and she wanted more, stronger, deeper and closer. She reached up, brought his lips down to hers, and inserted her tongue into his mouth with the same thrust he was pleasing her with. Suddenly her body began to shudder, as she screamed, "James!"

The sound of his name and the tightening of her muscles around him took its toll as he released his seeds of love into her. Still moving slowly, wanting to savor every ounce of her love around him, he continued to hold her hips beneath him as he collapsed on top of her. Ashley held his head against her breast and wondered at the sheer reality of what the two had just experienced. It was not just love making, it was a hunger that drove both of them to the breathtaking moment of ecstasy.

It was literally minutes before either of them could speak as they each savored the touch, smell and feel of their lovemaking. Ashley had to rescind her earlier conclusion. David would not stand a chance against James. Each of James strokes told her how far he would go to keep her safe. Knowing he needed to hear her say the words, she whispered in his ear, "I know you will protect me with your life."

James eased to her side and pulled her into his arms, "You are my life Ashley. I will kill Holt if he ever comes near you again." He felt Ashley tremble at his words. "Alright, I won't kill him. I'll just make him wish he was dead." He felt Ashley smile against his chest.

He sighed with relief as his mind wondered. The woman beside him was stubborn, willful and feisty as hell. She had a strength that matched his and he knew that was rare. He wanted ten little ones of her running around the house, to love and match wits with. He held her tighter and fell asleep with a smile.

Ashley closed her eyes and began to doze off to sleep as she thought of James' words. After the way he made love to her, she was certain he meant exactly what he said. He would kill David or die trying.

Chapter 7

Ashley was spending the day shopping in Georgetown with Nicki. There was no denying, shopping in Northern Virginia with no limits is the way every woman should live. Because she was about to become Mrs. James Brooks, Ashley now had that luxury. But the visit was not only pleasure, it was also business. The two were getting to know each other as friends as well as in-laws. And Nicki decided to use Ashley's agency, Next Level Consulting, to revise the set up for Brooks International offices which were located in Washington, D.C. Neither could resist the urge to shop along the way. Afterwards, they stopped in Union Station for lunch.

Both had filled themselves with the main course and were contemplating if they had room for desert, when

Ashley noticed a couple being seated at a table near the window directly in front of them. She immediately recognized David and once they were seated knew the woman with him was Carolyn Roth.

Ashley looked shaken. "Nicki, would you mind terribly if we passed on desert. I think we should leave."

Nicki looked around, "Is something wrong?" she asked, a little concerned.

"Nothing that can't be fixed by us leaving the restaurant, now." Nicki got the attention of the server for the check. "I'll excuse myself to the ladies room and will meet you at the bar," Ashley said and quickly walked away.

"Okay, I'll see you out front," Nicki replied to Ashley retreating back wondering who had unsettled her to the point she had to leave the restaurant.

Ashley entered the ladies room. What was Carolyn doing with David? Ashley shook her head as her hand rubbed her neck where David had grabbed her. Dropping her hand down, she thought, *He should not have the power to affect her in this way.* Ashley knew how ruthless David could be at times. With the last encounter, she wasn't sure what would have happened if Brian had not appeared. Maybe he was working on Gavin's campaign again. That would explain them being together. Besides she was sure Carolyn would not do anything to cause a scandal with Gavin running for governor and the wedding coming up in a few months.

Nothing meant more to Carolyn than becoming the First Lady of Virginia and no one knew that better than Ashley. Hell, last year Carolyn had almost ruined JD's relationship with Tracy because of her dream to live in the governor's mansion. Carolyn believed JD was her ticket to the mansion. When he ended the relationship with her to be with Tracy, Carolyn pulled a stunt that was very damaging to both JD and Tracy. Luckily, their love was strong enough to withstand the event and now the two was happily married with a child on the way. Carolyn then turned her sights on

Gavin Roberts, who was at one time the district attorney and JD's superior. Ashley was sure Gavin's decision to run for governor, had something to do with Carolyn. Now it seemed Carolyn would be getting her wish, although she did not deserve it. All signs showed Gavin will be the next governor of Virginia.

Ashley had turned her attention to washing her hands at the basin when Carolyn walked in. Ashley looked up, shook her hands and accepted the hand towel from the attendant. "Thank you," she acknowledged the women's action.

"It's her job, Ashley. You don't have to thank her. You need to get used to these things if you expect to be accepted into the realm of the Brooks."

Ashley smiled at the woman and gave her a gratuity. "I don't know about you, but my mother taught me manners. It doesn't matter what realm I may be in."

"I'm sure that attitude will change soon as you become accustomed to our way of living."

"I don't think you can put yourself in the category of the Brooks. They are a kind and humble breed, unlike you."

"You could learn a lot from me Ashley. I know how to get what I want, whether you like my methods or not."

Ashley knew she should have walked out the door but she could not resist. "Oh, you mean like you getting JD. How did that work out for you?"

The statement irked Carolyn, but she shrugged it off. She felt it was her duty to give as good as she got. "Why are you hiding out in the ladies room, Ashley? Could it be David's presence that sent you for shelter?"

"I'm not here with a man who's not my fiancée, you are. If anyone should be hiding, it's you."

"I'm simply having lunch with a political associate, nothing more."

Ashley smirked, "Nothing is that simple with you, Carolyn. If it were, you would not be in here with me trying to cover yourself. But you don't need to be concerned with me mentioning this perfectly innocent meeting to Gavin."

"I'm not concerned" Carolyn smirked. "I will simply walk out there and mention to David you are here. I am sure that will start some fireworks, that Nicole Brooks would enjoy witnessing. What do you think?"

Ashley smiled and stepped closer to her. "Nothing about you intimidates me; not your money, your name or your threats. Neither you nor David is a concern of mine. Now move out of my way, before I forget I'm supposed to be a lady."

"If that's the case why did you run in here the moment you saw us?"

"It was your imagination Carolyn. However, you are more than welcome to tell David I'm here. He will do something stupid and possibly cause a scene. You, being a public figure at this time, would make for good press coverage, don't you think. I can see it now; the fiancée of the projected next governor of Virginia involved with a brawl in a local establishment." Ashley folded her arms across her chest and waited for Carolyn's response.

Carolyn knew a public incident would not play well in the media, for her or Gavin. She stepped aside and Ashley stepped towards the door.

"Ashley don't think that marrying James is going to exempt you from my wrath. You interfered in my life when you introduced JD to Tracy. One good turn deserves another."

"Bring it on Carolyn, but remember I'm not Tracy and James is not JD. You interfere in our life and there will not be a hole deep enough for you to hide in. Enjoy your lunch." Ashley smiled and walked out of the door.

Carolyn rolled her eyes upward. She hated Ashley almost as much as she did Tracy. Unlike Tracy, Ashley had the Brooks money and influences to protect her. "But there is always a way to make someone pay for their actions," Carolyn mumbled to herself. "Always a way."

Carolyn returned to her table. She smiled at David. "I just ran into an old friend of yours in the ladies room."

David looked up at Carolyn. She was a beautiful ruthless woman, which was what he liked about her. Carolyn went after what she wanted and it did not matter to her who she had to step on to get it. If he was able to care about someone other than Ashley, Carolyn might be it. She was definitely a contrast to his wife, that's for sure. "Who?" he asked.

"Ashley Harrison."

The vein in David's neck began to throb. He wanted to jump up to find Ashley, but knew that would tilt his hand with Carolyn. With the outcome of his meeting with Stanley still in question, he needed to make sure he secured a position with Gavin's camp and Carolyn was his guarantee for that. "Really? What is she doing so far from Richmond?"

"Apparently getting to know her future in-laws." Carolyn watched David's reaction. She knew there was some type of connection between David and Ashley. On one or two occasions, David and James had harsh words with each other, but she never asked what the connection was. Previously, Ashley was of no interest to her. Tracy was always on her radar. Now that Ashley had pissed her off, what the hell. She will make both of their lives miserable. "What's your connection with Ashley?" she asked David.

David was not going to tilt his hand to Carolyn. He would give her enough to satisfy her curiosity and nothing more. "I took her virginity while we were in college. She's never gotten past it," he shrugged his shoulder nonchalantly.

"Really?" Carolyn snickered. "What are you a modern day Lexington Steele?"

David looked up at her without a smile or a hint of humor. "I satisfied you," he said raising an eyebrow.

Carolyn stared him down. "So I led you to believe. But it takes more than a healthy rod with the right movements to satisfy a woman like me. Tell me more about you and Ashley."

"Why?" David asked as he sat back in his chair.

"Let's just say, neither Ashley nor Tracy is on my Christmas card list."

David smirked, "But Tracy's husband, JD, is."

"Just as Ashley is apparently on yours." Carolyn sat forward. "You want to be on Gavin's campaign again. I will make that happen, effective now. I want whatever you have on Ashley and Tracy as repayment of my generosity."

David smiled inwardly. "What do you have against Ashley? It was Tracy who took Harrison from under your nose."

Carolyn frowned slightly, "It was Ashley who introduced them. But that's unimportant. I don't like either of them and I plan to make both of their lives miserable until I find something more amusing to do."

David smiled. "I have no doubt that you will do just that. But I have a suggestion. You handle Tracy and I'll handle Ashley."

"What do you have in mind?"

With some of the information received from Carolyn, David began formulating plans for Ashley. A simple piece of information was all he needed. He was certain that Carolyn had no idea that something so irrelevant was all he needed to get to Ashley. He smiled as he drove back to Richmond. The trip had been more of a success than he could have imagined. Covington had encouraged him to stay on, indicating he would find a position for him. Carolyn had stepped in and given him a position with Gavin's campaign, plus the in he needed with Ashley. Yes, it had been a very successful trip.

Carolyn knew there was no love lost between James and David. But she never knew the depth or cause of it until today. It seemed Ashley had one or two skeletons in her closet. The information from David, gave her an idea on

how to repay Ashley and Tracy for interfering in her plans
with JD. She would use the insight received from David
about the two friends to ruin both of them. Tracy she would
handle herself. Ashley was going to take the help of an old
friend. For a moment, Carolyn's conscience made her think
about her plan. It would take using a friend's vulnerability to
get to Ashley. "What the hell," she said while sitting in the
back of the limousine headed back to Richmond.

Ashley called Tracy on her way back to Richmond. She
gave Tracy all the details regarding the contract with Brooks
International. The two friends discussed the new contract
and the possibility for the company. They were one of the
top consulting firms in the state. This contract would open
doors for them to be recognized outside of the state. If all
goes well, it could open doors for them to establish an office
in DC or NY.

"Before we take this any further, we need to meet with
Monica. After all, she will be the one handling this company
once JD demands you to stay home to play Mother Goose
to his twelve children." Ashley's laugher echoed in the car.

"That's not funny, Ashley. He has actually mentioned me
staying home after the baby is born. He believes I could
handle the business from home." Ashley laughed again.
"Ashley, I'm concerned Jeffrey will not understand my need
to stay with the company. I mean, it's been my baby since
college. I don't know if I can give it up."

Ashley became serious. She wanted to comfort her
friend, but she knew JD well enough to know he was very
possessive of Tracy and her time. Once she has their baby,
that possessiveness is going to double. "I don't envy your
position, Tracy and I'm not sure what advice to give you on
this. I'm just glad James is not a caveman like JD. He would

never ask me to leave my job to stay home and raise children."

"Jeffery is not a caveman. He just likes having me home," Tracy countered.

"You don't have to defend him to me. I just hope you are ready to name Monica CEO. Lord knows she has more than proven herself capable. She's better at it than I am." Ashley hesitated than said what she felt she had to. "Tracy, I love you and I love that archaic brother of mine, but once you have the baby, JD is going to want you at his disposal day and night. Now, think about that. If he asks you to stay home, is he going to give you the same? With all these meetings and committee commitments he has, it seems you are spending a lot of time in that big empty house by yourself. It would be different if he was there with you some of the time." Nothing was said for a moment and Ashley realized she had spoken a little too bluntly. "Tracy, I'm sorry. I didn't mean to hurt your feelings. Next Level is more a part of you than me. You conceived it, started it and built it into a million-dollar business. I can't see you walking away from that or for that matter JD asking you to. And when all of this comes to a head, that's exactly what I'm going to tell that big headed brother of mine."

"Jeffrey doesn't have a big head," Tracy sighed, "and he hasn't asked me to give it up, yet. Just make sure you and your mom are in my corner when it happens. That's the only hope I will have to convince him I can do it all, take care of him, his political needs, the baby and the business."

"Oh speaking of political needs, guess who I ran into in DC?"

"Who?" Tracy asked.

"Carolyn Roth and you will never guess who she was with."

"Who?" Tracy asked again.

"Girl, you are beginning to sound like an owl. Stop asking who," Ashley laughed. "David."

Surprised Tracy asked, "What in the hell was she doing with David?"

"I don't know and I didn't stay around long enough to find out. Would you believe she had the nerve to threaten me?"

"Threaten you for what?"

"Because I interfered with her life by introducing you and JD. The woman needs to get a grip. JD was never that serious about her."

"Ashley be careful with Carolyn, I know firsthand the depth she would go to hurt someone."

"Tracy," Ashley paused, "do you believe for one moment that I am concerned about Carolyn? I will beat her green eyes black and pull every strand of weave out of her head if she tries anything with me."

Tracy laughed, "She does not have weave in her hair."

"Then I'll have Penne put some in there the next time he does her hair, just so I can pull it out."

Later in the week, Tracy received a call from Audrey Middleton, president of the Women's Business League. They were inviting the wives of each of the political candidates to come in and speak with their group. Tracy accepted the invitation after talking it over with JD. JD immediately called James and advised him of the function. James assured him the situation would be handled and Tracy would not be disappointed.

James first called Pearl Lassiter and set up an appointment for her to meet with Tracy. He wanted to make sure Tracy was well prepared for her first public speaking engagement. The next call went out to what he considered his secret weapon.

It was late in the evening and Avery Brooks was doing one of his favorite things in life, holding his wife in his arms.

When the telephone rung, he thought first to ignore it, but the number on the Caller ID was one he never ignored. "This better be good son, you are interrupting me and your mother's attempt to conceive another child."

James laughed heartily into the telephone, "I'm sorry Pop," he said still laughing, "I need to talk to mother."

Avery handed the telephone to Gwendolyn, "It's your son; I disown him for the moment."

"Tell Vernon to call back later." Gwendolyn smiled as she kissed her husband's neck.

Avery smiled at the sensuous touch, "It's not Vernon; it's James."

Gwendolyn pulled the cover over her naked body as she took the telephone and sat straight up. "James?"

"Hello mother. I'm sorry to interrupt you and Pop, but I need your help on something."

"Oh, don't worry about your father, we weren't doing anything. What do you need son?"

Avery looked at his wife astonished that she referred to their lovemaking as nothing. Lovingly he smiled at her reaction to the call. Lord knows he has been praying for an intervention with the situation between James and Gwendolyn. It's just that the timing was a little off. Avery looked at his wife talking intently with James. When the call was over, Gwendolyn proceeded to put her gown on. Avery reached out to her, "Where are you going, woman? Are you forgetting I'm lying here in a state of duress?"

"You'll get over it. James needs my help. I have to go to Richmond."

"Right at this moment?" was all Avery was able to convey before Gwendolyn retreated.

A week before the luncheon, Tracy, Ashley and Pearl were at the house working on her speech. Tracy's nerves were getting the best of her when Ms. Middleton called and indicated the turnout would not be what they had hoped for. The organization thought that JD's popularity would transfer to his wife. However, it seemed the people who have accepted an invitation would not have the economic impact the organization hoped. Ms Middleton indicated she only mentioned this to make sure JD's campaign would not anticipate a high return on any fundraising activity. Tracy thanked her for the call and assured Ms. Middleton, she would be there regardless of the turnout.

Pearl, who was advised of the situation and the remedy by James, encouraged Tracy to use this as her pilot. Since it seemed the expectations would be low, that would give her an opportunity to speak with a small crowd on any topic she choose. Tracy and Ashley decided, since the crowd would be from a low to middle income level, why not take the opportunity to show them how to invest what they can to improve their financial picture? It was a topic Tracy knew inside and out and would assist anyone who was interested in starting a portfolio. Pearl liked the idea.

Upon hearing the first run of Tracy's speech, she decided to change her media strategy. With the plot Carolyn had put in place, Pearl was going to downplay the event with the media, have as little coverage as possible. Now, after spending time with Tracy and hearing the plans for the events she decided not to only increase the media coverage, but to have the event videotaped for possible airing later.

For the next few nights Ashley and Tracy put the final touches on her speech. The night before the event, Tracy spent the evening discussing her speech with Jeffrey and Ashley. It was late when Ashley left for home, so she decided to go back to her place, instead of James' house.

The telephone was ringing as she entered the condominium, so she ran up the stairs to answer it. "Hello."

"Why aren't you answering your cell phone?" James asked.

Ashley smiled. "Because I didn't hear it ring. What are you doing up so late?"

"Waiting for you."

"I decided to come home since it was so late and I didn't want to wake you."

"And exactly what is it you anticipate doing at your place?"

"The same thing normal people do in their home, take a shower, relax, and go to bed." Ashley replied as she placed her purse on the dining room table. She noticed the morning paper was on the table. She distinctly remembered having the paper in the den and did not remember refolding it. "That's odd," she mumbled to herself.

"I have no intention of you and I sleeping under a different roof. I strongly suggest you get back into your car and come home."

"Mr. Brooks, this is my home. That is your house until we get married; then it becomes our house." Ashley smiled as she placed the paper back on the table.

"Ashley, I'm not having this argument with you. It's late, come home."

Dismissing the thoughts on the paper, Ashley turned her full attention to the conversation with James. "It is late and I'm tired, I'm not coming back out, James. However, you are more than welcome to join me here. If not, then I will talk to you in the morning. Love you. Bye."

Ashley pulled her shoes off and walked into her bedroom. She pulled out a gown for the night and jumped in the shower. When she emerged she was truly tired and ready for bed. She applied lotion to her body, put her gown on and fell across the bed. She immediately frowned; the smell wasn't right. She couldn't put a finger on it but it just wasn't right. She got up and changed the bed linen. It had been a while since she slept in her own bed. Afterward, she crawled under the Egyptian cotton sheets and fell asleep. It didn't seem she was asleep for long before she sensed a presence in the room. She sat up without turning on the lights and stared into the darkness. At one point, she felt as if there was movement in the living room. Ashley reached for her phone to call Tracy. At second thought, Tracy is almost six months pregnant, she can't help her. Ashley got out of the bed and picked up one of her shoes with a spiked heel. Then she looked at her shoe and shook her head. She can't mess up her shoes. She then grabbed the hair spray from the bathroom. She tiptoed out of the bedroom and looked around. As she walked through the living room she looked around but did not see anything. She walked towards the kitchen and peeped in. As she turned to go towards the guest bedroom and bath she noticed the newspaper was now in the trash can, not on the table. Then she heard someone at the front door. She stood at the top of the stairs and waited for the person to appear. Just as the person reached the top of the stairs Ashley flipped on the light switch and jumped out but before she could push the button on the can her hand was deflected. She found herself wrapped in James' arms. "Did you plan on setting my hair with that?" He smiled as he took the can from her hand and kissed her cheek.

"James, you scared the hell out of me," she said as she hugged him. "You should have called me to let me know you were coming."

"I wouldn't have to call you, if you were where you are supposed to be," he replied. "Why are you walking around with a can of hairspray?"

"I thought someone was in the house," she said as she looked up at him.

James turned the light off, put his arms around Ashley's waist and began walking towards the bedroom. "The hairspray was going to do what?"

"Detain the person until I could call someone." Ashley crawled back under the sheet as she watched James undress. "I had an uneasy feeling, something woke me up."

"Did you hear something?"

"No—just a feeling." James stopped undressing then proceeded to walk through the condominium. After checking each room he returned to the bedroom.

James joined her in the bed and pulled her into his arms. "Everything seems quiet on the home front. Nevertheless, I'll have Brian set up a security system tomorrow. Remove the key you have above your entrance. I put it back when I came in." Ashley settled her head on his chest and snuggled in. Once she was comfortable, she smiled and closed her eyes. "Your bed is too small. Like it or not, it's time for you to move into my place."

"Martha Harrison is not going for that, not until we are married." Ashley replied as she snuggled closer.

James kissed the top of her head, "And exactly when will that be?"

Ashley smiled, "Anxious, are we?"

"Damn right," James replied as he closed his eyes. As the two settled in, a figure emerged from the laundry room, quietly descended the stairs and exited.

Chapter 8

Ashley woke the next morning, jumped into the shower and dressed for Tracy's big day. She went into her kitchen and found James sitting at the breakfast bar drinking a cup of coffee. He pointed to the pot sitting on the cabinet, "It's nice and fresh," he said with a grimace. She smiled at the sight of James being in her home. Come to think of it, this was the first time he had spent the night at her place. She walked over to him and kissed him on the cheek, "Would you like some real breakfast?"

James reached out as she walked past him, pulled her back into his arms and kissed her until she relaxed into his lap. As he ended the kiss he looked into her eyes and smiled, "If we were home, breakfast would be waiting for us on the table."

Ashley exhaled as she placed kisses on his neck and replied, "Well you're not at home and you need to learn how to cook anyway." She hit him lightly on the shoulder then turned and walked over to the refrigerator. She pulled out bacon, eggs, cheese, fruit and juice then placed them on the counter. She picked up the remote to the television and turned on the morning news. Within a matter of minutes, breakfast was ready.

As they sat eating breakfast and comparing plans for the day, the newscaster mentioned the luncheon being held with Tracy as the guest speaker. The announcement surprised Ashley. "I thought we were down playing the luncheon. Give Tracy a chance to get accustomed to speaking in public," she said looking at James.

"That was the plan, until you and Tracy came out with this awesome speech, as Pearl called it. She felt this event may do better than expected." He said and then added as if an afterthought, "Oh, by the way, your mother-in-law will be there along with Nicki and a few friends."

"Nicki is coming from New York for this?"

"Yes. She said she wouldn't want to miss seeing you in action. This will also give my mother a chance to meet your mother."

Ashley looked up at James. "I suppose that's a good thing, but I'm not sure this event would be the right place. I mean Tracy is ready, but she is in no way comfortable about the turn out for this event. It will take all my attention just to keep her from backing out."

James stood up and kissed Ashley on the cheek. "You can handle it; you can handle just about anything." She smiled as she watched him walk into the kitchen. When she looked down she noticed the paper from yesterday in the wastebasket. She knew that was not where she put the paper the night before. She shrugged her shoulders and just assumed James had put the paper in the wastebasket. "Are you going to get Brian to check on a security system for here?"

"Yes," James replied. "But with everything going on, he may not get to it today. Speaking of security, I don't think it's a good idea to have a key outside your door. Anyone could reach above the door and use the key to get in. I would think the incident at JD's old place would have taught you that."

"I know, but it's an old habit. JD and I use to lose our keys all the time, so my mother would keep one above the door so we could get into the house. Tracy would do the same thing when we were in college. I would have to call her to let me in the room all the time."

"Times are different now. I prefer you calling someone to let you in, rather than the key being available to anyone." James walked over to where Ashley sat, picked her up as if she was the weight of a child. "Actually I prefer that you not need a key to get into this place. The only key you should need is the one to our home." He smiled as he proceeded back to the bedroom.

"You do realize it's after six and we have a big day ahead of us," she purred as she kissed the side of his neck.

"Precisely why I need you, to jump start my day."

She exhaled as he laid her on the bed. As he removed his slacks and joined her in bed she watched and wondered if all their mornings would be like this. She smiled up at him. "September 16th."

James pulled her on top of him and smiled. "That's four months away, it's too long," he said as he gently lifted her at the waist and guided her down, embedding himself firmly within her. He closed his eyes savoring the feel of her surrounding him. There had never been a time that she has not been ready for him. Even during her sleep, when he entered her she was always a perfect fit, always moist and ready. He opened his eyes and watched her body move above his. He moaned as he pulled her down within a breath's touch from his lips, "four months is too long," he managed to get out before losing his senses to her movements.

Two hours later, James and Ashley walked into campaign headquarters. Because of the day's events, the office was abuzz even at eight on a Saturday morning. The luncheon with Tracy and the appearance later with all the candidates had everyone multi-tasking to ensure both events went off without a hitch. At least fifty of the two hundred volunteers were at the office preparing signs, posters, banners, balloons and more to identify their candidate. James smiled as he walked through the office and thanked everyone for their assistance. He led Ashley toward his office and whispered, "This is going to be a good day." He opened the office door. Ashley walked through first, facing James. Her back was to the office as she smiled up at him and replied, "It's not going to be as good as this morning was."

James' smile began to slowly fade when he stepped into the office and looked beyond Ashley. David Holt was sitting in a chair at the far end of the office. "Good Morning," he said as he uncrossed his legs and stood. James immediately and possessively took Ashley's waist and maneuvering her behind him. He turned and closed the door ensuring the volunteers did not witness any incidents. "What in the hell are you doing here?" James asked as he attempted to progress closer to David.

"James," Ashley called out while holding his arm and pulling him back.

"Brooks, this is business. I did not come here to cause any problems for you or Ashley. I actually came to apologize," David said in a very calm, convincing voice.

James crossed his arms across his chest, then stepped backwards shielding Ashley away from David. "Is that so?" he asked, as the veins in his neck begin to throb.

"Yes it is." David replied as he looked around James to Ashley. "Ashley, I was completely out of line last month and I do apologize. You had a few harsh words to say to me that I never thought I would hear from you. I'm not using that as an excuse, I reacted badly and I hope you can accept my apology. I wish you every happiness in your marriage."

Ashley looked around James who was standing directly in front of her and was so close when she breathed in, his shirt connected with her nose. She placed her hand on his back pushing the shirt away from her face then looked around his shoulder. "You should not have come here, David," she said.

"I agree, but I was ordered to speak with both of you this morning, prior to tonight's rally." David looked from Ashley to James. He could tell, by the look in James' eyes, he was not buying the bull. David kept face and smirked to himself, he really didn't care if James accepted his apology or not. "Brooks, you and I will never be friends. But both of us are professionals and we know a united front is needed in this campaign. You have your reasons to dislike me, I give you that. We need to be, at the very least, cordial to each other during the campaign. If the battle lines need to be redrawn afterwards, then we will draw them at that time."

Ashley could not see the look on James' face because his body still had her pinned between the door and him. But she could tell by the tension in his body that he did not believe David's sincerity. "Ashley step outside," James said.

"No!" Ashley replied.

"James never took his eyes off of David, "Ashley step outside now!" he demanded.

"I'm not leaving you in this room alone with him." James turned and stared down at her. She was certain fire was coming from his nostrils and was just as certain the flame was directed at her. She would much rather that flame be directed at David instead of her. "I'll step out, but you have people in this office, behave yourself," she said as she slipped out the door. When she heard the lock turn on the door, she immediately pulled out her cell phone and called Brian. She told him to get downstairs with the key to James office immediately.

Meanwhile, James turned back to David. He put his keys on the desk and removed his suit jacket then put it on the back of his chair. David stood there and watched James' meager attempts to calm himself down. Any other time, David would have gone for the kill and said anything to set the man off. But Gavin ordered him to clear the air or leave the campaign. So David was willing to endure whatever he had to, to stay on the campaign.

"I'm trying to remember our previous conversation." James began speaking with a ghostly calm. "I distinctly recall telling you to stay away from Ashley. Apparently you were too stupid to understand my meaning or chose to ignore my warning." James moved to stand directly in front of David. He put his hands into his pocket to keep them from going around David's throat. James, at six feet four, stood three inches over David. The two stared each other down, neither giving an inch.

David smirked at James, "You know what your problem is Brooks? You really are not sure if you have her. That's why I'm a threat to you. If you truly had her, nothing I did would pull her away." He looked directly into James eyes. "Are you sure, Brooks? Are you sure you have her?" he asked, then displayed a sheepish smile.

It seemed something in James erupted at that moment. His hands went around David's throat in a flash with a force that shook the room. David's body slammed against the wall and began to move upward. David's hands went to the arm of the hand that was constricting his airflow.

Brian unlocked the door and entered the room. He stopped. The sight of David against the wall with his feet dangling was interesting. Then he noticed James still had his left hand in his pocket. He was holding a two hundred pound man up by his throat with one hand. There wasn't any indication that he was straining in any way. *Damn, I'm glad he's my friend,* Brian thought. In no hurry to interrupt the action taking place, he turned, locked the door then leaned against it. He crossed his arms over his chest then looked up at David. "Man will you ever learn?" He then looked at James, "If you are not going to kill him at this moment, and I prefer that you don't, put the man down."

James pulled David forward by the throat and slammed him back against the wall as David continued to struggle to free himself. "Don't ever touch her again. Do we understand each other?" he asked David, who was physically incapable of responding.

Brian walked over to James and tapped him on the shoulder. "I don't think he can answer you with your hand around his throat."

James looked at Brian, "That puts him in one hell of a predicament since I have no intentions of releasing him until he is able to communicate, with me, that he understands."

The look in James eyes indicated he was serious. Brian exhaled and looked up at David. "Wiggle your feet if you understand the man, asshole." David kicked his feet out as much as he could. Brian looked at James, "I don't believe him, but he indicated he understands. Now, let the man down." Brian stepped back as James released David and he fell to the floor, gagging to catch his breath. The thump caused Ashley to begin banging on the door. Brian walked over to the door then cracked it open. He looked at Ashley and smiled, "He's still alive," then closed the door.

James stooped down to where David landed. He never looked directly at David, but stared at the wall just above his head. "My patience with you has come to an end. The next time you touch her in anyway will be the last time you breathe." James stood and calmly walked around to his desk and took a seat. Brian smiled, and then helped David to his feet. He knew he could not let David leave the room with all the volunteers wondering what in the hell was happening. Brian unlocked the door once David took a seat in the chair the furthest away from James. Ashley rushed into the room and looked around. Other than the vein that was about to explode in James's neck, and the color that was not in David's face, things appeared to be calm.

She looked at James and knew he was trying hard to stay composed. "James," she began in the sweetest voice, "I love you. Will you be around to marry me on August sixteenth?"

James looked up at her and smiled. "That's three months away. It's still too long." Ashley smiled then turned and walked out of the room. She noticed the people staring with questions on their face, "Can you believe they are in there arm wrestling?" Ashley shook her head then pulled out her cell phone and dialed Tracy's number. It was time to refocus on the task for the day.

Ashley arrived at JD and Tracy's home a full hour later than planned. As she entered through the front door she found herself being pulled forward by her brother and led into his study. Once JD quietly closed the door he turned to her and frowned. "Ash, what in the hell took you so long to get here?"

"There was a situation at headquarters with James and David," she explained as she placed her purse on his desk and leaned back against it.

"David Holt?" JD asked.

"Yeah," Ashley sighed.

"What is it with you and that guy?"

"Nothing important. Where's Tracy?"

JD sighed with worry, "In the shower for the second time this morning."

"She's nervous, that's all. She'll be alright."

"She did not sleep well last night," JD said. "I'm not sure this is a good idea especially with Carolyn being behind it."

Ashley frowned, "What do you mean, Carolyn is behind it?"

From the look he was getting from Ashley, JD realized James had not shared the details of origin of today's luncheon. As he told her what he knew of the situation, he could see the anger beginning to build in her. Not only did he understand it, but was glad it was there. Ashley was just as protective of Tracy's feelings as he. There have been times when Ashley had sided with Tracy against him. He would never forget or live down the words she assaulted him with the night Tracy walked in on him and Vanessa. "Does Tracy know about this?" Ashley asked.

"No, I couldn't tell her. Although she's apprehensive about speaking in public, she wants to do this because she thinks it will help me in the campaign."

"Which it will," Ashley said. "But if Carolyn sabotaged this event, it could harm you politically and Tracy mentally." She walked over to the window and shook her head, "A woman scorned," she exhaled.

JD stood next to his sister, "I don't know, Ash. Carolyn and I were not serious. We were there for each other physically. I can understand this type of reaction from Vanessa, not Carolyn." Ashley put her arms around her brother's waist and put her head against his chest as his arms circled her shoulders. JD put his head on top of his sister's and sighed. "I hate the thought of Tracy being a target because of me. I got into politics to keep that from happening and here we go again."

"No you didn't JD. You may have made the decision at the time Tracy was attacked, but this was where you were going to end up, regardless, and Tracy was meant to be with you. Hell, momma and I are waiting for the day you and Tracy move into the White House."

JD laughed, "You know, I can't help but laugh every time I hear one of you say that. I haven't won any political elections and you and momma already have me winning the biggest election in the country."

"Hey, we believe in you. We don't like you very much, but we believe in you," Ashley laughed.

JD smiled, "You know you love me," he said as he hugged his little sister.

"You have the nerve to have your arms around a thin gorgeous woman, while your wife is in the room with a fat round stomach, carrying your son." Tracy smiled from the doorway.

Both of them turned and folded their arms over their chest and stared; she was radiating. Her skin was smooth, her eyes were glowing and her smile was captivating. JD's only thought was he wanted to keep her pregnant for the rest of their life. "Girl you look good, stomach and all. I like the navy blue pantsuit. You know you actually look sexy," Ashley said as she looked over at her brother. "Don't you think so JD?"

JD continued to stare at his wife. He would love to take her right back upstairs, undress her and make love to her for the rest of the day. "She looks sexier with no clothes on. But there's something missing," he shook his head as if he was trying to determine what it may be. Tracy looked down to make sure she had everything on. "I know what it is." JD said as he walked over to his desk. He opened the top drawer and pulled out a burgundy velvet box. Ashley walked over to the desk as he opened the box. She exhaled and smiled at her brother. JD pulled out a strand of cultured pearls, then walked over and kissed his smiling wife. "No true politician's wife would ever find themselves without a strand of pearls." He stood behind Tracy and placed the pearls around her neck. Ashley reached into her purse and pulled out her cell phone, with a camera. She snapped a picture of the couple as JD put his hands around his wife's protruding stomach. Tracy smiled up at her husband while she touched the pearls. Ashley thought it was the perfect moment for the two and smiled. She hoped to share a moment like this with James one day.

"Okay you two, that's enough of the mushy stuff. Both of you have appearances to do today and we are already behind schedule," Ashley stated. The front door opened and Pearl stepped in. "We're in here," Ashley called out.

"Good morning," Pearl smiled brightly and looked at Tracy. "You appear to be ready for your close up."

"As ready as it gets," Tracy replied as she held on to her husband's hands that still circled her stomach.

The front door opened again, and Brian walked through. "JD?" he called out.

"In the study," JD replied. "You are late."

Brian looked at Ashley, and then noticed Pearl standing next to the desk. "Good morning," he smiled at her. Ashley and Tracy looked at each other then back at Brian. He was dressed impeccably well, which was very unusual for him. Brian turned to JD, "I was delayed with an incident at headquarters."

"Was it the same incident that delayed Ashley?" JD asked.

"One in the same," Brian replied.

"Is everything in order there?" Pearl asked.

"Yes, everything is in order," he smiled and held it.

Ashley raised an eyebrow and looked over at Tracy. Tracy smiled and lowered her eyes. They both recognized the signs of a man smitten. Ashley cleared her throat, "Well it's after ten, what time are the cars due here?" she asked Pearl.

"The drivers will be here at eleven. Mr. Harrison, you and the other candidates are scheduled to do your microphone checks and stage presence at twelve and Tracy you are scheduled to be at the hall by twelve. Mr. Thompson, I hope you are not the only security for this event?" Pearl questioned.

Brian eyebrows drew together, "I'm very capable of handling the protection on this family," he replied, a little insulted.

"I'm sure you are. However, as competent as you may be, you cannot be in two places at one time, therefore, my question still stands. If you are the only security, then I need to contact someone to cover Mrs. Harrison's event, since I'm sure you will insist on covering Mr. Harrison." JD, Tracy and Ashley all looked at Brian for his response. It wasn't often they witnessed a woman speaking to Brian in the dictating tone Pearl used.

The front door opened and Magna Rivera walked in. "Magna!" Tracy called out surprised. "My security is here," Tracy exclaimed joyously as she walked over and hugged Magna. It was Magna who handled security on Tracy after the attack and the two became very close. Then Magna returned to D.C. When James asked Tracy to do the research on Brian's Agency, Magna was the first person she contacted. "It's great to see you."

Ashley walked past Brian and whispered, "Saved by the door," she grinned.

"Don't you think you have caused enough trouble for one morning?" Brian snapped back. His attention turned back to Pearl. There was something about the woman that put his nerves on edge. But he was certain he would get over that real soon. "As you can see, security arrangements were made for Mrs. Harrison. You will soon learn not to question my competency." He stated with hands on his hips and a tone that would make grown men back down.

"I'm glad to see it." Pearl replied. As she walked out of the room she continued, "You will have more opportunities to prove yourself to me, Mr. Thompson."

Brian watched as she walked out the room. JD watched Brian watching Pearl and smiled, "I believe you have been bitten," he smirked as he hit Brian on the shoulder.

"There's not a woman around who is capable of provoking that particular feeling in me. And that one's mouth needs to be tamed." Brian replied as he took a seat at JD's desk.

JD smiled, "Of course you are the man to tame her."

Brian ran his hand down his face, "I have been known to tame a lion or two," he crooned.

Precisely at noon, the car containing, Tracy, Ashley and Pearl pulled up to the hall where the luncheon was being held. Tracy looked around and noticed there weren't a lot of cars in the parking lot of the very stylish building. "Don't worry about the turnout," Pearl said as she noticed Tracy's expression. "If it's a small crowd that makes it more intimate and meaningful for those who attend."

"But the low turnout will not help JD in the polls." Tracy smiled shyly.

"It will if he wins by one vote and the vote just happened to be from one of the women you speak to today," Ashley stated as she pushed Tracy forward.

Pearl smiled at the two friends. She had spent a lot of time around the two over the past month and found they complimented each other. Ashley was outgoing, feisty and wise beyond her years. Tracy was quiet, reserved and had a deep understanding of people. She was meant to be the woman behind a strong leader. The more time she spent with JD and Tracy Harrison, the more she began to believe James' theory on where their futures lie.

The three women walked into the reception hall. It was elegantly decorated with tables dressed in white linen tablecloths with a navy blue overlay. There were small crystal holders with blue and white flower pedals surrounding white floating candles. The chairs were covered with alternating blue and white linen covers with bows on the back. There were two long tables on the stage on both sides of the podium decorated in the same manner. "The ambiance is nice, but it lacks the TNT touch." Ashley stated then walked towards the back of the stage.

Tracy smiled at her friend, "It's lovely, be nice. Everyone doesn't support the same businesses. It's called free enterprise." Tracy and Pearl went to the podium. Tracy looked out over the room, "If they are not expecting a big crowd, why did they set up so many tables?"

Pearl knew the answer, but did not want to tell Tracy, this was supposed to be a set up. Once the media noticed the low turnout, Carolyn would have her proof that Tracy is not capable in assisting JD in his political aspirations. "We are not going to worry about that. The only thing we are concerned with is allowing some of the public the opportunity to get to know you as a person," Pearl smiled.

Ashley walked further into the back of the building towards voices she heard. Since there were cars outside, she was sure someone was in the building. When she reached the office where the voices were coming from, she immediately recognized Carolyn sitting in the chair, but did not know the other two women. "Hello," the woman behind the desk stood and extended her hand.

"Good afternoon," Ashley replied then turned to Carolyn. "May I speak with you in private Ms. Roth?

"Yes, of course you may. Ladies, this is Ashley Harrison, JD Harrison's sister. Ashley this is Audrey Middleton, president of the Women's Business League and this is," she hesitated for a moment, and then continued, "Katherine, a friend of mine from the D.C. area."

"Hello," Ashley said to the very attractive, stylish woman sitting next to Carolyn. She looked back at Carolyn. "A moment in private?"

"Of course. Ladies would you excuse me for a moment?" Ashley turned and walked away from the door as Carolyn followed. "Yes, Ashley, what can I do for you?"

"Carolyn, I don't like you--never did. But you were a friend of JD's and I respect his opinion. What you planned to do to Tracy today is cold hearted and calculating. I would have never thought you were capable of so much anger.

You have everything a woman could possibly want or need. What I don't understand is why you are angry with Tracy, when it was JD who dumped you?" She shook her head, "But that's neither here or there. In case you did not get the message before, I have Tracy's back on everything. From this moment on you have me to deal with, whenever you go up against her." Ashley began to walk away, "Oh, and I don't scare easily, nor am I a lady, like Tracy."

Ashley turned to walk away when Carolyn called out. "Ashley, believe me, after today you will have issues of your own to deal with. I will be the least of your concerns." She stopped, then continued, "Oh, and by the way I don't mind using anyone to hurt you or Tracy." Carolyn smiled then walked back into the room.

Tracy was scheduled to speak at one o'clock. Mrs. Middleton indicated earlier that the program must proceed as scheduled. Therefore they would not be able to wait for people to arrive. Around twelve thirty, people began to filter in. Mrs. Middleton informed Tracy since the turnout was low, she would place the few people at the tables directly in the front. By twelve forty-five, Tracy's heart was about to drop. She was going to disappoint Jeffrey with a poor showing. Walking over to the window she hung her head.

"Hold that head up girl. You are a Washington, we don't hang our heads."

Tracy turned to see her mother standing in the doorway of the office. "Hey Mom," she had never been happier to see her mother, Lena Washington standing there. Except for when she showed up at the wedding, just in time to get Tracy to the altar. They did not have the hugging kind of relationship, but at that moment, Tracy was so relieved she could not stop the reaction. She hugged her mother, "Thanks for coming."

"Well, I came because I want to have a talk with this Carolyn Roth. But I thought you said a big crowd wasn't expected."

"Mom, ten tables out of fifty is not a big crowd." Tracy smiled nervously.

"There may be only ten tables filled at the moment, but there are at least enough people outside to fill up twenty more tables," Lena advised.

"What?" Tracy asked a little shocked.

"A few of those black sedans you see all the time on TV with important people in them pulled up when I was coming inside. Each one had a few people in them." Ashley and her mother walked into the room as Lena was talking. "Hello Ashley, Martha."

"Hi, Ms. Washington, I didn't know you were going to be in attendance today?" Ashley smiled.

"Well, I'm here for one reason and one reason only, Carolyn Roth. I need to give her a piece of my mind."

"Lena, I thought we talked about that and you said you were going to behave yourself," Martha stated.

Ashley smiled as Tracy frowned. "I gave her a piece of my mind earlier today, but I don't think it did any good."

"I'm sorry, but I have to give that girl a piece of my mind, Old School Style. Let's see if she can handle that," Lena replied

"Count me in. I like the sound of that," Gwendolyn Brooks said as she entered the room.

"Mrs. Brooks, it's good to see you." Ashley smiled as she hugged the woman. "Hey, Nicki, I'm glad you could make it." Ashley turned to Tracy, "This is James' mother and sister, Gwendolyn and Nicki Brooks. This is my best friend and sister-in-law, Tracy Harrison and her mother Lena Washington. And this is my mother," Ashley beamed with pride, "Martha Harrison."

"Which is which?" Lena asked.

"Oh, I like you," Gwen smiled as the other ladies laughed. "Whomever you plan on giving an old school beat down, count me in."

Mrs. Middleton came into the room a little flustered. "You will never believe who is out there!" She announced, putting her hands on her chest.

Everyone paused for a moment staring at the woman who was boarding on hysteria. "It's the First Lady," she spoke in almost a whisper.

"Oh, she made it, that's wonderful," Gwen exclaimed.

Tracy, Ashley and Lena looked from one to the other. "You are not referring to?" Ashley did not finish the question before Gwen answered.

"The one and only," Gwen smiled brightly. "Honey, when I support something or someone," she smiled at Tracy, "I don't half step."

"Oh I like you, I like you!" Lena smiled.

"Come along Mrs. Harrison," Mrs. Middleton reached out for Tracy, "we can't keep these women waiting. Now, I know Ms. Roth will not be happy with the turnout, but I'm thrilled," she exclaimed.

Tracy froze and stared at Mrs. Middleton, "Why would Carolyn care one way or the other?"

"Oh dear, we don't have time to get into this right now," she replied.

"Maybe we need to take a moment and get into it Mrs. Middleton." Gwendolyn stepped in. "Are you married to Arthur Middleton, who is up for re-election to the General Assembly for the Fifth District?"

"Yes." Mrs. Middleton replied a little bothered by the woman's question.

"We haven't met." Gwen smiled, "I'm Mrs. Avery Brooks," she said as she extended her hand with a smile. "We generally make a rather large contribution to your husband's campaign, frankly because there is no one else we like. But that can always change."

"Mrs. Brooks, it is wonderful to meet you." Mrs. Middleton smiled. "Arthur and I appreciate all you and Mr. Brooks do for his campaigns each term," she went on to say more, but Gwen cut her off.

"That's wonderful Audrey, may I call you that?" Gwen said as she guided the woman out of the room. The other ladies with the exception of Lena and Martha, who followed Gwen, stood watching the conversation exchange between the women. Tracy looked at Ashley wondering exactly what was going on.

Pearl walked into the room. "What's the pow wow about?" she asked.

"We're not sure," Tracy replied. "But it doesn't look good."

"Well, you can't worry about that. You, my lady, have a full house, with some recognizable faces out there. Are you ready?"

Tracy took a deep breath, "Let's do it." She grabbed Ashley's hand.

"I'm right behind you," Ashley smiled. "Come with us Nicki."

"I don't know Ashley. That look on Gwen Brooks' face indicates someone is going to catch hell," Nicki smirked.

Ashley smiled. "Well it seems Carolyn is about to feel the raw side of a mother's love for her child." Ashley looked back at the mothers. For a moment, she felt bad for Carolyn. Then a smile slowly appeared on her face. "That woman deserves whatever is dished out, believe that."

Ashley, Martha, Nicki, Lena and Gwen took the last empty seats in the room. Pearl stayed backstage with Tracy and held her hand while the introductions were being made. "When you go out to the podium, look up and straight back," Pearl suggested. "You got this Tracy. Do you. Just do you."

Tracy walked out to an overwhelming applause. Every table in the hall was filled. She looked out and saw Rosaline and Cynthia at the table with Ashley. Then she noticed Senator Roth was standing in the back of the room, which surprised her. She knew he always supported JD, but wondered why he would be at her function. Then she saw Mrs. Harrison, sitting center stage with a few of JD's aunts. Tracy's stomach began to flip flop. She needed to calm down. Taking Pearl's advice she looked up and straight back to the entrance of the hall. There she saw James, Brian, Calvin, Douglas and to her relief, Jeffrey standing there with his arms folded across his chest. With all the people in the room, she could feel the moment their eyes connected. She smiled brightly, then stepped back from the podium and exhaled.

Taking a deep breath, she stepped back up to the podium. Keeping her head down, she spoke softly. "Please be patient with me. I am not the public speaker in my household and my nerves seem to be getting the better of me or it could be the baby—I'm not sure which." The crowd chuckled lightly and then quieted down. "Take your time, baby girl," Lena encouraged.

Tracy nervously smiled. "I will Momma, I will." She cleared her throat and continued. "You may not believe this but, I did prepare a speech for you. It's not forthcoming at the moment." She hesitated, and then continued, "I did not expect to be speaking with such a large, distinguished group of women. Nevertheless, here you are, and I thank you for coming.

I know two things well. One is business, which is what I intended to speak with you on. The other is that tall handsome man standing in the back of the room, my husband Jeffrey Harrison." The crowd turned and applauded JD, who bowed his head graciously. "It doesn't seem any of you need my business advice," she said smiling. "Therefore, I'll tell you about Jeffrey, the way, I know him." There was little mumbling in the crowd. Tracy smiled and shook her head, "No ladies, I will not be sharing intimate details with you. Some of you may try to leave with him and I would like to keep him a little longer." The crowd of women laughed and turned in JD's direction." Tracy smiled, "But I will tell you this. When I say Jeffrey Harrison is a very loving man, I do mean it in every way." The crowd clapped and laughed then turned their attention back to Tracy. "I have resigned myself to the fact that I must share that love with others. Jeffrey loves the citizens of Virginia. He is dedicated, to a fault, at keeping them safe from crime of any kind and ensuring a good education to every child. Most of all, he is dedicated to ensuring everyone has the opportunity to improve their standard of living, wherever it may be. Now, I don't know about you all, but I know those are the qualities I need in my leader. Our opponents will tell you that he is young and inexperienced. I agree with that assessment to an extent. He is young and oh so good looking" she joked. "But he is also quite intelligent and energetic. Now, isn't that what we need to deliver a vision for the future: someone whose mind is open to all possibilities and not limited to the status quo. Don't you think it is time to have new ideas about the future? To have someone who is not intimidated by the old regime, but respectful of all they have accomplished in the past."

The crowd clapped and she continued.

"Isn't it wonderful to have someone who not only cares about his family and friends' well being, but your families and friends as well? Jeffery is a man of integrity and vision. He will not be swayed by partisan politics. He will be guided by what is right and good for the citizens of Virginia. I will be the first to tell you, I am not comfortable in the role as a public figure. Jeffrey, however, was born to be a leader. Since I fell in love with the man, and he wisely chose to fall in love with me, I will be out in front telling anyone who wants to listen and some who do not, the kind of man he is. Yes, he is young and yes in some instances he may have less experience than some. But, ladies I ask you: honestly, if you had a choice between young vibrant and willing to learn or someone set in their ways and not open to new possibilities, what would you choose?"

Women, young, old, Black, White, Hispanic, you name it, yelled out in unison, "Amen to that," and the crowd burst with laughter. Tracy couldn't help but laugh, too.

"I can see my husband blushing from here, so I think I will stop. Please take this bit of information with you. In case I did not say this or make this clear to you, I love my husband. However, I'm not supporting him in this campaign for that reason. I support him because I believe he will lead this state and with the grace of God, one day, this country in the right direction. We have a decision to make in November. We can stay with the old, or we can usher in the new. Roberts, Graham and Harrison is the ticket, please be sure to cast your vote. Thank you for coming and please enjoy your lunch."

The group of women stood and clapped for Tracy as she stepped off the stage. Walking through the crowd her only thoughts were getting to the security of Jeffrey's arms. As if sensing her need, he stepped forward with his arms stretched out to her. He was not able to express to her just how proud he was in words. Therefore, he showed her the only way he could think of, with a kiss. The kiss he bestowed upon her was sensuous, long and deep. Pleased with the show of affection, the crowd cheered louder.

The couple pulled away and stepped out into the lobby. They were immediately surrounded by cameras flashing and reporters with microphones pushed in their direction. A few questions were asked, but they declined interviews. James stepped in with Pearl and handled all questions. JD and Tracy shook the hands of those leaving and thanked them for coming. The ex-First Lady and now Senator stopped to speak with Tracy and all cameras were diverted towards them. "Unfortunately, I am unable to stay for lunch. Thank you for inviting me. You are adorable. Your honesty and love for your husband is very apparent. And from that kiss it seems the feelings are mutual. Don't let anyone change you." She smiled and waved at the cameras. Her Secret Service agents surrounded her and escorted her out the building.

The couple was greeting a few more people when Carolyn rushed into the building, furious. It seemed when she returned to the luncheon, she was not allowed in. She was told no one else could enter the building. The security at the door advised Brian that Ms. Roth was requesting entrance into the building. He advised the young man to tell Ms. Roth, capacity to the room had been reached and only the Fire Marshall could allow anyone inside. Carolyn marched over to Brian, "What the hell do you mean denying me access to this building? Have you forgotten who I am?"

"Carolyn," her father calmly called out. He whispered, "The cameras are on you. Straighten your face and shut up." He kissed her, then smiled at the cameras and reporters. He pulled her inside the hall where a few people were still eating lunch. "We are in campaign mode. Gavin cannot afford your emotions to run amok. Whatever has you pissed off will have to wait. Do I make myself clear?" The Senator glared angrily at his daughter.

"Her plan to embarrass Tracy failed. That's what has your daughter pissed off, John," Gwen said as the Senator turned in her direction.

"Gwendolyn, what on Earth are you doing here?" he smiled as he kissed her cheek, followed by a hug.

"Well, my son, James, is engaged to Ashley. We came to Richmond to support her friend, Tracy. Imagine my surprise to find out your daughter," Gwen looked directly at Carolyn, "attempted to sabotage this event."

John looked at Carolyn and wondered if she really knew how deep she had dug a hole for herself and Gavin by infuriating Gwen Brooks. "I'm sure there is some type of misunderstanding."

"There was no misunderstanding and this is not the first time Carolyn has attempted to intimidate my daughter," Lena said as she approached the threesome. She extended her hand "Lena Washington, Senator. We met before."

The Senator smiled, "Ms. Washington, I would never forget meeting you."

Lena returned the smile. "That's a wonderful sentiment Senator. It would be nice if you could pass some of that charm on to your daughter." Lena put her hands on her hips and walked towards Carolyn. "But since you did not, I would like a moment with her in private."

Senator Roth stepped in between the two women, "Actually, Lena, may I call you Lena?" he said as he placed his hand on the small of her back and turned her away from Carolyn.

Lena batted her lashes and smiled. "Of course you may," and allowed the Senator to steer her in another direction, knowing Gwen would handle Carolyn.

Gwen folded her hands in front of her and said, "Well, Carolyn, that gives us a moment to talk. We can do it here, where there's a possibility that we may be overheard. Or we can take this to the office in the back."

Carolyn turned to walk off, "I don't have anything to discuss with you."

Gwen caught her by the arm, "Then you will listen." She pointed in the direction of the office. Carolyn was not a fool. Snubbing Gwen Brooks would be political suicide, for Gavin. Carolyn gently pulled her arm away and entered the room. She placed her purse on the desk then turned and put her hands on her hips.

Gwen looked Carolyn up and down. She walked pass her and waved her hand in the air, "Child, take your hands off your imagination. No one is in this room except for you and me. And you know you don't scare me. Sit your little ass down."

Carolyn looked at Gwen, appalled at her tone of voice. "You are speaking with the next First Lady of this state. I would think you, of all people, would know how to respect that."

Gwen smirked at Carolyn as she took a seat behind the desk. "You better recognize that I am someone who can make that dream happen or make it disappear." Sitting forward, she folded her hands on the desk. "Do you want to try me?" Carolyn stared at Gwen for a long moment and decided not to try her. Carolyn sat in the same chair she was in earlier in the day. "Wise decision," Gwen smiled. She tilted her head and looked at Carolyn, "You have become such a bitter young woman and it's showing on your face, Carolyn. What makes matters worse; you are bitter about something that was fate. There was nothing you or anyone else could have done to prevent JD and Tracy Harrison from marrying. Any fool can look at those two and know they were meant to be together. What's truly sad is you are with the man you should be with and you are too blind to see it. You and Gavin could be a political powerhouse. But you are so intent on using your energy to destroy something you have no control over." Gwen stood up, walked around the desk, and stopped in front of Carolyn. "Gavin is in love with you. Every time Avery and I see him, he is singing your praises more than his own. And you know how he loves to toot his own horn. But you don't see his love because you are blinded by hatred. Until you release some of that hate, your heart will not have room for the love you are desperately seeking." Gwen walked over to the door. "Think about that. Oh and think about this. If you plot anything further against Ashley, Tracy or anyone connected with this campaign, you will have me to deal with. And believe me; the devastation of Katrina will be mild compared to the forces I will bring down on you."

Gwen opened the door and walked down the corridor leading to the main hall. As she entered she noticed Senator Roth and Lena seated at a table enjoying a private joke. "You two want to share?"

Lena looked at Senator Roth and smiled, "No I think we will keep this one to ourselves."

"Where's Carolyn?" The Senator asked.

"In the back office in need of her father." Gwen smiled.

Senator Roth shook his head. "How much damage has she caused the campaign?"

"None—if she listens," Gwen replied.

"I'll talk to her," Senator Roth said as he stood. "I will be calling you." He smiled at Lena.

"I'll be waiting." Lena smiled.

Gwen watched the Senator walk away then turned to Lena. "Did I miss something?"

Lena smiled back, "A little something." She stood, "Did you talk to that little heifer?"

"Yes I did."

"Did she get the message?"

"I believe she did. I'm just not sure she will take heed."

"Well, I guess it's time for me to step in. I may not have been there to protect my daughter when she was growing up, but I am here now. And I will be damned if I will allow the likes of Carolyn Roth to hurt my child in any way."

Gwen looked at Lena. Something told her this was not a woman she wanted as an enemy. "Whatever you have planned; count me in. I will do anything to help my child accomplish his dreams. Like you, I have not always been there for my son, James. He wants JD Harrison in office. Whatever James wants, is what he is going to get."

Lena smiled at Gwen, "Well alright then. Let the games began.

Chapter 9

James and Ashley were awakened by the sudden ringing of the telephone. The events of the night before had them out late and neither wanted to move. Reluctantly, James answered the annoying contraption as he pulled Ashley into his arms. It was Pearl indicating reporters were requesting interviews with the candidates and their wives. She thought it was a good idea to keep the momentum of the rally going in their favor. James agreed as Ashley stretched in his arms. He indicated he would meet her at the office within the hour. He knew the rally was a huge success and that they needed to build on that. But his body wanted to stay where it was, wrapped around his woman. He kissed Ashley's forehead. "Babe, I have to go into the office."

"So I heard," Ashley replied, as she snuggled closer. "You want me to go with you?"

"I always want you with me." He smiled as he pulled her closer.

"I need to stop by to see Tracy, and then I'll meet you at headquarters," she sleepily replied, and snuggled a little closer.

"That will work."

Thirty minutes later the couple still lay entangled. The telephone rang, again. It was the hospital. Karen Holt called indicating she needed to see him. James quickly showered, dressed and left. This did not sit well with Ashley. It was not the first time she had been set aside by him because of Karen Holt.

Ashley was feeling out of sorts when James left to see Karen. She decided to bypass church. Martha was not going to be happy with that, but that was just how she felt. A part of her was jealous and another was curious. All she knew was James got out of the bed with her to go to another woman. The thought of it pissed her off. As she told James, she stopped by to see JD and Tracy, to congratulate them on the rally. She knew they planned to attend morning service and should be home by now.

By all accounts the functions from the day before were all well received by the public. Tracy was receiving numerous requests to speak again and JD received thousands of dollars in support for the campaign. Overnight polling data showed tremendous gains and everyone was singing praises for the entire Democratic ticket.

Ashley walked through the side door and found Tracy in the sunroom with Pearl going over interview requests. "Hey," Ashley spoke solemnly.

Tracy looked up smiling brightly, "Hey Ashley." Then she frowned, "You don't look too happy. What's going on?"

"Hey Pearl. What did the reviews look like?" Ashley asked.

"Pretty good," Pearl replied nodding her head. "As a matter of fact, I think Tracy's popularity will take over Carolyn's."

Ashley smirked as she sat in the seat across from Tracy. "That shouldn't be hard. Carolyn can be a real bitch when she wants to."

Tracy looked at her friend and noticed the sparks that usually enter the room along with her was missing. "Where's James?" Tracy curiously asked.

Ashley threw her head back on the chair, covered her face with her hands, and muffled, "I think I might be pregnant." The room was silent as Pearl and Tracy looked at each other and then to Ashley. Pearl started to speak, but Tracy touched her arm and stopped her. Tracy waited until Ashley was ready to continue. "The only thing I can figure is when we went to meet James' family, we were suppose to only be going for dinner and ended up staying two days. I did not take my pills with me. When I came back, I really did not take notice of the missed pill or pills." She stopped talking and sighed loudly. "The truth is: I hope I am. I want to have James' baby. I'm not sure how he is going to feel about it." She put her hands down and pulled her head back up. Tracy was smiling at her waiting. "Oh shut up!" Ashley shouted as she threw the pillow from the seat at her.

Tracy blocked the pillow and began to laugh. "I think it's wonderful. Your child will have James' brains and your beauty. Have you taken the test?"

"No, I haven't," Ashley said smirking at Tracy with a fake grin.

"I'll go to the drugstore and pick up a test," Pearl offered as she stood.

"No need." Tracy smiled. "There are two upstairs in my bathroom. I'll get them." She jumped up and ran upstairs to retrieve the test.

Ashley slumped back in the seat. "My mother is going to freak."

Pearl laughed at the woman sitting across from her. She did not know Ashley well, but she really liked her spirit. "Your mother will not freak. She will be happy to have another grandchild to spoil on the way."

"Are you crazy? Martha Harrison is not going to like the fact that her daughter will be having a child out of wedlock."

"But you and James are planning on getting married, anyway. What's the problem?" Pearl asked.

"Planning and being married are two different things. The wedding is being planned. This is June. If what I suspect is true, I will be a few months pregnant before I walk down the aisle."

"From what I can see, you are the one prolonging the wedding, not James. Move the date up. Get married next month, that way your mother will not know," Pearl suggested.

Tracy reentered the room with the test boxes in her hand. "Here you go," she said smiling.

Ashley took the boxes. "Where's JD?" She asked.

"He had a meeting after church with Gavin and Dan. He will not be home for a while," Tracy stated to ease Ashley's concerns.

"This may just be wishful thinking. Yesterday when I took the picture of you and JD, I wished I was carrying James' child and he was holding me the way JD held you. Then this morning I couldn't understand why I was so irritable. Then I realized my "Aunt Ruby" had not arrived. To tell you the truth, I can't remember the last time. " Ashley said as she stood.

Tracy hugged Ashley. "I'm sure James will be overjoyed with this news. Now stop procrastinating and go take the test. I want to know if I am going to be an aunt soon."

"This could cause an issue for the campaign," Pearl mentioned to Tracy once Ashley left the room. Tracy looked at Pearl with a questionable smile. "Ashley is JD's sister and, like it or not, there are still people who stand on the higher moral ground regarding situations such as this."

"I'm not sure that it's anyone's business. What's happening should only concern James and Ashley." Tracy replied.

Pearl looked at her. Was she that naive about politics? "It's a political year; everything about your husband is open to the public, even your pregnancy."

Ashley walked back into the room. Pearl and Tracy turned to look at her. "I'm going home," was all she said as she picked up her purse and left the house.

Ashley walked up the stairs to her condo and sat at the dining room table. She reached in her purse and pulled out the pregnancy test. She stared at it and wondered why her life couldn't be simple like JD's? He met the woman of his dreams; they fell in love, got married and are now expecting their first child. She had to convince the man she loved that he loved her. When he decided he wanted to marry her, she finds out he had kept his identity from her and now this. Ashley answered the telephone as the chime interrupted her thoughts. "Yes, Tracy, it was positive. No, Tracy I have not decided if I will tell James or have the baby."

"Well, I think you should talk to James. I know you are still bothered with the fact he kept certain information from you about his family. But he had his reasons and you said you accepted it. Now, there's a baby in the future. Which, just in case I haven't said it, I'm very happy about. I think you are scared of what your mom might say more than you are of James' reaction. But whatever you decide you know I have your back. Just talk to James first."

A tear dropped down Ashley's cheek. "I really do want the baby, but I'm not sure how James will feel. We never discussed children, other than James Jr., of course."

"Do you love James, Ashley?" Tracy asked

"More than life."

"Then don't be afraid of having it all. Marry James and give me a niece or nephew and a cousin to play with JC."

Ashley laughed, "You decided on a name for the baby?"

"Yes, Jon-Christopher."

"JC, I like it. I wish my life was as simple as yours."

"Hey, I've been through enough drama, I deserve this simple life. Unfortunately, it will not stay that way for long. I believe JC will be the only child we have who will get Jeffrey's undivided attention. Once he is elected into office, our life will be anything but simple. So don't be so quick to want the life I have. Go and capture the life that was meant for you. Talk to James."

When Ashley hung up the phone she looked at the test again. The stick had a blue plus sign, shining brightly at her. She closed her eyes and said a quick prayer. She shook the stick up and down with all her might then stopped and waited for a full minute. Ashley slowly opened one eyelid and peeked at the stick. The plus sign was still there and Ashley could have sworn she heard the stick laugh at her. "Ahh sh..." she screamed kicking her legs like a child not getting her way.

An hour later, she decided to go to James' house. She would cook dinner and give Clair the evening off. That way, she and James could talk freely. Maybe Tracy was right, he might not be upset.

Ashley noticed a car in the driveway when she pulled up, so she parked on the street in front of the house. The set of keys James gave her opened the door leading from the garage into the kitchen. Normally, she would have used that entrance, but since she was closer to the front door she rung the doorbell. "Hello Clair," Ashley said as she opened the door.

"Hello Ms. Ashley, did you lose your key?"

"No," she replied. "Someone was parked in the driveway, so I parked on the front."

"Mr. Brooks is not home," Clair said nervously.

"Yeah, I know. I came to cook dinner and give you a night off"

"How sweet," a voice said from the kitchen doorway. Ashley looked at the woman standing in the doorway addressing her. The same woman was with Carolyn at the luncheon. Ashley looked at Clair. "You may excuse yourself now Clair," the woman ordered.

Ashley frowned, not liking the tone of voice the woman used to address Clair. "Clair you are welcome to stay," she said as she walked over to the woman. "We weren't properly introduced the other day. Hello, I'm Ashley Harrison and you are?"

The woman looked at Clair demanding her exit. Clair excused herself and left the room. "I'm not in the habit of speaking in front of the help," the woman stated.

Ashley raised an eyebrow and dropped her keys on the stand by the door. "Clair is a respected part of this household, not the help as you put it. Who are you?"

"I am Katherine Stallworth-Brooks; Mrs. James Brooks to you."

Ashley had never seen a picture but the image in front of her is exactly what she anticipated of the former Mrs. James Brooks. Ashley made a quick assessment as Katherine stood in the foyer. She stood about five-six in heels; weight approximately one hundred and ten to one twenty, smooth cinnamon skin with brownish red hair. She was tailored from head to toe. This woman made Ashley think twice about her appearance. Ashley was always immaculate, but there was something about the woman that made Ashley's five eight frame seem unfeminine.

"Now, I have a question for you. Why are you here?" Katherine asked.

"Let's try that another way; why are you here?" Ashley asked placing her purse on the table.

Katherine laughed, "You dare to question me? You are a bold one. James normally selects the meek and mild; someone he can handle; the very opposite of me."

"I'm so sorry to disappoint you, but I'm neither meek nor mild." Ashley replied, "Nor am I in the mood to play tit for tat. Is James expecting you?"

"I'm not in the habit of explaining myself to one of James' booty calls. However if you must know, I do have some business to discuss with my husband."

"There's an invention called the telephone. It's really simple to use. Just pick it up and dial."

Katherine smiled; there was something about this woman she liked. Normally James doesn't give keys to his house out or allow any woman to spend time with James Jr. But lately, her son had mentioned the friend of his dad and Katherine had to make sure this new friend did not interfere with her or her son. She did not know what to expect, but certainly not this young statuesque beauty standing in front of her. By all accounts, she was not easily intimidated.

Ashley smiled as she folded her arms across her chest. "I am losing my patience here. I will ask one last time, is James expecting you?"

"My, my, aren't you a little bitch." Katharine said as she walked towards Ashley. "Let me give you a little information. I don't know what your status is here. Nevertheless, this is my husband's home. If anyone is going to demand answers to questions it will be me. Fortunately for you, I don't care enough about who you are to waste my time. But whatever plans you had for tonight just got cancelled."

"Ex-husband's home Katherine," James said from the kitchen. "Now, you may not have to answer the question for Ashley, but you damned well better answer it for me. What are you doing here?" James asked as he placed his keys on the tray with Ashley's.

"Good evening James. It's good to see you," Katherine said without a hint of panic.

"Why are you here? Is James Jr. okay?" James asked, concerned.

"I need to speak with you in private concerning him," Katherine replied sadly.

Not believing Katherine, James turned and smiled at Ashley. "Hey, what are you doing here this early?"

"I came by to cook dinner and talk. Imagine my surprise," Ashley replied.

"Equal to mine, I'm sure. I really wanted to talk to you tonight. Can you hang around?" James asked with a longing look on his face. Ashley knew James well. He was worried about something, she just wasn't sure what. Ashley looked over at Katherine. "It looks as if you are going to be busy tonight. Why don't you call me when you finish; I'll be at home."

James wanted Ashley to stay. So much had occurred today and he needed to tell her about it. Now Katherine was here. This was the last thing he needed. "I'll call you later," he said.

Ashley walked past him and Katherine, picking up her keys. "Interesting meeting you Mrs. Brooks," she said as she walked out the door.

James looked at Katherine, for the first time in a long time he had no reaction to her at all. He was not angry to see her nor was he apprehensive. "What is it Katherine?" he asked.

"How have you been James?" Katherine asked sweetly.

Ashley was at her wits' end. What was Carolyn doing with James's ex-wife? More importantly why is his ex-wife here? She was trying to be gracious by allowing James time to deal with his ex, but she did not like it at all. Earlier, it was Karen Holt, now it's Katherine. Something had to give. Ashley called Tracy. When she did not get an answer she called her cell. "I went to talk to James and guess who shows up?"

"Who?" Tracy said recognizing Ashley's tone.

"The ex-wife."

"What?"

"Yes, Katherine the Great was at the house when I got there. She promptly advised me, she was Mrs. Brooks and any plans I had for the evening had come to an end."

"Why was she there?"

"I don't know Tracy."

"Where are you now?" Tracy asked, concerned.

"I'm driving around in the rain," Ashley cried.

"Ashley, why don't you head to the condo and I will meet you there."

"I don't want to go there and twiddle my fingers until James gets there. The whole time, I will be wondering what is going on at his house. Is JD home yet?"

"No, he's at a fundraiser with Gavin. I really don't want to be around Carolyn. Where are you heading, I'll meet you."

"I'm going to Momma's house," Ashley replied.

"Okay, I'll meet you there."

"I need a drink," Ashley screamed.

"You can't drink; you're pregnant."

"Damn, I need something to relax my nerves. I'll call Cynthia and Rosaline. Maybe they can meet us and we can have a girl's night out. Anything to get my mind off of Katherine the Great."

"Please, Ash, calm down. I'll meet you at your Mom's house in an hour. Okay?"

"Okay Tracy, I'll see you there"

Ashley went into her Mom's house. It seemed no one was home. She lay on the sofa in the sunroom. How in the hell did she get herself into this situation? Another man she loved was going to leave her; first her father; then David; then JD and now James. Not only was his ex-wife too beautiful for words, she seemed to know how to work James. To add to her problems, how will James react when she tells him she's pregnant? That will give him more incentive to leave.

James' child. For a moment Ashley smiled. The thought of it was somewhat nice. Lord knows she loved the man, but the question was, did he want another child?

Ashley closed her eyes and remembered the week following JD and Tracy's wedding, that was when she and James really got to know each other. That night, or should we say the next morning, because no one left that reception until the next morning, she stayed with James at his home. He did not want her to be alone. After all it was New Year's Eve, the time for new beginnings. They stayed at his place for days, talking, laughing and just enjoying each other's company. The only time they left the house was to meet JD and Tracy before they left for their honeymoon. Other than that, they spent the next two days talking about life and, of course, making love. It was then they developed a working relationship for JD's campaign. The two complemented each other well. The message "Rejuvenate the State," was formed by the two of them to emphasize JD's accomplishments at such a young age. James began to realize just how much of a diamond in the rough Ashley was. He had always been attracted to brilliant people. His initial attraction to Tracy was because of her business mind, which was evident. Ashley's brilliance was not as visual, but once they began developing strategies together it was clear that Ashley was far above average in her field. James already loved her free spirit and the way she had of handling difficult situations with humor and kindness.

Ashley turned over on the sofa and placed her arm on her forehead. Why did she doubt James' love for her now that Katherine was here? All those insecurities keep surfacing. Was it the fact that only four months ago when they were in Jamaica, he could not tell her he loved her? On the other hand, it could be the way she had to keep her feelings to herself when it came to James Jr.

On the few occasions Ashley was allowed around him, it seemed James was so intent on making the boy a man, he forgot to let James Jr. be a little boy first. When Ashley spoke on it; the display from James was worse than the first time she spoke about the little boy. This was the one area James did not tolerate any interference. The first time Ashley attempted to include James Jr. in their holiday plans, James made it very clear, no one interferes with his relationship with his son. So Ashley never broached the subject again. It was only recently, that James did not purposely keep her at a distance on the weekends James Jr. was over. Now, the two had formed a good relationship, but Ashley could still feel James' reluctance to look at the three of them as a family.

Then there was Karen Holt. Ashley believed James involvement was professional. However, there were too many times that the subject of Karen came to her attention. Not to mention the remarks David would make about James and Karen. Now Ashley knew anything that came out of David's mouth was suspect. David only wanted to cause problems for her and James anytime he could. But Ashley's insecurities about James let her imagination wonder and no matter how hard she tried to keep things inside, it always ventured out. Then there was this thing with Lena Washington. She knew the connection between James and Lena had to do with JD and Tracy. But there were times when James and JD would be discussing Lena, and the conversation would come to an abrupt stop when she entered the room. Still Ashley did not understand why James had to play such an involved role in the situation. Especially now that Tracy and her mom had an open line of communication.

Ashley sighed. There were just too many issues that had not been addressed with the two of them to bring another issue into focus. As much as Ashley would love to have the baby, it would cause problems between her and James. It was a sad situation to have to choose between having James or having their baby. Now was just not a good time for a baby. A tear escaped Ashley's eyes; she wanted both.

James' patience had been tested before, but never to the extent Katherine had just experienced. If she wasn't sure before, she was now: James had no love in his heart for her. He made it clear the part she had in his life was that of the mother of his son. Therefore, she had no choice but to use that to try to manipulate James. Carolyn pulled in her marker. She wanted Katherine to do whatever she could to cause havoc on the relationship between James and Ashley.

Katherine stood on James patio watching him and James Jr. in the yard throwing a football. She took a sip of her drink and wondered the best way out of this situation.

There was always the option of facing the truth. But at this point, would that cause more damage to James and his family? "Damn!" she exclaimed aloud. "Why did I ever talk to that woman?" She had no one to blame but herself. She gave Carolyn the upper hand. Now she had to find a way to take that hand away. Carolyn's wedding was in two weeks.

That's how long Carolyn had given her to break up James and Ashley. Katherine had no idea how manipulative Carolyn could be until she received the call threatening to expose her well-guarded secret if she did not comply. If she complied it could change life as she knows it for her and her son. James made sure neither her nor James Jr. wanted for anything. He had truly been good to her. She just could not bring herself to disrupt James' life, not after the loyalty he had shown her when any other man would have turned their back. "No Carolyn, you will not get your way this time. I will not be used." Katherine said aloud.

The situation called for tact if she was to pull this off without causing harm to herself or her son. "Who could handle the information and not use it against her or James? Who had the balls to stand up to Carolyn Roth without causing any damage to the campaign? Who had the finesse and persuasiveness to get Carolyn out of our life, Katherine thought as she watched James Jr. tackling his father. Suddenly, she smiled. She picked up the cordless telephone on the table and dialed a telephone number.

"Butchie, I love you, but if you are calling to pull my wife from this house again, I'm going to cause you serious bodily harm. She just got home from the last time you called." Avery yelled into the telephone. "Remember I'm your father. I brought you into this world and I will take you out if you keep interrupting my downtime."

"I apologize for the interruption, Avery, this is Katherine."

Avery hesitated then looked at the Caller ID, again; it did show James' home number. "Sorry about that, Katherine. What are you doing at James' house?"

"No need to worry, Avery, this visit is for James Jr., not me. By the way, I'm fine thank you for asking."

"You always land on your feet, Katherine. I'm sure it has something to do with having nine lives."

"Yes, well, Avery, we could toss insults back and forth all night. Unfortunately I don't have the time. I need to speak with Gwendolyn."

Avery snickered, "You're going from the frying pan into the fire." He handed the telephone to Gwen.

"Katherine?" Gwen spoke with uneasiness.

"Gwendolyn, do you know Carolyn Roth?"

"Yes I do. She reminds me of you."

"We need to put aside our differences and work together to keep her from destroying James. Are you willing to do that?"

"What does Carolyn have to do with James?'

"Nothing, its James' fiancée, and she's using me to do it."

Anger immediately entered Gwen's voice. "Don't you think you have caused him enough harm?"

Katherine exhaled, "Yes, I do. That's why I'm calling you. I don't want to be the person to crush James' heart again. Unfortunately, Carolyn knows details about our situation and has threatened to make them known if I don't cooperate with her scheme to break up James and Ashley. And to be frank, I don't want to be a pawn in her game."

"I'm not sure how Carolyn could know more than James, since he was there. The only way she could cause damage is if James has not told Ashley."

Katherine hesitated, but she was certain Gwendolyn's love for her sons was stronger than her hatred for her. "Gwen there is more to James and my break up than you know and Carolyn knows the whole story."

Gwendolyn closed her eyes and shook her head. Her son just came back into her life and had begun to reach out to her again. There was no way in hell she was going to allow the likes of Carolyn Roth or Katherine Stallworth-Brooks take that away from her. James had a light in his eyes again and Gwen was not going to see that light go dim again. "Ashley has put the love back in James' heart that you took away. If you do anything to hurt him again, life as you know it will end. I will start with the monthly living allowance, then I will take the house and last, but certainly not least of all, I will have the trust fund changed, irrevocably. So whatever your friend Carolyn has planned stops here."

"The threat isn't necessary, Gwendolyn. I called you to help me stop what Carolyn is trying to do. But remember, I have your only grandson. You don't want to piss me off. Fortunately for you, I don't want to see James hurt by anyone. I am content to let our dirty laundry remain in the closet, but we have to make sure Carolyn doesn't air it out."

"Alright, Katherine, you have my cooperation," Gwen replied calmly. But don't be fooled, I can have my grandson removed from your custody at anytime I wish. He is with you because we know you are a wonderful mother; on that you are beyond reproach. Don't ever use that threat against us again. Now that we have dispensed with all the niceties, tell me what Carolyn knows on my son."

As James climbed the stairs to Ashley's condo, he sensed uneasiness in the air. The last few days had been hectic on all fronts and had demanded his attention. The campaign was beginning to pick up its activities with events planned daily. Brian's agency was in full bloom: his staff now consisted of ten private security personnel, five private investigators and a receptionist. The other offices throughout the building were being leased faster than they were completed.

Then there was the situation with Karen Holt. On the day of the kickoff, David was not too pleased with the way James had manhandled him. He, in turn, took that out on Karen. She thought the abuse would stop now that David was working on a promising campaign. James knew better. Karen now believed David needed help and so did she. She called James the morning after the rally when she found herself in yet another emergency room and advised him she had enough, and decided to leave David. James turned to Brian and Douglas to help him get Karen situated in an apartment and to give her protection until David accepted her decision.

In addition to those circumstances, James accidentally ran across Senator Roth and Tracy's mother, Lena Washington out on what appeared to be a very intimate dinner. He knew he was going to have to mention it to JD, but for the life of him, he would not be able to explain why the two of them would be together. However, at the moment, none of those concerns took precedence over the woman scowling at him the moment he reached the living room.

"Hello beautiful," James smiled as he attempted to kiss Ashley.

Ashley turned her head. "It's been two days since I left you with your ex-wife. This is the first time I have seen or heard from you. Do you mind telling me what was so intriguing and urgent?" Ashley had crossed her arms over her breast and had raised an eyebrow.

James smiled. Something stirred within him. It was amazing the love he felt for the woman in front of him. He could not remember why he hesitated getting involved with her in the beginning. Oh yeah, fear, the fear of someone having a piece of his heart again. Well it was too late for that now; she had his heart down to the depth of his soul. James told Ashley why Katherine had stopped by. It seemed Katherine was in the midst of building a new home. The house would not be complete for another two months. Her current house sold quickly and since the new house was not complete, she and James Jr. needed a place to stay. Katherine suggested they stay there until the new house was complete. That way James Jr. will have the opportunity to get used to the neighborhood and school.

Ashley could not believe what she was hearing. She began to laugh and could not stop. "I just don't believe this," Ashley said. "Please tell me you are not considering Katherine and James Jr. staying at your place."

"Katherine suggested she would be on the east side of the house and I will be on the west." He hunched his shoulder, "It would give me an opportunity to spend more time with James Jr." James said as he walked over to the fireplace. Ashley knew she had to tread lightly here. "James Jr. was not my concern. Katherine living under the same roof with you is."

"Well, James Jr. is my concern. No matter what, I will not allow him to be displaced or uprooted from what he knows"

"Children are resilient; he will adjust to whatever is put before him."

James frowned. "I don't want him to have to adjust. I want him to have the best of everything I can give him. I thought you understood that."

"James, I do understand that. I don't have a problem with anything you want for your son. I do have a problem with Katherine possibly manipulating the situation, because of your love for him."

"I am not being manipulated by Katherine," James yelled. Ashley stared for a minute, and then walked into the kitchen. If the conversation continued, she would not be able to control what she might say. One thing she has learned from being with James was how to control her mouth.

"What?" James asked. "Whenever you get that look and walk away you are holding something back. What is it?"

Ashley shook her head and exhaled, "Nothing babe, would you like a drink?"

"No, I want you to tell me what you are thinking."

"I don't think it's a good time for that. Let's just let it go for now."

James took the glass off the counter top. "You know, Katherine said you would have a negative reaction to this, and I told her, that would not happen, because you understood how I feel about my son. It seems I was wrong."

That remark sent Ashley overboard. "James I don't have a problem with the way you feel about your son. When it comes to James Jr., I am to listen and not be heard. Okay, I accept that. But, I refuse to be put even further on the back burner with you. First it's James Jr., then Lena Washington, then Karen Holt, then the campaign and now you want to add Katherine to the mix. When exactly do I come in as a priority, can you tell me that?" It seems James could not answer fast enough for Ashley. Ashley voice raised another octave. "You know what, don't bother to answer, I'm not sure I want to know." Ashley slammed the glass she was holding on the counter top. "Katherine said I would have a negative reaction," Ashley repeated aloud. "You damn right I have a negative reaction to your ex-wife moving in with you. I don't care if it's in the south end of the house; it's under the same roof. And for the record, James, I don't give a damn what Katherine the Great may think about my reaction to anything. And at this moment I don't really give a damn what you think. You and Katherine the Great both can go straight to hell as far as I am concerned. I believe you know your way out." Ashley stormed off into the bedroom and slammed the door behind her.

James stood there for a moment not really sure what just happened, but he was too pissed to try to filter through it. James made it clear to Katherine that her plan would not work. James Jr. could stay, but there was no way he and Katherine could stay under the same roof. If Ashley had given him the opportunity he would have explained that to her. But there was also no reason for Ashley to react the way she did. Did she really think that little of him to condemn him to hell without reason? And what in the hell was she referring to about Lena Washington and Karen Holt? He did not understand her reaction and at the moment did not care. He loved Ashley beyond reason, but there was no way he was going to deal with her moodiness, not after the last few days he had to deal with. He left the condo and headed home.

Gwen sat in her favorite chair in her office. The information Katherine shared with her a few nights ago would devastate her recently reunited family. There was no way she could allow that to happen. She sipped her tea and pondered the question of the moment, how could she put a stop to Carolyn's threat without interfering in the campaign. There was information she had on Gavin and Senator Roth that would end both of their political careers, and she was not prepared to do that. Neither of the men did anything to her family, it was Carolyn who needed to be taught a lesson.

Avery stood in the doorway observing his wife. He knew something was going on that concerned James, but was waiting until Gwen was ready to bring him in. The news of her calling in favors for the luncheon reached him, but he did not ask any questions. In fact her actions helped Harrison's current campaign and just about sealed his future fundraising efforts. The murmurs of him advancing in the Democratic Party were already surfacing. In addition to that, JD and Tracy impressed the wives of the political powerhouse so much they were talking to their husbands about him. Just the mention of one's name in that circle could propel you to higher office. Whatever Gwen was contemplating since Katherine's call was personal and that concerned Avery. "Couldn't sleep?" he asked from the doorway.

Gwen looked up and smiled, "No, my love, I couldn't." He walked over to the chair and picked his wife up as if she was a child. He sat in the chair and positioned her in his lap. She held the cup up in the air so it would not spill and giggled like at child. "You never had a problem moving me."

Avery smiled. "And I never will," he kissed her cheek. "Now, tell me what's bothering you."

Gwen placed her head on his shoulder and shared all that Katherine had told her with him. A tear dropped from her eyes when she mentioned James Jr. and the effect all of this would have on him if it became public knowledge.

Avery wiped the tear from her face. "The wedding is a week from this Saturday, right?"

"Yes it is. That is when Carolyn expects Katherine to complete this plot."

"That's why Katherine was at James' home."

Gwen nodded, "Yes. Unfortunately, it's working. James and Ashley are not talking to each other. Nicki spoke with Ashley today, apparently she and James had an argument about Katherine the other night and they have not spoken since." She hesitated, "Avery, I'm so afraid that Ashley will not be able to forgive James if he does not tell her the truth. She forgave him for keeping us a secret from her; I don't know if she can do it again. I'm not sure I could."

"Let me handle Roth. You handle James and Ashley. Make sure he tells her everything. I don't want you to be concerned with this any longer."

Gwen kissed his throat, "Will you take me to bed now?" she said as she tighten her hold around his neck.

Avery smiled down at her, "Why do we have to go to bed?" He shifted her body in his arms to straddle his legs.

Gwen placed the teacup on the table and smiled at her husband, "You dirty old man."

The next morning Avery placed a call to Senator Roth. He realized it was terribly early, but this could not wait. "John, I need a few moments of your time today, are you in The District or Richmond?"

"Neither. I'm in Norfolk. I will be in Richmond, later today. Carolyn has planned a number of appearances for Gavin and me today in connection with the wedding."

"Ironically, that's the reason I'm calling." Avery said. "There may not be a wedding. I value your friendship, John, but your daughter has crossed a dangerous line with Gwen. You and I need to talk before this interferes with Gavin's political future."

Senator Roth pushed the end button on his cell and placed it back on the nightstand. He turned over to the warm body lying next to him and pulled her into his arms. "I have to leave sooner than expected." He kissed her shoulder and stood to get dressed.

Lena pushed the hair from her face and sat up in bed, pulling the sheet up to cover herself, "What has Carolyn done?"

The Senator smiled at the woman he recently had come to care deeply for, "I'm not sure but from the sound of what Avery Brooks just mentioned it's not good."

Gavin sat in his office staring at the message that was given to him two days ago. He knew there was no choice; the call had to be returned. He also knew returning the call meant the woman remembered who he was. The last time he saw Lena Washington was at JD and Tracy's wedding. At the time, he was not sure she recognized him and, thankfully, Carolyn stepped in and interrupted them. That was also the last night he made love to Carolyn. He stood up and walked over to his bar. Pulled out a bottle of Remy Martin and poured a hearty drink. He sat back at his desk and sighed. "Let's get this over with." He dialed the telephone number on the message and waited to see what his fate would be.

"Hello Gavin," Lena smiled. The call acknowledged her suspicions. The man on the other end of the telephone was connected to her husband's disappearance years ago. The last night Lena saw her husband, William "Billy" Washington, he was drunk. He had made the unforgivable mistake of putting his hands on Tracy, who was eight at the time. Lena's son, Al had warned Billy before about Tracy; unfortunately he did not heed to the warning. She left the house as soon as she was able to get Tracy out of the bedroom. Al and his friend Gavin, who was a police officer at the time, were there when she returned, but there was no sign of Billy. All Al said to her was Billy would not be coming back. Her life was never the same after that night, neither was Tracy's.

"Mrs. Washington, how may I help you?"

"I'll cut to the chase. I want you to get your fiancée off of my daughter."

"When did you become concerned with your daughter's well being?"

"Gavin, we could sit here and go tit for tat on our past, but I don't think you want to do that. See I am not running for public office. My past is not of interest to anyone. Can you make the same claim?"

"What do you think you know about my past that would be of interest to anyone?"

"Since you returned this call, more than you would want me to know. However, that is not important. This call is not aimed at you. I want Carolyn to stop interfering with JD and Tracy. I do not know the history there, but I would think this request would benefit you too. I do not intend to cause any problems in your personal or professional life. I haven't done a lot for Tracy in the past and this is an opportunity for me to make that right."

"How do I fit into your plan to make things right?" Gavin asked.

"All I want you to do is to make sure your fiancée marries you, regardless."

Gavin was very curious with the request. One, there was nothing in it for her. The Lena he remembered would not bother with anything she did not have a stake in. Two, with everything that Carolyn had put him through, he loved her and wanted her as his wife. The thought of having a child even crossed his mind. "Will what you are planning hurt Carolyn?" he asked.

"Just her feelings. She is going to face the same fate she attempted for Tracy. All your major contributors will be there. Moreover, if Carolyn marries you, a reporter will rave about the intimate wedding the Governor and the First Lady had. The press will be very complimentary, but Carolyn will be taught a lesson. She will not have the grand event she planned."

Chapter 10

A week passed and Ashley was still not speaking to James. Tracy explained as much as she could to JD without telling him why Ashley was so moody. At the same time, she was trying to get Ashley to see that James had not really done anything to deserve the anger she felt towards him, but she was not receptive. Tracy decided to call in reinforcements to help with the situation. She invited Cynthia, Rosaline, Brian, Calvin, Douglas, Ashley, and James, his sister Nicki and his brother Nick to the house for a cook out. For good measure, she also invited her mother-in-law, Martha, Avery and Gwendolyn Brooks, just in case the siblings were not successful. Both James and Ashley were being stubborn and it would take a full fledged intervention to bring those two back together.

JD, Brian, Douglas, Calvin, Nick, Avery and James were in the study having a rather heated conversation regarding the situation. Of course, it was James' position that he had done nothing to warrant an apology. It was Avery's and JD's position that James should apologize, anyway, to end the stalemate. "Hell no, he should not apologize," Brian argued. "I think he had every right to have his wife and fiancée under the same roof. It cuts down on the confusion of keeping them straight in your mind," he laughed.

"Man, it's bad enough having one woman under the roof, there is no way in the world you can handle two," Calvin laughed. "Don't listen to Brian."

"If you step up first and apologize it gives you the upper hand on the next argument," Avery offered. "That way, even if you are totally wrong it will not matter; it will be her turn to apologize."

"You seem to be missing the elementary point. I did nothing to apologize for," James stubbornly stated. "If anyone needs to apologize it would be Ashley and I don't intend on spending another night in bed alone waiting for her to come to her senses."

JD, Brian and Calvin laughed, "Man, I hope you have someone else to sleep with you tonight. I have never known Ashley to apologize for any reason," Calvin said laughing.

Douglas, who was sitting quietly with his own thoughts, sat forward in his chair and looked at James. "Let me make sure I understand what happened. Your ex-wife came into your home and it was Ashley who left. You did not speak with her for two days due to circumstances beyond your control. When you did talk to her, you told her your ex-wife wanted to move back into your house. Then you told her that the woman you were once married to said she would not like the idea of her moving in said house. Does that about cover it?"

Everyone in the room thought for a moment, as did James, who agreed, "That's about right."

Douglas stood and looked at the men in the room. "I know I've never been married or involved in a serious relationship, but I know women. The one thing you never do is tell your current woman what your ex-woman said. You should apologize." He placed his glass on the desk and walked out to the patio with the women.

Brian looked at Calvin, JD and then at James. "Yeah, he's right. You should apologize, for being stupid."

Avery stood and patted James on the shoulder. "You are going to apologize for letting her think you even considered allowing Katherine to stay under your roof. On the other hand, you can continue to allow your pride to keep you in a cold bed. The choice is yours."

JD stood, "Let's join the women and give James the opportunity to think over his decision. But do me a favor. Please end the standoff soon. Ashley has not been in a good mood since this all started. This morning, she put my bagel in my coffee then told me to stop my whining, all because I wanted to kiss my wife. I want her out of my house until my real sister returns."

James walked out onto the patio and all eyes turned to him. Ashley, who had avoided him the entire evening, was standing between her mother and his. JD was sitting in a lounge chair with Tracy sandwiched between his legs. Nick, Brian, Douglas and Calvin were standing at the grill. Nicki, Cynthia and Rosaline immediately stood next to Ashley to let James know, right or wrong, they had her back. Avery looked at James and whispered, "Bite the bullet son," then walked over to stand next to his wife.

Noticing the women's stance, Nick went and stood next to his brother, and then Douglas joined them, followed by Brian and Calvin. The lines were drawn. With the exception of JD and Tracy, it was clear where everyone stood. For a moment Martha wanted to take both Ashley and James over her knee for acting like children.

Seeing the separation in friends, Gwendolyn spoke first, "James, do you have something you need to say?"

James looked at his mother. He knew without a doubt she loved him and would not jeopardize their re-established relationship. With everything that happened between them for her to take Ashley's side told him two things. One, Gwendolyn Brooks liked Ashley Harrison and had already accepted her as her new daughter in law. Two, it was he who needed to take the first step to end the standoff. "Ashley, may I speak with you in private for a moment?" James asked through clinched teeth.

"No. Whatever you have to say to me can be said here." Ashley replied with her hands on her hips. She hoped her voice was not shaking like her insides were. The last week had been hell without James. She wanted to tell him how much she loved him and missed him, but most of all she wanted to say she was sorry for saying what she said. She didn't want him to go to hell, just Katherine.

James looked at Ashley and knew she was being stubborn. He could see it in her eyes; the tears were there on the brink. The argument was not that serious and although he had to admit, once Douglas spelled things out, he could understand why she had become upset with him. But now she was taking this too far, he took the first step, but that didn't seem to be enough for her. Well, since she wanted to be stubborn, then so would he. But not to the point of losing the one thing that made his life right. He didn't know why she was so emotional, but it was time for it to come to an end. James put the glass he was holding in his hand on the table and walked over to her. He folded his arms across his chest and stared deeply into her eyes, "Ashley Renee Harrison, it's time for this nonsense to end. I love you and you are going to marry me. You have thirty days to plan the wedding. Enough is enough."

Avery held his head down and shook it; his son had lost his mind talking to an angry black woman like that. A collection of moans echoed around them. The women gasped at the tone James had taken with Ashley. Ashley gave James a look of defiance and stomped her foot. "When hell freezes over James Brooks."

James reached out, grabbed her shoulders and kissed her until he believed the fight in her had diminished. Ashley was sure her legs were about to give out and was grateful James was holding her up. When she began to relax in the kiss he pulled away and held her at arm's length. "Then you better get a winter coat and a pair of snow boots, it's going to be a cold July." He turned and stormed out.

For a moment no one said anything. Martha looked up at her daughter, who was standing there with her mouth open. She wanted to laugh at the man that reminded her so much of her husband. It was at that moment she knew James Brooks was the man for her daughter. "Well, dear, I better start shopping for a dress. Is there a particular color scheme you want to work with?"

Ashley looked at her mother and repeated, "I'm not marrying him!"

"Of course you are dear," Martha said as she kissed her cheek and walked into the house.

"You know Ashley," Rosalind stated, "I will handle the menu, just let me know how many people to prepare for. Wait up Mrs. Harrison; we need to plan a menu." Rosalind ran to catch up with Martha.

Cynthia looked at the men standing together watching things unfold. "Why are you all still standing there? Tuxedos need to be ordered, get to it."

"Cynthia, I'm not marrying James!" Ashley stated and put her hands on her hips for emphasis. "Hum hmm," Cynthia replied as she sat her glass on the table. "I will be with your mother, working on the location and planning a theme," she smiled and ran behind the departing women. As she reached the men Cynthia gave them a look that made it clear they needed to make a move. "I only have thirty days to put this wedding together. Don't make me repeat myself, go get your tuxedos ordered," she commanded and walked away.

Nick, Brian, Douglas and Calvin looked at each other. "Damn, we are going to have to wear a tuxedo again, aren't we?" Brian asked.

"That is the traditional attire for a wedding," Nick replied. "Who is that?" pointing to Cynthia.

"The Wicked Witch of Weddings," Brian said.

JD laughed and Tracy gave him a look. She stood and then walked over to Ashley. JD changed his expression, "Hmm, you guys get with James and see how he wants us to proceed."

Ashley looked at them and stomped her foot again, "Is anyone listening, I am not going to marry him."

Gwen looked at Ashley and knew it was only pride keeping her standing. "No dear, we are not listening. See we all know you love James. We can tell by the swollen eyes from tears you been shedding all week. I don't like the way he did it, but he let you know he loves you and is ready to move on. Nicki, can we get Vera on short notice?"

Nicki looked at Ashley and smiled. She loved seeing James like this. "I'm so glad you came into his life."

"I like you Nicki, but I am not going to marry your brother," Ashley exclaimed.

"Okay." She hugged her new friend and then turned to her mother, "I'll have the jet fueled and ready to take us to New York within the hour. I know all her sizes, down to her shoes. Let's see what Vera has in stock, just in case she changes her mind."

JD walked over to Ashley, kissed her forehead and smiled. "I will be with you, whatever you decide."

Ashley hugged her brother; she knew he would have her back. "I love you JD."

"I love you, too, Squirt. That's why I will be there to give you away." Ashley hit JD in the chest and pushed him away. JD smiled. "Mr. Brooks, what do you say we go inside and get something to toast the happy couple?"

"That sounds like a winner to me," Avery said, and followed JD into the house.

The tears Ashley was holding back began to fall. Tracy waited until they were completely alone and turned to Ashley. She hugged her as the tears flowed. Once Ashley began to settle down, Tracy wiped her face with a napkin and then picked one up for herself. Whenever her friend hurt, so did she. She smiled at Ashley and gently said. "Ashley, you love James with all your heart. I know because you told me so. You are also carrying his child. I know for the last two weeks you have been a ball of nerves with everything you have been dealing with. Hell, to tell you the truth, the last three months has been a rolling snowball for you—from learning about James' family, to the mess with David and now this situation with Katherine. But through it all one fact remains. You love James and he loves you." She stopped and looked at her friend to make sure she was listening.

"Doesn't anyone understand how pissed I am with him? He was the one who left our bed for Karen Holt. He was the one who let Katherine back into his life. And he was the one who got me pregnant!"

"Well, I think you helped with that, at least I know I did with my pregnancy."

Ashley laughed, "I enjoyed it, too," she said wiping the tears from her eyes.

Tracy laughed with her. The two sat there holding hands. "Life is so strange. Here we are crying when we should be smiling. You are getting married and we are going to have babies this time next year."

"Tracy?"

"Yeah"

"Do you believe James loves me the same way JD loves you?"

Tracy thought for a moment, "I don't think any two people love in the same way. Do I believe James loves you with the same intensity Jeffrey loves me? Yes. I believe that man would move Heaven and Earth to be with you." Ashley exhaled, releasing a heartfelt smile. "Now, as much as I would like to continue this conversation, I think you and I need to find a gown fit for the queen that you are. And one that will fit the whale I have become," they both laughed.

In all the years Clair worked for James, the house never seemed so alive. It was wonderful to have the house filled with people. The entire Brooks clan with the exception of Vernon and Constance were gathered in the family room discussing the events of the day. Surprisingly, everyone was in good spirits including James. He was actually relieved. The last week without Ashley had been hell, but he now knew without a doubt he would not live without her in his life. He also knew he was going to have to face her before this night was over. And when he did, she would have a few choice words for him, which he would accept graciously. "Well James, what kind of ceremony will it be? Do I need to pull out the shot gun for Ashley?" Nick laughed.

James smiled, as he stood behind the bar preparing drinks for his houseguests. "No, I don't believe you will have to go to the extreme. You may have to come to the ceremony in the emergency room. I'm sure Ashley is going to kill me for my outburst today."

"That was a rather interesting way of apologizing," Avery smiled.

"I would have resorted to violence if you had spoken to me in that manner. And I agree, you better wear some armor when you talk to Ashley tonight," Gwen stated as she took a seat.

"I don't know," Nicki chimed in, "I think it was a little romantic, declaring your love for her in front of her friends and family. I would have never believed you were capable of such passion, if I hadn't seen it for myself."

"I know you shocked the hell out of me," Nick laughed. "I thought JD and his friends were going to jump you there for a moment when you grabbed Ashley."

Avery shook his head, "No, they know you love her and she knows it too. But you need to clear the air just like your friend Douglas said. Ashley has no way of knowing what went down between you and Katherine the other day."

Before they could go any further Gwen broke in, "Actually none of us knows what went down with Katherine. James would you like to share?"

James exhaled and took a seat next to Nicki, "Katherine has decided to move to Richmond, to allow me better access to James Jr. She asked to stay here while her home is being built."

"I hope you told her no!" Nicki stated.

"I hope you told her hell no!" Nick added.

"In no uncertain terms; Katherine and I will never live under the same roof again."

"If you told her no, why is Ashley upset?" Nicki asked.

"Bad communication on my part; I haven't told Ashley I said no."

"Well, it's time to clear the air." Avery said. "It's been just about a week. That's too long to keep this going. I'm glad you finally took a stance. Now, what type of wedding will it be?"

"Whatever Ashley wants," James replied with a very satisfied smile.

"Excuse me Mr. Brooks, you have a call, a Mr. Holt."

"Thank you Clair," James replied as he picked up the telephone with David Holt on the other end. James excused himself from the family and took the call in his office. "What do you want Holt?"

"Where's my wife Brooks?"

"I'm not at liberty to say, Holt. If she wants to talk to you she will call."

David gave a cynical sneer into the telephone, "You have gone too damned far Brooks. You had no business interfering in my marriage. You tell me where she is or you will pay the price."

"Go to hell Holt," James said and hung up the telephone. James dialed Brian's cell and found he was still at JD's house. "Brian, is Karen tucked safely away?"

"Yeah, why?"

"I just received a call from Holt. He's mad as hell. He wants to know where his wife is."

"It's on you. Do you want her to stay put?"

"Let it be her decision. Tell her he's asking about her and go from there."

"I'll handle it on this end," Brian replied.

James hung up the telephone. He wondered if he was doing the right thing. When Karen called last Sunday, she told James she wanted to leave Holt, but knew he would come looking for her. She did not think she would have the strength to say no to him and asked for James' assistance. That Monday James met with Karen and arranged for her to take a six-month leave of absence from her position at Special Services. He asked Brian to make living arrangements for her. Brian asked Douglas to allow Karen to stay at the apartment above the Renaissance until she decided what she wanted to do. Brian also asked Douglas to make sure she was not disturbed by Holt. He placed a call to a friend at Virginia Domestic Violence Alliance to counsel her. Only Brian and Douglas knew where she was being placed. It was up to Karen if she wanted to contact anyone else. Based on the call from Holt, James knew Karen had not been in contact with him. He exhaled. For a moment he felt for Holt. If anyone tried to keep him from Ashley it would drive him crazy. At that moment, James decided it was time to face Ashley. He needed to hold her and tell her in a more personal way how much he truly loved her.

Ashley was sitting in her den going over the list of things Cynthia left for her to make decisions on. For some reason the mood wasn't there. Trying to decide on colors, invitations, music and food was not foremost in her mind. Well, maybe the food part was since she was hungry at that moment. For the past week it seemed like she needed to eat every minute of the day. It crossed her mind to make an appointment with the doctor to verify the pregnancy, but she wasn't in the mood for that either. Actually, the only thing she was in the mood for was James. But since he demanded she marry him, she had not heard from him. Ashley put the list aside and went into her bedroom to change clothes. She put on a pair of jeans and a midriff top, and then put her hair up in a ponytail. She smiled at her reflection in the mirror and remembered Tracy and her ponytail. She slipped her feet into a pair of flat sandals and headed to the kitchen. The telephone rang on the way. "Hello," she said into the receiver.

"Hello," she said again when no one answered. She looked at the Caller ID. It read "UNKNOWN." She hung up the telephone and pulled the cherry vanilla ice cream out of the freezer. She grabbed a spoon out of the kitchen drawer, sat in one of the chairs at the table and placed her feet up in another. As she ate her ice cream, she wondered what she would do with the condo once she moved in with James. She and Tracy purchased the condo right after college. Tracy always believed in investing well. It never dawned on her to rent an apartment; she always said there was no return on putting money in someone else's pockets.

That was six years ago. Last year when Tracy and JD got married she signed the condo over to Ashley, paid in full. The value of the condo had tripled to a little over $300,000. Maybe she would sell it. Ashley sighed as tears began to form. She laid her head back and closed her eyes. She let the tears flow freely; her life was changing for the better, why was she so sad?

After a few minutes she brought her head back up and dug into the container of ice cream. She opened her eyes and was stunned to find James standing before her. She stared up at him with the spoon midway to her mouth, but did not utter a word. He took the spoon and put it back in the container. Lifting her feet, he sat in the chair placed them across his legs and then preceded to pull her chair closer to him. He positioned his hands on both sides of her face and wiped the tears away with his thumbs. He lowered his lips to hers and whispered, "I am sorry for everything that has happened with us this past week." He gently kissed her lips, "There are some things I need to tell you about Katherine."

Ashley put her arms around his neck as they sat forehead against forehead. "I don't care about Katherine or Karen. I care about you. Tell me about you," she said as tears streamed down her face.

James took her hand and led her into the den. He sat on the leather sofa and pulled her into his lap. Ashley was amazed how easily she fit whenever he held her. She snuggled as close to him as she could. It was wonderful to smell his cologne, feel the stubble on his chin, the warmth of his arms around her and the gentle beat of his heart.

"Katherine and I were married right after grad school. Everyone thought we were the perfect couple, both coming from prominent families. For a while, I thought we were too. But not soon after we were married I found Katherine was more interested in the status our family name could bring than she actually was in me. It seemed the prestige of being a

Brooks was the attraction. She loved the jet setting of our lifestyle; it was an aphrodisiac to her. Unfortunately, it did not appeal to me. I always enjoyed working and indulged in making a name of my own. As a result, Katherine began to feel neglected. I came home from a trip to New York earlier and planned to surprise her with a shopping trip to Paris. I asked the pilot to stay on standby and had the driver to take me home. When I entered the house, I asked Charles if he knew where Katherine was. He indicated she was visiting Constance in their suite.

Not thinking much of it I entered their suite without knocking. I went into the living area, but did not see her, but I heard voices. I followed the voices and found Katherine in the bedroom with my brother, Vernon. Katherine was ashamed enough to jump up and begin putting her clothes on trying to explain, but not Vernon. He sat up in bed with this smug smile on his face and asked, "Are you looking for your wife?" Before I knew anything I had him by the throat dangling from the balcony of their bedroom. It took my father to talk me out of dropping him. When things settled my mother didn't uphold Vernon's actions, but she relentlessly stood by him against me. At least that's how I felt at the time. Now I realize she could no more turn away from Vernon than she could me. We are both her sons, she could not banish either of us. I left the house that night; Katherine came with me. I couldn't look at her for weeks. But she was my wife. So I gave her the option of moving to Richmond and she took it. I moved here and started a new life. A month later, Katherine told me she was pregnant. I never asked who the father was, I'm not sure I wanted to know. Nevertheless, there was no way I could turn my back on her, therefore, I accepted the child as mine, without question. I believe she gave James Jr. my name because she desperately wanted him to be my child. To be honest with you I don't know for certain that he is mine biologically. But in my heart he is and will always be my son, regardless of what a DNA test may or may not show. "

Ashley hadn't realized how tightly she was holding on to James or how wet his shirt was from her tears until she shifted her head to look up at him. "James Jr. could be your son, you can't be sure."

James looked down into Ashley's eyes. They were filled with tears. She was hurting for him the same way he was hurting for her when she told him about David Holt. He pushed her hair aside and kissed the tip of her nose. He swallowed hard and said, "I never touched Katherine after Vernon. In all probability James Jr. is Vernon's son," he said calmly.

Ashley reached up and put her arms around James neck. He pulled her close and buried his face in the cradle of her neck "I'm so sorry James. I'm so sorry."

James held her there long enough to compose himself, and then he sat her back on his lap and cradled her head in his arm. "You don't ever have to be insecure about Katherine, Karen or any other woman. You are the very heart of me. Don't ever doubt that." He kissed her with such passion that Ashley was convinced he was making love to her with her clothes on. And if it wasn't for the fact that she was already pregnant she was certain that kiss could have impregnated her. James broke the kiss and was content to hold her in his arms.

"Hmm, James," Ashley said as she closed her eyes. "The day we went to your parent's home was the first time you had gone home since the incident?"

"Yes," he replied wondering why she asked the question.

"You went back for me?"

"Yes"

"Why?"

"I felt I needed to clear the air with Vernon and my mother before I made you a part of our family. I didn't want you to marry into a hostile family and that's what we were for a while."

Ashley smiled. Then she began to giggle and that giggle then began to turn into laughter. She sat up in his lap, smiled, and then exhaled. "James Avery Brooks you are going to be a daddy; again." The expression on James face was one of confusion. So Ashley explained further. "When we went to your parent's home we planned to stay the day only, but we ended up staying two days, remember."

"Yesssss," James replied hesitantly

"Well, I didn't take my pills with me and we had a lot of fun in your suite. You noticed I said suite and not any particular room? We were all over the place the last day we were there."

"You're pregnant?" he asked calmly.

Ashley closed one eye, looked at him, and positioned her fingers together. "Just a little bit."

"You're pregnant?" he grinned, "You're pregnant?" he chuckled and hugged her. "You're pregnant."

"Well, we're pregnant. " Ashley smiled as he leaned down to kiss her.

James froze and looked at her with a frown. "Your mother is going to kill me. Does she know?" He stood up and put Ashley on her feet. "My Lord, woman, we have to get married now, your mother is going to kill me. I promised her I would protect you."

"Next month will be fine James. My mother will not know before then."

James stood there gazing lovingly at her. There was nothing she could have told him that would have pleased him more. Surprisingly, the more he thought about it, the happier he became. He cupped her face in his hands. "We're going to have a baby." A broad smile creased his face as he gently kissed her lips. Then he pulled away and frowned again.

"Oh Lord." Ashley said then dropped in the seat behind her. "What now?"

"We have to get married now; this could affect the campaign."

"Lord forbids anything would impact the campaign."

Brian followed James instructions. He met with Douglas at the Renaissance to talk to Karen. While in the elevator to the penthouse apartment Douglas asked Brian. "How long do you anticipate I will have a house guest?"

"Man, with the asshole we are dealing with, it's hard to say. I can tell you this, James is on the verge of murdering this man," Brian replied. Douglas looked at him with a question on his face. Brian threw up his hands, "Don't ask. I have no idea. He said no, he is not, nor has he ever been involved with Karen Holt. Every so often, I wonder, but I can see he truly loves Ashley. Hell, he's as bad, if not worse, than JD is about Tracy."

Douglas laughed, "I believe that. Holt met James here one night and if I had not stepped in I'm sure James would have given him an ass whipping he would never forget."

"Yeah, well at least you were able to stop him. The morning of the rally, James had the man by the throat, dangling from the damn ceiling." Brian laughed. "Man, I swear, I never thought I would run across a man who I would think twice about tangling with. I'm not ashamed to say James Brooks is one."

Douglas knocked on the door. Since one of Brian's employees brought her to the apartment, neither had met Karen. They were both shocked and appalled at the vision that met them at the door. Karen did not remove the chain from the door, "Yes" she said through the door.

"Mrs. Holt, my name is Brian Thompson. Mr. Jones, who escorted you here, works for me. I have been employed by James Brooks to ensure your safety until you make a decision on the next step you want to take. This is Douglas Hylton. He owns the building and this apartment. May we come in to speak with you for a moment?"

Karen closed the door and removed the chain. She opened the door and immediately turned her back and walked away from them. She sat in the chair looking out of the window. "Please don't think I'm being rude. I'm just not very presentable at the moment."

Douglas sat at the table in the dining room, which was close by the door. He did not want to intrude on this matter. "Mrs. Holt, could you tell me in your own words what transpired between you and your husband?" Brian asked as he stood opposite her.

Karen pulled her feet up into the chair and wrapped her arms around them. "From what I could understand, David and James had some type of confrontation last Saturday. When he came home from the rally, he was very upset. I made the mistake of thinking he would be in a good mood, since the rally was such a huge success." She hesitated to wipe away a tear that escaped her eyes. "I'm sorry; I thought I was all cried out." She continued, "I was dressed to celebrate the occasion, a white Victoria's Secret silk teddy; the one with the thong panties." She placed her head on her knees and smiled, "I looked pretty good." She stopped as if trying to remember each detail. "I popped the champagne as soon as he walked through the door and said here's to a great start on the campaign trail." Brain stepped closer. Tears ran down what he could see was a bruised cheek. "He walked over to me and ran his knuckle down my cheek. I could see in his eyes that something was wrong. Before I could move away he lifted me by my neck and slammed me against the wall. He pushed me up the wall as high as he could reach and told me to dangle my feet. The pressure on my throat was too much and I couldn't do anything. I was about to black out when he dropped me to the floor. I wished I had blacked out. He began hitting me in my face with his fist. Between hits, he said James' name several times. I never really got heads or tails on what he was mumbling about."

Brian looked at Douglas and wondered what would make a man do such a thing to a woman. Karen stood about five four and might weigh one hundred twenty. David was six three and weigh at least two hundred twenty. A blow from him at the right angle in the right place could have killed the woman. Brian sat as Douglas put on a kettle to make tea, then he turned back to Karen. "Mrs. Holt, this wasn't the first time David has hit you. Why are you leaving him now?"

Karen held her head up and looked at Brian. He almost wished she hadn't. Her face was badly beaten. The incident occurred a week ago and the bruises were still vivid. "He never hit me in my face before." She said as she put her head back down on her knees. "Please, call me Karen."

Brian smiled and gently replied, "Alright, Karen. Are you sure, this is what you want to do? Before you answer you should know your husband has contacted Mr. Brooks demanding to know where you are. He asked me to make you aware of the request and to let this be your decision."

Karen smiled, "James is such a good man. I wish I had met him years ago." Brian and Douglas looked at each other. "I'm sure this is what I need to do," she said. Douglas walked over and placed the tea on the table that was between the two chairs. "Thank you," she said without looking up.

"Then know I will do all that is within my power to keep him away from you," Brian stated with a firmness that comforted Karen.

"It's not me that you should be concerned with, it's Ashley Harrison."

Brian sat forward, quiet gripped by what she said. "Why should we be concerned for Ashley?"

"He's been stalking her. Even to the point of entering her apartment when she is not there."

"How do you know that, Karen?" he asked.

"It's in his log sheets."

"What log sheets and how do you know about them?"

"When he left the house the other night he did not close the door to his room. I know he told me never to go in there, but I did. He keeps a log on her. He also knows you are following him. There were one or two times he asked me to dress in sweats and put on a hat. He even went as far as to put a telephone book in the driver's seat of his car. He asked me to drive out of town for about an hour. He told me not to get out of the car, but to pull over and make a call on his cell telephone and then return home."

"Karen, do you know how David is getting into Ashley's apartment?"

"Ashley leaves a key at the top of her doorway. According to David's log, she used to do the same thing in college."

"Did you read anything in his log that we should know about to protect Ashley?"

"I know he plans to try to get her pregnant. It seems Carolyn Roth told him some story about James' son. David thinks getting Ashley pregnant will be his ultimate revenge on James."

"Karen," Brian said to her, "Ashley would never let David within ten feet of her. How could he possibly get her pregnant?"

Karen looked at Brian, "He did something with her birth control pills a month ago. According to his calculations, within thirty days she should be able to conceive a child. He has it all planned out in his log book."

Brian was getting a little frustrated at this point. He knew he had to keep Karen talking to get the information she read. "Karen, I know this can't be easy for you. But do you know where David's log book is now?"

"Yes," she replied as tears streamed down her face.

"Would you tell me, where it is?" Brian asked in the kindest voice he could. He was not feeling calm inside. A number of things were running through his mind. He knew David attempted to rape Ashley before. He also knew James would kill David if he put his hands on Ashley now, not to mention how all of this would affect JD's family and campaign.

Karen reached down between the cushions of the chair she was sitting in and pulled out the logbook. She then handed it to Brian. "This is the most recent one. There are several at the house that go back to the day he attempted to rape Ashley at Harmon." Brian saw the look of unbridled hurt in Karen's eyes. She was forced to face the worst humiliation a wife could ever imagine at the hands of her husband. The man that was supposed to love, protect and honor her was the very one who caused her the pain. He took the book and placed it on the table, but held on to her hands. He pulled her to him and held her as she quietly cried on his shoulder. He held her until she fell asleep in his arms. He placed her on the bed and covered her.

"Do you have plans for the night?" Brian asked Douglas as he came out of the bedroom.

"I did. However, they have changed. You handle Ashley. I will stay here with her until I believe she is better," Douglas replied.

"Don't leave her alone in a room for more than a minute," Brian said.

"I have you covered here. You get to Holt before we have a murder charge against James and JD."

Chapter 11

Brian called the employee who was following David Holt. He told the employee to do whatever he had to, to pull the car over to make sure it was David driving. He hung up the cell phone and called James. His housekeeper indicated James was not there. Brian called James's cell phone, but did not receive an answer. When Brian was about to try Ashley's number a call came through. It was the man following David. He indicated David had apparently loaned his car to someone. The person he was following was not David. After cursing angrily, Brian instructed the man to meet him at Ashley Harrison's condominium. Brian was more upset with himself than with the man who lost David. James mentioned Ashley and that damn door key to him before the rally and he never had a chance to get an alarm system in place. It was the key above the door that caused JD problems last year. "Damn!" he exclaimed aloud as he pressed the gas pedal, accelerating to get to Ashley's place.

James turned off his cell phone while he was trying to reconcile with Ashley. He did not want anything to interfere with the conversation they needed to have. He was driving home as one of the happiest men on the planet. Not only was he about to marry the woman that made his life worth living, that same woman was pregnant with his child. James smiled to himself. "I'm certainly a blessed man." He would be a happy participant in this pregnancy, unlike his first child. "Hmm," James sighed. How will James Jr. react to all of this? He knew his son and Ashley had formed a wonderful relationship and he was not concerned with that, but a baby would certainly change the dynamics of their life.

He pulled into his garage and parked. He stopped at the entrance to his kitchen and smiled. His family would be thrilled with this news. Hell, he would even share this happy news with Vernon, without malice. James opened the door and walked in. Clair greeted him with a smile. "I like your little brother Mr. James. He is so handsome and fun to have around. But I think your sister Ms. Nicki, is going to seriously hurt him if he throws her into the pool again" she laughed.

"Well, get use to having people around doing silly things Clair, this family is growing," James smiled and kissed her on her cheek. "Where are my parents?" he asked while walking away.

Clair stared in shock at his retreating back and replied, "They retired about an hour ago. But the twins are still out by the pool. "Oh, Mr. Thompson called for you earlier."

"Thank you Clair," James replied still in a state of euphoria. He went out to the pool and found Nick and Nicki seated on the side talking.

"It's good to have the family back together again like this. I hope Vernon and Constance come to the wedding," Nicki said.

"I'm sure if James extends the invitation, Vernon will come because he would not want to upset mother. If not for that reason, Constance would not miss the event and will force him to come. Either way, he will be here."

"I'm so glad to see James happy. Just goes to show you, you never know what is around the corner in life."

James decided not to disturb the conversation his younger siblings were having. He really wanted to talk to his parents and get back to Ashley, so he headed upstairs. He turned his cell phone back on and noticed two messages, both from Brian. He made a mental note to return the call after he told his parents they could expect a new grandchild.

At the door of Ashley's condominium Brian reached up and felt around until he touched the key. "Damn!" he exclaimed and rung the bell.

Ashley buzzed him in. "Hey Brian. What are you doing here this time of night?" she asked smiling.

Brian walked up the stairs, looking around as discreetly as he could. "I was looking for James. I called his cell and he did not answer."

Ashley was smiling so brightly, Brian couldn't help but to ask. "Okay, who gave you unlimited shopping privileges?"

Ashley smiled brighter. "Actually James did in a roundabout way, but that's not what has me smiling."

"Okay I'll bite, what is it?" He smiled back.

"James and I are getting married."

Brian started laughing. For the life of him, he would never understand women. When James told her that she was mad as hell and swore hell would freeze over before she married him. Now, she was smiling about it. "Do you have some type of alcohol in that glass?"

"No, it's my tea that I drink every night, why?"

"Well, I guess hell must have frozen over."

Ashley was puzzled for a moment, and then she remembered her words and began to laugh. "Yeah, I guess it has. Did you still need to reach James, I'm sure he is home by now."

Brian looked around, "No, I'll try to reach him at home. Do you mind if I use your bathroom?"

"No, of course not. I'm going to call Tracy."

Brian went down the hallway leading towards the bathroom. He looked inside each room to make sure no one was there. He then checked the laundry room and last the bathroom. He wasn't too concerned about the other half of the house because that was open and he could see through those rooms, with the exception of Ashley's bedroom and bath. He did not want to concern her with his probing but he also did not want to take a chance of Holt being in her house. "You ran out of toilet paper in there. I'll get some out of your bathroom." Ashley watched as Brian walked through the living room to her bedroom. She watched as she continued her conversation with Tracy while drinking her tea, which seemed a little bitter to her. Brian came out of the room satisfied no one else was there. "Okay I'm out Squirt," Brian said as he walked down the steps.

Once outside the building Brian got into his car. He called the employee assigned to Holt, who was sitting in the car across from him. "The house is clear and I have the key from the top of the door frame. Make sure no one enters that condo. I am going to Brooks' house to talk to him. Brian pulled off never noticing the shadowy figure standing behind his employee's vehicle.

Ashley finished drinking her tea after she hung up the telephone with Tracy. She was tired, but she had to tell Tracy about the conversation with James and how happy he was about the baby. Things were finally falling into place. Ashley was amazed how much Cynthia and Rosaline had accomplished on the wedding plans. They decided the wedding would take place at Gwen's home, which was perfect. Ashley was sure Cynthia could not wait to get into Gwen's house to begin setting things up. After talking to Tracy, Ashley called James and found his mother had filled him in on the plans. "They are not wasting any time are they?" Ashley laughed into the telephone.

"We don't have any time to waste. I want you to become Ashley Brooks as soon as humanly possible," James replied.

"I know it may affect the campaign." Ashley replied.

"Hell no woman, I want you and my child under the same roof with me so I can watch your body grow."

That was the sweetest thing Ashley had ever heard. She smiled and yawned into the telephone. "That is what I want, too," she replied close to tears. "But right now I'm about to fall asleep on my feet. I don't know why I'm so tired."

"It's because you are carrying my child. That's enough to wear anyone out."

"You are right. Oh by the way, Brian came by here looking for you. He said he was going to catch you at home."

"I'll call him. You get some rest and I'll be over as soon as I wrap things up here."

"I love you James Brooks."

"You are the heart of me, Ashley Renee' Brooks."

James hung up the telephone and called Brian. "Brian, I see you have been trying to reach me. What's going on?"

"I'm at your front door." Brian replied.

James went downstairs to let him in. He looked at the clock on the wall. It was after midnight. Whatever was going on must be important. He opened the door and Brian walked in, "We need to talk. Where are your folks?"

James looked concerned, "They're upstairs asleep. We can talk in my office." The two walked into the office and James closed the door. "What's going on Brian?"

"The situation with Holt is more serious than we anticipated. I spoke with Karen tonight and she gave me this." He placed the book on James's desk.

James picked up the book, "What is it?" he asked.

"It's a log book. Holt has been keeping track of Ashley for years. Read the last page in the book."

James began reading and looked up at Brian. Ashley just told me tonight she's pregnant. She thought she had missed her pills last month when we went to my parent's home."

"Wait a minute, she's already pregnant?" Brian asked.

"Yes," James replied.

"But David hasn't completed his plan yet. He knows her habits. His plan is to drug her tea and then have sex with her hoping to impregnate her." Brian looked up at James.

"Do you realize the number of flaws in that plan? How can he believe he can get into her place? How?" James asked as he continued reading.

"He's been using this to get into her condo," Brian said as he threw the key on the desk.

When James saw the key, the blood seemed to drain from his face. "Holt was inside Ashley's home?" He yelled as he stood.

"According to that log book, he's gone as far as sleeping in her bed."

James picked up the telephone and called Ashley, there was no answer. Nick walked into the office just as James grabbed the key. "What's happening?" he asked seeing the anger in James eyes.

"I don't have time to explain," James said as he ran out the door.

"James, wait!' Brian called out but he was no longer in earshot. Nick ran out the front door and reached the car just as James was pulling out of the driveway. But James never stopped. Nick stopped Brian and jumped in the car with him.

Ashley was dreaming that James was taking his time making love to her. He was slowly removing her clothes. She felt his hands touching her legs and moving up her thighs. Somewhere in the back of her mind, his touch did not feel the same. He was hovering over her and as if he had not seen her body in a long time. When he caressed her breast, it was with a roughness that startled her. She opened her eyes and saw the top of his head and she called out to him. "James?" she said groggily.

He ran his tongue down her stomach and she felt his hands at the very core of her. It was something in his touch that did not arouse her, she closed her legs, and tried to sit up, but she couldn't. She called out again "James?" But the person who appeared above her wasn't James.

"Hello Ashley," David smiled.

Ashley was willing her body to move, but she did not have control. She closed her eyes and reopened them, but found she was not dreaming. She was not completely awake, but she was aware enough to know it was not James in her bedroom, but David. What she couldn't understand was why she was just lying there not moving. Her mind was telling her body to move but it didn't.

"You are so beautiful lying there Ashley." David smiled. "After tonight I will always be a part of you. Don't you remember I never let something that belonged to me go." He began removing his shirt. He took her face in his hands kissed her lips gently. "You can't fight this Ashley. Tonight is the night we are going to conceive our child." He stood and went into the bathroom. Ashley moved, not as fast as her mind was telling her to, but she was able to get to the other side of the bed before he grabbed her from behind by putting his arm around her waist. "I'm glad you are able to move some. I want you to participate in the conception of our child," he laid her back down on the bed. "I wanted to oil you down. Remember the way we used to do in college? You oil me down and I would do the same to you." He began rubbing his hands over her body.

Ashley closed her eyes as tears began to escape. How could David be there in her bedroom? How did he get her gown off? How could he be doing this to her?

David saw the tears and gently kissed them away. "I'm excited to tears, too, Ashley. I have planned this for a long time. I know we are going to have a child and once we do, James Brooks will never want you again and you will always have me with you. Don't you see Ashley, this is the only solution." David stood to remove his pants. He was ready to make love to Ashley, more than ready. He had gone years making love to Karen and each time imagining it was Ashley beneath him. Now, he didn't have to imagine, here she was. He placed his knee between her legs and gently pushed them apart. Ashley kicked out with her legs weakly and began to swing her arms to try to hit him. But he grabbed her arms in mid air. "You always were feisty, that's why I love you so much." He held her hands over her head and kissed her lips. As he lowered his body down to hers, he heard the front door open.

"Ashley!" James called out. "Ashley!" James ran into the bedroom and saw Ashley in the bed under her sheets with her eyes open and tears falling. She looked to the left of James and when he turned in that direction, he was hit with a hard object, which propelled him backwards into the living room. David stepped from behind the door and stood above James who was momentarily out. David put his foot at the base of James throat. "You have interfered in my life for the last time Brooks," he snarled.

As he began to apply pressure, Ashley called out "David!" David turned to see Ashley standing with the sheet wrapped around her and a hair spray can in her hand. She sprayed directly into his eyes, which caused him to bring his hands up to shield his face. He yelled out, "Bitch," then swung and hit her with so much force she hit the wall and fell to the floor. James kicked out and tripped David to the floor. He grabbed a stunned David off the floor by his throat and swung his body against the wall. James stood over David and punched him again and again and again.

Hearing the commotion, Brian and Nick ran up the stairs and pulled James off David. James swung backwards knocking both men to the floor. He went back to David, picked him off the floor and repeatedly slammed him into the wall. Brian grabbed one arm of James while Nick tried to pry James fingers from around David's throat. Nick called out to James several times to no avail.

"James, think of Ashley and the baby!" Brian yelled out.

He turned with turmoil in his eyes and looked at Brian who was still holding on to his arm. "Butchie please let the man go," Nick pleaded. James then turned to the other side and looked at Nick. He released David's throat and his almost lifeless body fell to the floor. James sprung around when he remembered Ashley was in the room. He pulled away from the two men and went to her. She was in the corner of the room wrapped in the sheet in shock. He picked her up and carried her into the den. He sat on the sofa and held her protectively in his arms, the same way he had the first time she told him about David. His only wish was that he had killed the man then.

When the police arrived, they indicated James had to be taken into custody on the charge of attempted murder or possible murder depending on David's condition. The EMTs on the scene wasn't sure David would make it to the hospital. Brian asked that it be done after Ashley was in the ambulance and on her way to the hospital. Unfortunately, Ashley wasn't able to speak; she was in shock. She clung to James as if her life depended on his strength. But at the moment she could not tell anyone exactly what happened.

Brian called JD prior to the police arriving. When he ran up the stairs, he stopped at the top. The scene rocked the very foundation of him. It reminded him of the scene when Tracy was attacked. It was his responsibility to take care of Ashley when his father passed away. Just as it had been his responsibility to take care of Tracy. "JD," Brian called out; bringing his mind back to the present. "We have a situation. They need to examine Ashley and take James into custody. He's not letting her go. We need you to talk to him, and now would be a good time to use your influence with the officers. Once they know the whole story, I'm not sure if it will help or hurt James' case."

JD who was still a little shocked himself inhaled, "Tell me everything that happened," he said. "Did Holt," he swallowed before he asked the question, "did he ---?" JD was too emotional to finish the question.

"We don't know." Brian answered. "When we arrived Ashley was in the corner in shock and James was literally killing Holt."

JD nodded his head and listened to the details, as he knew them. When Brian finished, JD walked over, said something to one of the officers, and then went into the den.

He closed the French doors behind him and looked at Ashley sitting in James' lap. James looked up at him and exhaled, "They need me now?"

JD nodded, "Yeah. Based on what I heard it should only be a formality." Ashley had not moved or blinked her eyes. She looked up at James and tears began falling. She put her head on his shoulders and hugged him tightly. James smiled, "I won't be gone long." He squeezed her tightly as he looked up at JD. He was the only person that James knew he could trust to take care of Ashley. His eyes pleaded JD to help him to release her, because he was sure he could not do it on his own.

Understanding from personal experience what James was feeling, JD sat down on the sofa next to him. He put Ashley's feet in his lap and began rubbing them the way he used to do when she was a little girl and he needed her help. "Squirt," he whispered in a brotherly tone, "I need to know how far did Holt go. Did he--?" JD could feel James body tense and wondered if he knew the answer.

Apparently so did Ashley. She touched the side of James face and brought his head around to look directly into her eyes. "No," she said and sweetly kissed his lips. "James came in before he could."

James exhaled and began to breathe again. He kissed her gently on the lips and without breaking eye contact with Ashley he asked, "Is he dead?"

JD remembered asking the same question when Tracy was attacked, and wished he could tell James yes. He remembered the relief he felt when they told him the men that attacked Tracy were dead. "No."

James swallowed and closed his eyes, "I meant to kill him."

JD inhaled and thought to himself, if James makes that statement to anyone else it could be interpreted as premeditated murder if Holt dies. "Let's keep that comment between us. The information I have indicates you will not or

should not be charged; they just need to look further into
the situation. Nick has called your father and he will be at
the station when you get there. In the meantime, we need to
get Ashley examined." JD looked up and saw the EMT's
with a gurney outside the door. He stood, "I'll take her now,
James."

James stood and shook his head, "I'll take her." For a
moment, JD wondered if James would be able to let go. He
opened the door and surprisingly James placed Ashley onto
the gurney. He pulled the sheet over her, gently kissed her
and said, "I'll be there as soon as I can."

She held on to his hand and replied, "I'm going to marry
you as soon as I can."

He smiled as JD followed Ashley out with the EMT.
When they were no longer in sight, James turned to Nick,
"You called Pop?"

Nick crossed his arms over his chest and stood tall ready
for the onslaught of James' questions. "Yes I did."

James shook his head, "You always telling Pop on me,
man. Did you forget about brotherly loyalty?"

"Yeah, just like your forgot about, "Thou Shall Not Kill."

"Two totally different things. You don't always have to
tell Pop what happens."

"No, he can just read about it in the morning paper."

Brian looked at the two brothers and wondered if either
of them knew there was a room of people listening to this
ridiculous argument. "Excuse me. I hate to be the one to
break up this truly interesting confrontation. But we really
need to make moves. "

James looked at Brian, "You of all people know Holt
should not be breathing."

Brian raised an eyebrow at his friend, "I know you don't
have an attitude with me, Butchie! I just saved your ass from
a prison term. Let's go." Brian said as he walked off fully
expecting James to follow. As they walked out of the condo,
an officer went to place handcuffs on James. Both, Brian

and Nick jumped in between James and the officer. "That's not going to happen here," Brian, ordered. "You should count your blessings I'm letting you take him in for questioning."

When James arrived at the police station, not only was his father there, but so was Vernon. Avery Brooks' name carried a lot of weight, but he was a civil rights attorney. Vernon Brooks was a defense attorney who specialized in high-profile cases. Usually his clients were the wealthy kids whose parents wanted them to remain clean and could afford his services. Whenever an arrest was made in major criminal cases, Vernon's was the first name mentioned as a defense attorney. He was the best of the best. "So, you still are trying to kill people for touching who you consider your woman?" Vernon said smirking.

James looked at Vernon and for the first time in years, he smiled at his words. "Yeah, I guess you would know."

A tip of Vernon's lips curved into a half smile. He ran his hands down his chin and said, "Yeah I guess I would. Sit down and tell me how all of this came about."

James looked around the interrogation room. "It's a hell of a place for us to have our first sensible conversation in ten years."

"Yeah, wouldn't Mom be proud," Vernon replied.

"Hum Hum, you two smiling now, but you won't be when Gwen Brooks finishes with you," Avery stated.

James relayed all the events of the evening to his brother and father. He knew if he told them about the attempted rape at Harmon, that would clear him quicker, but he promised Ashley he would never tell anyone and he will not break that promise. Vernon arranged for James' release and indicated he did not anticipate any problems with the case if charges were filed. It was a clear case of self-defense.

Avery caught Vernon before he went back into the room with James. "Son, I'm not going to intervene with your case but, are you sure it's a good idea to have your brother released at this time?"

Vernon frowned and looked at his father. "You can't want James to stay here over night."

"Vernon do you remember the first night you tried to sleep after James caught you with Katherine?"

Vernon thought about that night and knew there was no way in hell James would let Holt continue to breathe if he is in that hospital. "Maybe its best that he stays put until we know about David Holt's condition."

Martha stood at the door of her daughter's hospital room, relieved that Ashley was physically stable. But there were a number of other issues that upset her. She watched as Tracy sat on the side of Ashley's bed talking to her. It was clear the friendship between the two women was deeper than anyone had ever imagined. Not only had Tracy kept Ashley's secret, but she protected her when she and JD could not. Martha was upset that her daughter did not feel she could come to her with the attempted rape in college, but was glad someone was there for her. Now that Ashley had revealed the whole truth, it was Martha's task to inform JD. She looked up, "Lord, give me the strength." She stepped outside the room and looked down the hallway. JD was talking with a number of people. The only one she recognized was Pearl Lassiter. When she got her attention, she motioned for her to come over.

"Hello Mrs. Harrison. Do you need JD?" Pearl asked.

"Yes, I will need to speak with him privately. First I need to know what effect all of this will have on his campaign."

Pearl nodded her head, "Well," she sighed, "I have to be honest, the opposition is going to put their own spin on the events of the night. However, we will make sure the public knows this was a clear case of James protecting himself and Ashley from a not-so-stable person. I believe once we put this fire out—and believe me we will—JD's record is going to speak for itself."

"Will JD have to let James go?" Martha asked.

"Mrs. Harrison you and I both know JD will never remove James as his campaign manager. His loyalty runs deep, sometimes to a fault."

"Are you going to recommend that James step down?"

"No. I believe in my heart that James is the man to get JD through the circus we call politics and allow him to stay true to who he is. Any other manager will be out to get to the top regardless of the damage to the man. James, Calvin, Senator Roth and even that pain in the butt Brian are the foundation JD needs around him. I would not change any of the dynamics of this team."

Martha smiled, "When you were younger we worried about John and Sally being able to raise all twelve of you children without some of you turning out to be hellions. I can't speak for the rest of them, but I certainly am happy you are on JD's team. You be sure and tell your mother I said thank you for number four of the dozen."

Pearl laughed. The joke in the neighborhood was always *which one of the dozen are you?* At home, for a while, all her brothers and sisters would refer to each other as the number in the birth line. "I will tell her that. In the meantime, don't be concerned with this. That group of people standing with JD is a part of my staff. Our job is to make things like this go away. I'll get JD for you and make sure you have some place quiet where you can talk."

"Would you get Calvin and Brian and have them stand outside the door where JD and I will be talking?"

"Sure," Pearl replied as she walked away.

Martha sat in the room as she revealed the story and watched JD's expression change from surprised, to concern and then finally to anger. It was hard to determine exactly who JD was the angriest with, Holt, Ashley, Tracy or himself. Understandably, he wanted to kill Holt. The thought of this man attempting this, not once but twice angered JD. The thought of Ashley not telling him this when it first happened hurt him. He always believed she would come to him for any reason. Unfortunately, the brunt of his anger was directed towards Tracy. After clearly dismissing his mother's words of warning, JD left the room and headed towards Ashley's room. Brian stopped him in the hallway. "I can't let you go down there at the moment." Brian said calmly.

Martha stood at the door, "JD, you are angry with the wrong person. It was not Tracy's place to tell you what happened with Ashley. And frankly, it was Ashley's choice not to tell anyone, including me."

JD turned to his mother and hugged her. "It wasn't your responsibility to keep Ashley safe. It was mine. It's the one thing Daddy asked me to do." He walked away and entered Ashley's room. He loved his wife deeply, but could not believe she kept something of this magnitude from him. "Tracy I need to speak with Ashley alone," he said in an abrupt tone.

Ashley, who laid on her side facing Tracy with her back to JD looked up at Tracy and gave her an encouraging smile. Now six months pregnant, Tracy eased out of the chair. "Okay," she spoke softly. She looked at her husband and could actually see the anger in his eyes. And for the first time in her marriage she knew that anger was directed at her.

Tracy stepped outside with Martha, Calvin and Brian. They all could see how nervous she was once JD entered the room. Brian looked at his watch, "It's late. Do you want me to take you home, I'm sure you are tired?" he said to Tracy.

She smiled nervously, "No, I'll wait for Jeffrey."

"I don't know, Tracy, maybe it would be better if you wait at home for him," Calvin said.

She shook her head. If her husband was upset with her, she would handle it. They would handle it together. It seemed the clock on the wall grew louder with each tick. Tracy knew the conversation going on in that room was going to anger Jeffery more. Not only had she kept the Harmon incident from him, but the most recent ones as well.

"James, man, it's good to see you." Calvin shook his hand as he entered the hallway. "Did they clear everything up.?"

"Yes," James nodded his head. "The statement Ashley gave in conjunction with Karen's statement, helped."

"Karen gave a statement against David?" Brian asked.

"Yes," James exhaled a little frustrated. "I apologize, but I need to see Ashley." He said as he walked towards the room.

James walked into the room to the sight of Ashley arms around JD and her softly crying. A deep crease formed in his forehead and then he relaxed. He folded his arms across his chest. "It's a good thing you're her brother." Ashley turned and the tears in her eyes caused his knees to buckle at the sight of anguish on her face. She pulled away from JD and James immediately pulled her into his arms. JD watched on as the two consoled each other. He then realized, it was no longer his responsibility to take care of her. JD smiled and left the room.

James rubbed Ashley's back trying to calm her. "Everything is alright. This nightmare is finally over. David is being placed under arrest as we speak. Of course, they will have to wait until he heals to put him behind bars." Ashley smiled a little but continued to cry harder. James was at a loss; he thought his words would calm her a little. He held her tighter "Shh, shh, baby," he cooed. "I'll never let anything happen to you or our baby." He brushed her hair from her face and looked into her eyes, "You know that, right?" She nodded her head, but continued to cry. "Then, what is it Ashley? Why are you so upset?"

Ashley was heaving as she tried to speak. "I...." she inhaled "I told momma I was pregnant and now she's going to kill you." Ashley cried hysterically into James shoulders.

James started laughing as he tried to console her, "No baby, she won't kill me," he said.

"You want to put a bet on that?" Martha Harrison said from the doorway with her hands on her hips.

JD stood outside the door of Ashley's hospital room and stared at his wife. He was beyond angry with her. While talking to Ashley he found out not only what Holt did at Harmon, but things he had done since he and Tracy were married. JD wanted to hit something, but he knew that something would never be his wife. He walked over to Brian and Calvin. They had a few words and they left. JD turned and looked at Tracy. She was beautiful, with her stomach round and full with his son. He closed his eyes and exhaled, how was he going to handle this. He felt betrayed by her. Tracy should have told him about the incidents that involved her even if she did not tell him about those with Ashley. He walked towards her and stopped in front of her. Tracy sat there with her hands in her lap and refused to look up at him. She could not stand to see the angry look in his eyes again; it hurt too deeply.

"Tracy," JD said with his hands in his pockets. "Why did you keep this from me?"

She never looked up as she continued to watch her thumbs as they twirled. "It wasn't my place to tell."

JD exhaled, trying to keep his temper in check, "Look at me Tracy."

Tracy didn't want to look up at him, but she would never refuse her husband's request. She sat on her hands and looked up with tears in her eyes. The moment JD saw the tears roll down his wife's face his heart skipped a beat. He never wanted to cause her distress, especially while she was carrying his child. He bent down to her and gently kissed her lips. Tracy put her arms around his neck and cried against his shoulders. He pulled her up into his arms and held her tight, while she cried. "Just because I fell for those tears, doesn't make me any less angry with you," JD said as he kissed her neck. "You are my wife. When things happen to you, I expect to be told about it, no exceptions. Do I make myself clear?" Tracy nodded her head against his shoulder. He pulled her away from him and looked into her eyes. He used his thumbs to wipe her tears from her cheeks.

"I love you Tracy. I can't deal with you of all people keeping things from me. James, Brian and Calvin do enough of that. I don't expect it from you."

Tracy lowered her eyes and then looked back up at him. The last thing she wanted was for JD not to trust her. She thought long and hard for anything she had not told him. Her eyes grew large. "I wrote Turk a letter once a week and put them in a box in my closet. And I took some money out of our joint account and brought some furniture for the baby." She inhaled and then continued. "I was rude to Carolyn one day on the telephone."

He looked at her with a slight frown on his face. "Why are you telling me these things?"

"Because I don't think that I have and I don't want you mad at me," she cried.

JD smiled and wondered how he could ever stay mad at her. As he hugged his wife, Pearl approached them and advised the media had arrived.

Chapter 12

For the first time since James purchased his home, it was filled to capacity and Clair found herself managing an unruly household. The Brooks family was in a quandary over James' possible arrest. The Harrison family was in a quandary over the attack against Ashley; which to be honest was at the forefront of Clair's mind. There was nothing she wouldn't do to help Ashley get through this difficult time. After all, Ashley has brought happiness into this house. Clair was thrilled when James told her about his engagement. She was concerned when the other Mrs. Brooks showed up unannounced and the disagreement that occurred between Ashley and James. But things seemed to have worked themselves out. Now this, just when Mr. James' life was coming together. Lord knows the man had been sad enough for an entire lifetime. The sound of someone coming down the stairs interrupted Clair's thoughts. She stepped into the dining room from the kitchen and found Ashley heading in her direction.

"Ms. Ashley you should not be up. Mr. James is not going to be happy about this," Clair stated animatedly.

"I know," Ashley sighed, "But there is no way you can handle breakfast for all of these people by yourself. I'll help you."

Clair looked at the bruise on Ashley's face and almost broke into tears. How could someone want to hurt such a thoughtful person? "Ms. Ashley I can handle this. I cook for five children and seven grandchildren every day. This is a piece of cake." She turned to walk back into the kitchen. "You come with me. I have a hot cup of French Vanilla cappuccino, just for you."

"You have no idea how good that sounds," Ashley said, smiling and walking behind Clair.

Clair reached for the cup as Ashley entered the refrigerator and began pulling out breakfast items. As she placed them on the table, Clair moved them to the countertop. "Sit, Ms. Ashley. If you insist on being here, you can watch, but you will watch from that chair. Is that understood?"

Ashley stared at Clair with tears in her eyes. "I can't sit and do nothing. I have to keep busy."

Clair's heart tightened at the look in her eyes. In the year they had known each other, Clair never saw anything but joy and happiness in there before. Now she saw tears. She took Ashley in her arms and hugged her tight. "All of this will go away. Mr. James will see to it. Don't you fret."

"I don't want James to go to jail because of me," she cried.

"He won't. I'll make sure of it," Vernon said from the doorway.

The two women looked up at him. Neither heard him come down the stairs. "Good morning sir," Clair said as she stepped away from Ashley. "If you have a seat at the table in the dining room I will bring you a cup of coffee." Ashley took a seat at the table where Clair placed her cappuccino. She took a drink of the smooth hot liquid and tried to hide the tears in her eyes from Vernon. "I'll take that coffee here. I hope you don't mind Ashley."

Ashley held her head up. "No, I don't mind," she replied hoping her voice did not give away how stressed she was.

Vernon sat at the table as Clair placed a cup of hot coffee in front of him. "Cream and sugar is on the table," Clair announced and began preparing breakfast.

Vernon watched Ashley intently. He could certainly see why James was attracted to her. She was a beautiful woman. Self assured confident and very protective of her man. The first time the two met was not pleasant and he could understand her coolness towards him, now. Nevertheless, his instincts told him Ashley had answers that would clear this situation up. He sensed James did not disclose all he knew regarding David Holt. Since James would not tell him all, maybe she would. "That's an ugly bruise. How are you feeling this morning?" he asked.

Ashley never looked up, "I'm fine," she replied.

"Are you sure? You seem to be a little nervous. Did the doctor indicate if the drugs would have any side effect?"

Remembering the fifth degree Vernon took her through the first time they met, Ashley was in no mood to play games with him. "Why are you here Vernon?"

"Because my brother needs my help. And I intend to do all I can to ensure he does not go to jail," he bluntly stated. He sat forward, drank some of his coffee and stared at her. "I believe James withheld information last night that could have cleared him of all charges. I'm not sure of it, but I am almost willing to bet my checkbook it has to do with protecting you in some way. Would you like to share?"

Ashley looked shocked, "I thought the charges were dropped."

"No, they are being withheld, pending an investigation." She sat forward and placed her hand on her forehead, contemplating her next words. "Ashley if there is anything you could share with me that would clear James, tell me now before this goes any further."

"What did James tell you?"

"Only that Holt was attempting to rape you when he entered the apartment. He was hit with an object and momentarily rendered unconscious. When he came to, Holt had turned back to attacking you at which time James attempted to kill him." Ashley shook her head. She pushed away from the table and looked out the window. The view from James's window was always peaceful, but today it did not bring her any comfort. Tears streamed down her face as she crossed her arms over her stomach. "Ashley was there any past history between you and this man?"

Ashley nodded her head. "We went out when I was in college. When James and I started seeing each other David began showing up almost everywhere. At functions, my job. I have no idea how he got into my condo. All I know is James showed up just as he ..." She hesitated.

Clair moved towards Ashley to comfort her, but Vernon stood and stopped her. "Ashley, when was the last time you were with Holt?"

Ashley turned angrily, "What are you trying to say? I haven't been with David since college."

"Okay," Vernon said as he walked towards her. "Is there anything you can tell me that will help James. What unfinished business did you have with this man that would make him stalk you in this manner?"

"You don't have to answer that." James said from the doorway. He walked past Vernon over to Ashley and gathered her into his arms "You shouldn't be out of bed. How are you feeling this morning?"

"I'm okay. I talked to Tracy a little earlier. She'll be over in a few minutes." Ashley smiled as she returned his hug.

James shook his head, "I guess my kisses weren't good enough."

"It's not that," Ashley jokily hit his arm as Clair and Vernon looked on.

"I know. You want your friend here. I understand. " He frowned as he rubbed the bruise on her face and kissed it. Turning his attention to Vernon, he said, "Vernon, I told you all you need to know last night."

"No, Butchie, you didn't. You told me what you wanted me to know. Now I need Ashley to tell me what I need to know. Ashley?"

"It's time for all secrets to end. If I had been open about all of this years ago, this would not be happening now." Ashley sat back at the table. Vernon joined her. Clair handed James a cup of coffee and he sat next to Ashley. She inhaled, "David attempted to rape me in college. It was covered up by the university and no one other than my roommate knew about it."

Vernon sat forward, "You mean to tell me this has happened before and it's documented somewhere?" Ashley nodded. Vernon sat back almost in disbelief. He slowly smiled and looked at James. "That clears this up."

James shook his head, "No, it doesn't. This information does not leave this kitchen."

Vernon looked at James in disbelief. "James, this man has a history of attacking her. It clearly strengthens the case of stalking and self-defense."

"I made a promise to keep this information confidential and I have no intention of breaking that promise."

"A promise to whom?" Vernon asked. When James did not reply, Vernon looked from James to Ashley. "Will you release him from that promise?"

Ashley looked up at James. "Yes."

"I don't wish to be released."

Vernon shook his head and stood up. "Well, you know what? I didn't make any promise, but one. That was to clear you of all pending charges and that's exactly what I am going to do." He walked out of the kitchen and headed towards the stairs.

"Vernon!" James followed calling after him raising his voice. "You will not do this."

"Do what?" Avery asked while heading down the stairs.

Vernon continued to walk until he was standing behind his father. "Pop, James is purposely interfering in his own defense and I refuse to let him."

Avery looked at James, "Butchie is that true?" he frowned"

James looked passed his father to Vernon. "There is a thing called client/attorney privilege and Vernon is about to break it."

"No Pop. No, I won't. I will not be revealing anything James told me." By this time, the rest of the family had gathered on the stairs responding to the raised voices.

"It is six o'clock in the morning. What's all this yelling about?" Gwendolyn asked concerned.

Since it seemed Vernon had taken refuge behind his father, James turned to his mother. "Mom, Vernon is breaking client/attorney privilege and telling Pop things he shouldn't. And Nick did the same thing last night."

"Why you got to tell mom on me?" Nick yelled from the hallway.

Ashley stood in the doorway of the kitchen. Shaking her head in disbelief, she whispered to Clair, "Do you see what I see: two grown men running behind mommy and daddy, telling on each other? Well, at least they are a family again."

"Yeah, a crazy one," Clair said and retreated to the kitchen.

Ashley walked over to James and put her arms around his waist. "Vernon you have my permission to use the information in any manner necessary to clear James' name."

She smiled up at James. "I'm sure Tracy will testify also if you need her to. How soon can this be resolved?"

Everyone in the room seemed to relax at Ashley's words, especially Avery. He wasn't sure he would have been able to keep James off Vernon this time. "I'll have it cleared by noon on Monday," Vernon declared and ran up the stairs.

James turned to Ashley, "I think you should go back to bed. You should take it easy at least for today."

"No, I'll be okay," she replied. "I'll sit with you while you have breakfast."

The doorbell rang as everyone moved into the dining room. Clair answered the door and Tracy rushed through. She went straight to Ashley who was seated next to James at the table. Ashley pulled away from James and hugged Tracy. "It's finally over Tracy. We don't have to worry about David again."

"I know," Tracy sighed with relief. "How are you feeling? Did the doctor check everything? Should you be up this early? I think you should go back to bed and stay there for the rest of the day."

"You are probably right," Ashley replied as she headed toward the stairs.

"Good morning everyone," Tracy greeted as an afterthought. "James, I'll talk with you after I get Ashley to bed."

James smiled as he watched the two friends walk up the stairs. His family turned to him with a questioning look. "Yes, I just suggested the same thing. And no, I don't have a say when it comes to those two."

"As long as you know that and understand when to be quiet you will be just fine," Avery advised. Vernon came down the stairs fully dressed. "Where are you off to?"

"I just spoke with the Assistant District Attorney handling this case. He spoke with Mr. Harrison, who has excused himself from this case for obvious reasons. Both will be here within the hour." Vernon took a seat as Clair came through the kitchen door with several platters in her hands. "This smells wonderful," he said as he took a platter from her hand.

The doorbell rang, again. "Boy this sure is a busy house this morning," Clair said as she headed towards the door.

James looked around the table. This was the first time his entire family had been in his home. He lowered his head and wished it could have been under different circumstances. But for whatever reason, the Lord saw fit to bring his family here during his time of need. When he looked up Vernon was looking in his direction. The two had a lot of work to do on their relationship. He took the first step and now Vernon had taken the second. James nodded acknowledging all that Vernon was doing on his behalf. He looked past Vernon and saw Martha walking towards the dining room. James stood and began to walk towards her, "Please don't get up James. I just wanted to check in on Ashley. Good morning everyone."

"Good Morning. Ashley is upstairs and Tracy is with her," James replied. Martha nodded, "Thank you, James, I can find my way. You might want to give JD a hand. A number of reporters have surrounded him out front."

"What reporters?" James asked as he walked towards the door. Vernon and Avery got up from the table and joined him. Martha was right, reporters and news crews were in the front of his home.

James started to go out the door, but Vernon stopped him. "No, you can't go out there James. I'll speak with them." Vernon and Avery stepped out of the door. Avery maneuvered JD away while Vernon took over media.

Once inside the house JD spoke to everyone and then turned to James. "Where is she?" he asked angrily. "I told her not to leave the house without me. I can't believe she came through that crowd and there's one just as big at our house that Pearl is handling."

"I take it you are referring to your wife." James grinned. "It's good to know you have no more control over your wife than I have over Ashley."

"How is Ashley?" JD asked a little frustrated.

"She's trying to show a strong front, but this has shaken her. Come into my office. We can talk there." James, JD and Avery went into the office, while everyone else went back into the dining room to finish breakfast.

Twenty minutes later, Calvin, Brian, Douglas, Vernon, Avery, Nick, JD and James all sat in the office going over the effects all of this may have on the campaign. Vernon and Calvin discussed the handling of the case. Based on all the information provided by Karen in addition to Ashley and Tracy's testimony, they were certain, no charges would be filed. Now, the case against David had to be built. As District Attorney, normally JD would assign this case; however, to ensure the defense would not be able to claim any improprieties, Calvin would be handling the assignment of the case, but not the case itself. He was too close to the family.

The men came out of the office just as Tracy and Martha were coming down the stairs. JD walked over to Tracy and stood in front of her. Martha cut in between them. "JD, now you know there was no way you were going to keep her from coming over here today."

JD looked at his mother and exhaled. "Mother this is between Tracy and me. Step aside." Martha looked at Tracy with sympathetic eyes, then back to JD as she walked away.

"Jeffrey, I just wanted to make sure she was alright," Tracy said with sad eyes.

"I told you not to leave the house without me or Brian. What did you think they were going to do to her over here?" he asked angrily. "Did you come through that crowd of reporters outside our house?

" Yes." Tracy replied meekly, "But I was very careful. I did not say anything to anyone."

"Tracy I'm not worried about you saying anything. I could care less what you say. I don't want you to get physically hurt. You are caring my child; I don't want anything to happen to you or him," JD said raising his voice. "I'm going upstairs to see Ashley. Do not leave this house until we can both leave together." Tracy looked around nervously at the people in the other room. JD placed a finger under her chin and turned her face back to him. "Do I make myself clear?"

"Yes." Tracy replied as she walked towards the kitchen. JD watched her walk away and was sorry he yelled at her. He climbed the stairs two at a time. As the other people at the table pretended not to hear the exchange, James went into the kitchen to console Tracy. He knew it was her love for Ashley that made her go against JD's wishes.

The media were consumed with the arrest of David Holt. The spin-doctors on both sides of the campaign were at work. Pearl was winning out. It took some doing, but she was able to convince James to allow Ashley to go public with the entire story. With Karen's help the Harrison campaign wasn't as marred by the chain of events as the Roberts campaign. To show a united front some of the background bickering had to stop. Some of the polls were showing Gavin's single digit lead was dwindling because of Holt's connection to his camp. The opponents were waging a media bliss directed towards women, indicating the Democrats respect for women was questionable. With the rape arrest and the spousal abuse allegations, the public's trust was wavering.

The spokesperson for all three camps met with the candidates and their wives. Pearl felt the upcoming Roth-Roberts wedding was a good opportunity to show a united front. However, with everything that had happened over the previous month, JD and James were both hesitant to meet with Carolyn. Her actions against Tracy were more than JD could tolerate. Trying to set her up to fail in public would have been devastating if it had succeeded.

James lost control when he learned Carolyn was the one who brought Katherine into his relationship with Ashley and encouraged David's actions.

Pearl had to find a way to get the men to sit down and talk or at least make an appearance together soon. She asked Senator Roth to intercede. When Senator Roth arrived at James' home, he was shocked at the depth of anger toward Carolyn. Roth listened to all the men had to say regarding both the situation with the luncheon and the situation with David Holt. He had no idea Carolyn was involved with Holt in any way, much less giving him information about Ashley. Her interference with James' family was beyond reasoning or explanation. However, she was still his daughter and he felt compelled to smooth things over on her behalf.

"Well, if everyone is finished I would like to speak." Both men sat quietly and listened. "James you certainly have reason to be angry with Carolyn. She had no right to involve your ex-wife or your son in this vendetta against Tracy and Ashley. Please know if I had even an inkling of her involvement with the Holt man, I would have intervened myself. Ashley is the daughter of the best friend I could have ever had in this world. I would not want to see her harmed in any way." He then turned to JD. "Son," he said as he shook his head, "I know you are about at your wits end when it comes to Carolyn and her antics. The only thing I can say is you know how she hates to lose, but that does not excuse her actions." He leaned against the mantel and crossed his arms over his chest. "With that said, let's look at the entire picture. All that has happened is not campaign ending and nor should we let it be. We are talking about what is best for the Commonwealth of Virginia and, frankly, neither of you can say, even in your anger, that Gavin and

Carolyn are not the answer. Of all the things she has done, Gavin has not been a party to any of it. He should not have to pay the price for Carolyn's actions, nor should the state.

Now, JD you have to stand with Gavin and Daniel to get all of the ticket over the hump. The fact that David was a part of his campaign has caused more damage than expected. A united front is not only needed, but is crucial. To be blunt, if you two are not able to put aside personal issues you are in the wrong line of business. Politics is not for you. So, gentlemen, decide now, will you allow Carolyn's actions to prevent you from accomplishing the goals you have set for yourself?" He sat his glass down on the mantel and walked towards the door. "When you have an answer to that, let me know. In the meantime, I'm going to have a talk with my daughter."

When the door closed behind him, James looked at JD. With all that had happened, James was still committed to getting JD elected. Roth was right; this was a personal issue and should be handled in a personal manner, not in the political arena. "He's a very convincing man, isn't he?"

JD looked at James and shrugged, "He is a politician."

"What do you purpose we do about Carolyn?" James asked.

"I'm not sure any of us could do anything with Carolyn, but this madness must come to an end."

Still angry, James stood and looked out the window. "She called Katherine and threatened to expose information regarding our son. She gave David information to help him bring his plans for Ashley to fruition. I don't know if I can let that go."

"You know, sometimes it takes a woman to handle a woman. Neither Tracy nor Ashley has the mean streak needed to handle someone like Carolyn, but we know someone who does," JD said raising his eyebrows.

James turned, stared at JD and began smiling. "We know two people." James walked over to the door "Mom, could you step in here for a minute?"

Gavin Roberts sat in the study in his home and listened intently to the report from one of his advisors. The tale being revealed caused him to shake his head. It was difficult for him to believe the depth of Carolyn's involvement with David Holt. He walked over to the window. The capitol could be seen in the distant background. Gavin's dream was to be Governor of the Commonwealth. Marrying Carolyn would guarantee that dream being fulfilled. Not only will he become Governor, he would be marrying a woman he loved very much. That feeling was not reciprocated and he knew that. The events of the last twenty-four hours reinforced that. What he did not know was how far Carolyn had taken the revenge against Tracy. Knowing she would go so far as to threaten a child's well being was more than he felt his pride could take. He tried to understand how hurt she was when JD married Tracy. But he was offering her everything she wanted. Becoming the First Lady of Virginia and all the love a man could offer a woman. Apparently, it wasn't enough. He exhaled and continued to listen to the polling numbers. They were lower than what he considered comfortable. Carolyn's involvement with Holt not only caused physical injury to Ashley, but damage to the campaign as well, not to mention his pride. Gavin excused himself from the meeting, but asked the staff to continue with the strategy session and he would return shortly.

Gavin arrived at the Roth Estate twenty minutes later and his decision had not wavered. He entered Carolyn's suite. She decided to move back to the estate the week before the wedding. Carolyn was old fashion in many ways. Sometimes Gavin wondered if Carolyn knew herself how much traditions meant to her. She was raised in a political family. You learn early that losing at anything is not acceptable. Unfortunately, Carolyn had taken losing JD to Tracy to a whole other level. If they had any chance of making a marriage work, it had to stop now.

"Gavin, what are you doing here?" she asked.

"Have you seen the news?"

Carolyn stared at Gavin for a moment before answering. He had warned her about lying to him and from his appearance, this was not a time to take a chance. "Yes. I saw the news coverage earlier today."

"The polling numbers have dropped. The drop for JD and Daniel was not as significant as the drop in my numbers. The team is holding a strategy session at the house."

Carolyn smiled. For a moment she thought he was angry about her involvement with David. "Do you need my input? I'm pretty good at putting a spin on things."

Gavin looked at Carolyn and smirked, "That you are Carolyn. That you are." He walked over to her and kissed her forehead. The bittersweet kiss sent a shiver through her. She stepped back and looked at him. "No, I don't want your input on strategy." He put his hands in his pocket, stood with his legs apart, and looked intently into her eyes. "I'm calling off the wedding."

A frown marred Carolyn's forehead. "Calling off the wedding!" she shook her head in total disbelief. "You are joking. You can't be serious." She watched and for the first time in a long time she could not read Gavin's thoughts. "Tell me you are joking!" she yelled.

Gavin did not move or alter his expression. "I warned you last year not to let your antics hurt anyone I cared about. I made it clear JD was one of those people. Your actions against Tracy and Ashley have affected my campaign and my relationship with a man I admire and respect. Moreover, your relationship with Holt has damaged the little pride you afforded me at one time." He shook his head in disbelief.

Carolyn desperately walked over to Gavin, "We can still win the campaign and JD will survive whatever happens with Tracy, he always does. We are just months away from getting everything we want Gavin. Don't be foolish and throw all of that away over something that won't even be remembered after next week. Think about what you are doing."

Gavin looked at Carolyn and smirked. "I have thought about it. I can't live with a woman whose main purpose in life is to hurt other people. Look around you Carolyn. You have everything a person could ever want or need. Money, power, beauty and the love of a good man: Hell Carolyn, I'm even taking you to the mansion and it's not enough." He turned and walked out of the door.

As he descended the stairs, Carolyn ran out after him. "Gavin, the wedding is planned. The invitations are out. We are expecting five hundred guests on Saturday. We can't call this off," she exclaimed with all the anguish the last twenty minutes had caused. "Please," she grabbed his arm. "Please don't do this Gavin. I'll make it right," she pleaded. "Just tell me what I need to do to make it right with you."

Gavin looked at her with a frown then calmly said, "You don't have to make it right with me. You have to make it right with JD and Tracy. Then you have to make it right with James and Ashley. Then you have to make it right for the little boy whose life you were willing to turn upside down, just to get revenge." Gavin pulled away. He walked down the stairs and out of the door without looking back.

Carolyn stood on the stairs trying to clear her mind. Tears ran down her cheeks as she realized she was about to lose the one thing that meant the world to her. This couldn't be happening to her. Gavin would not walk away from her or the mansion. It was what they both wanted. The longer she stood on the steps the more she realized he was not walking back through that door. Carolyn sat on the step and cried. A few minutes later she stopped. She had to clear her mind and think. There was no way in hell she was going to give up her wedding or the mansion and certainly not Gavin. She got up, ran down the stairs and grabbed her car keys. She was not going to lose another man and her dreams again.

Carolyn walked into her father's townhouse in the city which was near the capitol. Since she was staying at home until the wedding, it seemed her father spent most of his time here. His car was in the garage so she knew he was home. Upon entering the house she wondered why he wasn't answering his cell phone. "Daddy," she called out frantically as she ran up the stairs to the master suite. She pushed open the door to the bedroom and froze in her tracks.

"Carolyn! What are you doing here?" He sat up in the bed making sure the sheet covered his naked lower body.

The look on Carolyn's face was one of pure shock. Then it changed to disgust, then anger. "What in the hell are you doing here?" She yelled at the woman in the bed next to her father.

Lena threw the blanket to the side and stood there, naked as the day she was born, "A women's place is next to her husband," she smirked as she walked into the bathroom.

Carolyn looked at her father as he stood and put on his robe. "What are you doing here Carolyn?" He asked again calmly.

A shake of her head did not clear the scene or the words she was sure she misunderstood. Carolyn looked at her father. "Did she say husband?" She asked in disbelief.

John Roth walked over to his daughter. He reached out for her and she stepped back. "Did she say husband?" She angrily asked.

He stepped back and walked over to the closet. He pulled out a pair of pants and stepped into them. Carolyn walked over to the closet. She stood directly in front of her father. "Daddy," she said in a shaky voice, "she called you her husband. Please tell me she is wrong Daddy. Please. Tell me she is wrong," she cried.

"Carolyn, go home to Gavin. I'm sure he has some issues to discuss with you."

The heart in her chest stopped. She couldn't breathe. Her father, whom she loved, who was supposed to love her without limits was sending her away. Lena walked out of the bathroom in a robe and stood in the doorway. Carolyn stared at the woman. "You're throwing me out for her?"

Roth could hear the hurt in his daughter's voice. He loved Carolyn, but he could not live his life for her. "I'm not throwing you out Carolyn. I'm sending you to the man you are suppose to marry. You have things you need to clear up with him before the wedding."

Carolyn looked at him with tears streaming down her face. "There isn't going to be a wedding on Saturday. Gavin called it off." Roth reached for her, but she stepped back. She looked at her father and then at Lena. She walked out of the room, down the stairs and out of the townhouse without saying a word.

It seemed James had just settled in beside Ashley and pulled her sleeping body into his arms when the telephone rung. It was Gavin's campaign manager. A meeting was being called within the hour at Gavin's place. A development that will affect all three campaigns needed to be discussed.

Chapter 13

Carolyn was lost and felt completely alone for the first time in her life. There was always someone for her to turn to when she was hurt or upset. Her mother was always too busy with her society life to care one way or another. But her father was always there for her. How could he marry that woman, was all Carolyn could think. Of all the people in the world, why Lena Washington? First, there was JD and now her father. Tears continued to roll down her cheeks. She drove with no particular destination—No one she called a friend. "A friend" she said to herself aloud. There was only one person she could always call a friend and that was Jackie.

Jackie was her childhood friend. They did everything together from elementary school through adulthood, until last year. JD's best friend, Calvin, asked Jackie to marry him. Carolyn remembered how excited Jackie was that night. It was New Year's Eve and JD's wedding day. Carolyn was too busy with her own pity party to acknowledge her friend's happiness. Since that time, Carolyn and Jackie had parted ways. In fact, Jackie did not invite Carolyn to her wedding. Jackie and Calvin flew to Aruba with close friends and family. They were married on February fourteenth. Now Calvin and Jackie were expecting their first child. To this day, Jackie had not forgiven Carolyn's reaction to her engagement. Nevertheless, Jackie never turned her away when she needed a friend and Carolyn was certain, she would not turn her down now.

Carolyn rang the doorbell to Jackie's home. When Jackie opened the door, Carolyn could not speak. The emotions of the past few hours poured out of her in tears. Jackie pulled her into the house and sat her down on the sofa. Calvin walked into the room and looked at the distraught Carolyn who had slid to the floor and was crying hysterically into his wife's lap. Not wanting to be a part of Carolyn's antics Calvin looked at Jackie and rolled his eyes. He turned and walked out of the room.

Jackie rubbed the top of Carolyn's head. "What have you done?"

"Why does it have to be something I've done?" she yelled.

Jackie was used to Carolyn's temper tantrums, and did not react. She simply replied, "Because you are your own worst enemy. I've seen you do things to hurt yourself repeatedly. So what have you done this time?"

Carolyn looked up, began to cry real tears, and told the whole story. Jackie got up to get a box of tissues from the table. She walked over to Carolyn, drew her hand back and smacked her across her face with all the strength she had within. She then sat down on the floor next to a very shocked Carolyn who slid away quickly. Jackie pulled tissues from the box and handed them to Carolyn, who hesitantly took the tissues from her hands, but continued to stare at the woman who was supposed to be her friend.

Jackie exhaled, "Carolyn, you are a blind fool. You have everything a woman," she stopped and thought, "no, any person could possibly want in life. You are beautiful, intelligent, wealthy and powerful. You have a man who loves you—God only knows why. But you are so busy trying to chase a dream, and that's all it has ever been was a dream, that you cannot see or appreciate what you have. Gavin loves you so much he was willing to marry you knowing, you did not feel the same way about him. Did you ever ask yourself why? No you didn't. Well, let me shed some light on it for you. Gavin decided to run for Governor, because all you have ever wanted was to be the First Lady of Virginia. In order to give you what you wanted he had to become Governor of Virginia, and that is precisely what he set out to do. While he was trying to accomplish your dream for you, you were out making a fool of yourself over JD, who you knew did not love you. To further stomp on Gavin's pride, you take up with the likes of David Holt. What did you expect? I'm surprised it took him this long to call the wedding off. You claim you care so much about JD, but you have tried everything under the sun to ruin his happiness. Then to threaten your friend with exposing a secret she shared with you regarding her child was a new low. I'm truly surprised James Brooks did not try to kill you along with David."

Carolyn's' tears had stopped flowing a while ago. Jackie's words were not soothing at all. If this was how her friend was talking to her, she definitely did not want to confront any of her enemies. "Is that all you have to say?" she asked.

Jackie looked at Carolyn, wondering if anything she said sank in. "Do I need to say more?"

"Yes Jackie. You have to tell me how to fix this. I can't lose Gavin. What should I do?"

Jackie looked back as she heard Calvin from the doorway. She smiled at her husband, who had showed her how to love. "That all depends," Jackie replied as she turned back to Carolyn. "Do you love Gavin? I mean truly love him?"

Carolyn did not respond for a while as she thought back to the night of JD's and Tracy's wedding. She was so hurt that night. Gavin knew she was mourning over the loss of another man, but that did not stop him from wanting to comfort her. That night was the first time that Carolyn was ever made love to. Oh, she had had sex many times before, but that was the first time a man made love to her.

That night, when Carolyn fell asleep in Gavin's arms, she felt loved for the first time in her life. The next day when Carolyn woke up, Gavin was not there. For a minute, she wondered if she had imagined the whole night. But when she hugged the pillow, she could still smell his cologne and knew she was not dreaming. Carolyn got out of bed, put on her robe and walked through the house looking for Gavin; he was gone. "Well, do you?" Jackie asked pulling Carolyn from her memories.

"Yes, I do," she replied, surprising herself.

"Do you love him more than the thought of becoming the First Lady of Virginia?"

Carolyn had to think about that question. She lowered her head and smiled as tears began to roll down her face again. "Yes," she replied whimpering.

Jackie stood up. "So you have finally experienced your 'ah ha' moment. Congratulations, now you have to repair the damage you have caused." Jackie looked down at Carolyn. For the first time in her life, she did not feel the woman looking up at her was superior to her in any way. "Get up off the floor. You need to get your mojo back in gear. I'm going to start the shower and you will get in it. I want you to think while you are in there about everything we talked about. When you finish, if you still want to marry Gavin, because you love him, then I will help you get out of this mess, you have created."

Gavin stood at the head of the table in his library, surrounded by Stanley Covington, John Roth, James Brooks, JD Harrison and Daniel Graham. As the head of the DNC it was Stanley's responsibility to ensure the ticket is successful. That would mean, not just a win, but to create the beginning point for the next campaigns. Since all of this began with one woman, he believed that woman could mend this situation. Before he met with the men, he called Tracy Harrison. From what he knew, all of this transpired because of her marriage to JD. He asked her to intercede. He was certain whatever Tracy asked of JD, he would do. He was just as certain whatever Ashley asked of James he would do. It would be up to the men to get Gavin to forgive Carolyn and do what is best for the ticket. It was his belief that the men sitting at the table were meant to shape the future of the country, if not the world. Everything within him believed JD Harrison was meant to be the President of the United States, someday. He was equally convinced James Brooks was the man who would get him to the point. There was no way he was going to allow a woman to interfere with history. Carolyn had invoked so much disruption into the campaign. He wasn't sure how things were going to work out for the men personally, but there were two things he was very sure of. First, before they left that house, the union between Gavin and Carolyn would be on again and second, all three candidates were going to show a united front tomorrow during the morning news cycles.

"James," Stanley began, "how is Ashley?"

James smiled, "She is recuperating very well."

"I'm pleased to hear that. Please accept my apology for my part in this." He extended his hand to James and he accepted it willingly. "With that said, let's get to the business at hand. Should the actions of one person prevail over what is best for the country? Not just the state, but the country." He stood and walked over to where Gavin sat. "Let me tell you what I see in the future. Gavin, you will become the next Senator of this state. Once your term as Governor is complete, Roth will retire his seat in the Senate. Daniel, after your term as Lt. Governor you will become a Congressman and gather support for whatever policy the administration sets forth. JD you will become Governor of Virginia and then you will be the party's nominee for the President of the United States." He looked to JD. "I realize that is an insurmountable amount of pressure on you. The reality of it is the moment others in this country realize your potential, you will become a target for every racially motivated group inside and outside this country." He pointed around the room. "You see, this is not just about today, or this time. All of you in this room will play a major role in history. This base must be unbreakable. Your trust and dedication must be unwavering. Unfortunately, for you, that trust and dedication must also extend to the woman you chose to be a part of your life. I know each of you quite well. No one can convince me that Carolyn's actions would affect your patriotism." He hesitated and looked at the faces around the room. "Fix this tonight. I will see you all in the morning at six a.m. We are scheduled to do the Morning Show. Gavin you are angry, I truly understand why. But you and I know, you are going to marry Carolyn. We will all stand in support of you tomorrow and Saturday, when you exchange vows." He walked towards the door then turned back and smiled. "Then in January, we will all be at the Capitol taking the first step towards history. Just in case you men needed it, I called in reinforcements."

Stanley turned and opened the door. "Hello Tracy; Ashley. Thank you for coming." He hugged them both. "I see you brought backup," he said looking over their shoulders.

Tracy turned and saw Calvin, Carolyn and Jackie standing behind them in the entrance. "I'm afraid I can't take credit for that." She turned back wondering if Ashley could keep her cool.

Ashley walked over to Carolyn, as the men rushed from the office. James immediately grabbed Ashley. Pregnant or not Ashley was not one to hold in her temper. Gavin stood next to Carolyn. His anger with her had not lessened, but he would not allow her to be harmed.

Carolyn turned to James and JD, who was protectively holding on to Tracy. "Gentlemen, we need to speak in private."

JD shook his head. "No."

"Let them talk," Senator Roth said to JD.

JD frowned and began to speak when Tracy interceded. "Jeffrey, I promise not to let Ashley kill her," she reassured him.

JD smiled down at his wife, "Does that promise extend to you?"

Tracy kissed his cheek, "I don't make promises I can't keep," she smiled sweetly.

Carolyn looked at Gavin. He was standing beside her, even with all she had done. First, she was going to take steps to clear this mess up for him and then she was going to tell him, honestly how she felt about him. "Will we have a chance to talk later?" she asked him almost pleading. He hesitated, "Please," she added.

He nodded his head, "I'll be here when you finish."

Carolyn turned to Tracy and Ashley, "Ladies, let's talk in my sitting room." She led the way as Jackie and the other women followed. Tracy turned, winked and smiled at Stanley.

Stanley returned the smile, and wondered if JD realized the depth of his wife's understanding of the political world.

He had no doubts the women would emerge united. "You all should take a lead from that little lady." He bid each of them good night.

Gavin exhaled and looked at his colleagues. "We can stand here and watch that staircase, or we could step into the library and have a glass or two of brandy. What will it be gentlemen?"

John looked at Gavin, "Would you happen to have a few bottles of that around here?"

"As a matter of fact, I do," Gavin replied smiling.

"I believe we will each need a bottle," James said as he hit JD on the shoulder. JD's attention was still on the stairs leading to Carolyn's sitting room. He wasn't as convinced as the others that the situation was under control.

"JD," Roth called out, "I believe the news I have to share with you will take your mind off of what's happening upstairs."

JD raised an eyebrow at the senator. "Nothing is more important than my wife."

John smiled. That was the one constant in his life. JD has never wavered on his wife's position in his life. "Believe me, you and James want to hear this."

Gavin and John walked into the library. JD, James and Calvin looked at each other. "Whatever it is can't be as bad as what has already happened tonight," Calvin commented.

James looked at JD who had the same look on his face. "I wouldn't bet the bank on that if I were you."

Roth looked at the men and laughed, nervously. "You are going to find this amusing." He cleared his throat, "Lena and I were married in the Bahamas last week. The faces staring back at him were blank.

"Lena who? JD finally managed to ask.

James began to chuckle. "I do believe he is referring to your mother-in-law." He took one look at JD and knew he was not finding the amusement in Roth's announcement. He stood and closed the door. Other than Calvin, James was sure everyone else in the room knew the irony of the announcement. But he wanted to make sure no one in the house overheard the conversation.

"Did you tell her the truth?" JD demanded.

"No, I haven't, yet. But I do plan to."

"Senator, that admission is not only going to affect your life, but mine as well. Don't you think you should have at least talked with me about this?" JD asked angrily.

James looked at JD. "Let's calm down a little. I believe the Senator is trying to inform us of his intentions."

Calvin, who was sitting quietly decided to ask the question. "What truth are we referring to?" John looked at JD, as did James and Gavin.

JD exhaled, "Last year during the background investigation it was determined that the Senator is Tracy's biological father."

Calvin looked from JD to Gavin in disbelief. "Does Tracy or Carolyn know this?" he asked as he stood and began pacing.

"No," both JD and Roth said in unison.

"We want to keep it that way," Roth added.

JD looked at him "Well at least we agree on that."

James looked at Roth, "The question is, will Lena? And what affect, if any, will this have on the campaign?"

The men continued talking and concluded that each of them was committed to the campaign. It was evident JD was not completely comfortable with the announcement by Roth, but he wished him well in his marriage. James was concerned with the effect all of the events would have on the campaign. He made sure the conversation stayed positive by giving a toast to the marriage. JD turned to James and asked, "What could possess him to open that hornet's nest?"

James smiled "Love; pure unadulterated love." Privately he prayed the conversation going on upstairs with the women was progressing better.

It was close to three a.m. when the women joined the men in the library. It was immediately evident what they had spent the past few hours doing. Tracy looked around the room and put her hands on her hips. Calvin and Jackie had left earlier, but every other man in the room was intoxicated. "Jeffrey Harrison, you are due in front of cameras in less than three hours. Have you lost your mind drinking like this? All of you know better than this," she said angrily.

Ashley walked over to James, who seemed to be the most coherent of the four. She kissed him, put his arms around her shoulder and helped him up. "Come on big boy. Let's get you home."

James smiled up at Ashley, "I love you Ashley Renee' Harrison."

Ashley returned the smile. "That's what you say now," she replied as they headed out of the door. "Wait until I'm fat like Tracy."

"Excuse you," Tracy frowned at her.

"Love you Tracy. See you at the studio," Ashley walked away laughing

JD smile up at his wife. "You are the most beautiful pregnant woman I have ever seen, Tracy Harrison."

Tracy looked down at her intoxicated husband whose smile was as contagious as chicken pox.

"Alright, good looking, let's get you home too," she said as she attempted to pick her husband up.

Carolyn ran over, "Tracy you shouldn't be doing that. Here let me help," The two women looked at each other for the longest moment. Carolyn put JD's other arm around her shoulder, "I'll help you take him to the car." They both lifted JD together and walked out to the car. "Call Pearl Lassiter. Tell her to meet you at the house. Make sure JD is ready for the camera by six."

"He'll be ready," Tracy replied as she put the seat belt around him. "Carolyn, you know how to make Gavin listen. If you truly love him, let him see you are willing to give up on your life's dream for him. Let him know nothing in this world is more important to you than his happiness. Whatever you do, don't mention the mansion. He will only think you are still trying to fulfill your dream, not his."

Carolyn listened to Tracy's advice. After all, she accomplished exactly what she wanted. "I'll convince him. That's my specialty," she smiled encouragingly. "Wish me luck."

"You're a pro at this, you don't need luck. You got skills. This time, use them for something meaningful. I will not stand by and allow you or anyone else to cause any issues for Jeffrey or his campaign."

"You've made yourself clear," Carolyn stated coldly.

"No, Carolyn, I don't think I have. You may be the one marrying the Governor, but I am the one married to the future of this party. It is now incumbent upon me to establish a working relationship with all the wives of any candidate of any campaign Jeffrey is affiliated. Now, I didn't want that job, you put it in my lap with your escapades. If you want to remain an active part of this political party, you will start by cleaning up the mess you have placed all of us in. A good place to start is with the man you now claim you love."

Carolyn wasn't sure, but she believed Tracy had just declared herself the leader of the political wives. She frowned for a moment as Tracy walked around to get into the driver's seat of the vehicle. "I'm not sure I'm comfortable with your last statement Tracy. I am going to marry Gavin and he will be Governor. That action alone will make me the First Lady of Virginia, not you."

Tracy opened the door, and then looked over the top of the car. "When you start acting like a First Lady, I may consider relinquishing the reigns. However, until that time, you are taking a back seat. If you think, I'm wrong, pay close attention to the news media tomorrow. Every story about you will have Ashley or me defending you. It will be a hard sell, but we will get it done and the public will believe us." Tracy tilted her head to the side, "Think about that. Now, tell me, who is running the show?"

Tracy pulled off as Carolyn turned and looked at the doorway leading to the house she now called home. She walked inside and found Gavin still sitting in his office, with yet another drink in his hand. She walked over, took the glass out of his hand, and placed it on the desk. "You have three hours before we have to convince the people of Virginia you are the best man to be Governor." She pulled him up and put his arms around her shoulders as she balanced him against her.

"You know I love you, right?" Gavin slurred.

"Yes. But what you don't know is I love you, too." A single tear ran down her cheek. "I also believe in you. I know you are the best man for Virginia and me."

Gavin stopped when they reached the staircase and looked down at Carolyn. "Are you through with JD?"

"Yes."

He stared at her for the longest time, before he replied, "Is there anyone else?"

"No."

They resumed walking up the stairs. "I will marry you Carolyn, but I will not allow you to tamper with my heart again."

By six that morning Pearl Lassiter had organized the most direct media blitz that was the envy of the political world. All media were allowed unlimited access to the candidates. Each candidate was up front and honest regarding the events leading up to the attack on Ashley.

Gavin stood by Carolyn by publicly forgiving her indiscretions. Tracy was by JD's side declaring her support of Gavin and Carolyn during this turbulent time. James and Ashley answered every question imaginable regarding her relationship with David in addition to her relationship with James. By the end of the day, at least twelve hours were spent with reporters.

James and Ashley arrived home just as the evening news came on. They sat back and watched the reports and the commentary that followed. The opposition had put their own spin on the events, but it seemed all in all the public was accepting the information as truth. "It seems like ages since I asked you to marry me. If there are any more delays, I swear I'm going to kill someone," James exhaled, while sitting with Ashley in his arms.

Ashley looked up from the shoulder of the man she loved, "Your days of trying to kill people are over. My plan is to keep you busy raising our children."

James smiled into Ashley's eyes, "The word children implies we are going to have more than this one. I like that."

Ashley looked back and smiled at him. "I'm going to give you a house filled with little James Brooks."

Chapter 14

The morning of July sixteenth the sun shined bright, even at seven o'clock in the morning. James and Ashley awoke early to take their morning run. Going into her second month of pregnancy the only changes in her body were the subtle growth of her breasts, which James rather enjoyed.

The last month was a whirlwind of activity. The investigation into the attack was stressful for all involved, but none more than Carolyn Roth-Roberts. With all that Carolyn had done to Tracy and her, Ashley's heart went out to her during the week preceding her marriage to Gavin. Because of her involvement with David and her attempt to blackmail Katherine, Gavin initially called off the wedding.

Even now a month later, on her wedding day, Ashley wondered how Gavin and Carolyn were working out.

Ashley turned towards the path leading back to the house and noticed James was no longer striding beside her. She looked back and saw him running slightly behind her smiling. She smiled back breathing a little heavy, "What are you smiling about Mr. Brooks?" she asked as she slowed to a trout.

James stopped. He bent over and placed his hands on his knees, breathing heavily. He looked up at Ashley who had stopped and turned back to him. "I'm enjoying the sight of my wife's behind moving in front of me. Are you sure the spandex shorts are not too confining?"

Ashley had become very self-conscious about her appearance after finding out she was pregnant. "Do they look bad? I checked the mirror twice before leaving the room."

James stood straight. There wasn't a lump or bump anywhere on her body. She was just as lean and solid as ever. The only noticeable difference to him was the sparkle in her eyes every time he looked into them. He could see himself in her eyes and he liked what he saw. No longer was the bitter, loveless, withdrawn man reflected back at him. He saw a man full of love, joy and peace. The woman whose eyes he saw all of that in would be his wife before the day was over. "You have the legs of Tyra and the body of Halle. Nothing on you ever looks bad."

Ashley put her hands on her hips, "Good answer Mr. Brooks," she replied beaming.

"Why have we resorted back to Mr. Brooks' status?"

"It's the only way I can keep from jumping your bones," she replied seductively and turned to trot off.

James smiled and decided the imposed wedding day separation was not something he wished to continue to honor. He chased her down and enjoyed her giggles when he picked her up and placed her over his shoulders. "It's

been twenty-four hours since we made love. That's one hour
too long." He ran off the path into a heavily wooded area of
the property. He placed her against a tree and pressed his
body to hers.

"Ashley Harrison you are a beautiful woman and I can't
wait to make you my wife." She smiled as he fiercely
captured her mouth, entwining his tongue with hers sending
bolts of energy to his very core. The moan from Ashley
encouraged him to please her even more. Reluctantly leaving
her lips, he removed her top and captured one nipple that
was now firmly budding from his gentle touch. Ashley held
his head securely to her breast with one hand and tugged at
his sweat drenched T-shirt. Slowly he pulled away, removed
the shirt and spread it on the grass beneath the tree.
Reaching out his hand, she eagerly came to him and
wrapped her legs around his waist as he gathered her in his
arms. Easing down to the shirt, their bodies merged, but not
close enough to quench the need that was building up in
each of them. He removed their running shorts and eagerly
entered her with one loving thrust. They both exhaled with
pleasure. Neither moved, savoring the feeling of being one.
Bracing his weight with his arms, he looked down into her
eyes, "You are and will always be the heart of me."

Tears formed in her eyes along with a lump in her
throat. The words were touching, but the look in his eyes
told her all she would ever need to know. Unable to respond
verbally she allowed her inner muscles to respond for her.
She squeezed him tightly and smiled at the moan that
escaped him. He moved slowly within her allowing the
motion to entice her to join him in the rhythm, and she did.
No other part of their bodies touched, just the core of him
and the center of her. He bent his elbows and began to kiss
her sweetly. As the kiss intensified so did their movements.
The rhythm increased as they were both gasping to breathe.
Ashley positioned her legs over his shoulders and James

emerged himself deeper into her. Ashley screamed out his name as they exploded simultaneously.

James collapsed at her side and began to laugh. "You have turned me into a wild man."

Still breathing a little harshly, Ashley smiled. "You tamed me."

James laughed heartily, "You are not, nor will you ever be tamed. But that's alright. I love you tamed or wild."

Ashley smiled as she placed her head on his chest. He pulled her closer and held her near his heart and within a matter of minutes, they both drifted off to sleep.

Cynthia was in the midst of a whirlwind of activities. The foyer of the Brooks mansion was decorated in gold and black with red and white roses cascading down the staircase to the left and right. The center staircase was lined with a white silk runner and white roses with gold and black lace bows. The railings between each staircase were lined with gold and black lace bows with the tails hanging strategically down into the foyer. The baby grand piano that usually graced the family sitting room was located to the left of the center staircase and a harp was located to the right. The chairs with gold covers were dressed with black bows and the black covers were dressed in gold bows. The seats were placed ten feet from the bottom of the center staircase. The chairs were lined ten across with ten rows for the one hundred guests invited to the private ceremony. An archway was placed in front of the ceiling to floor windows that spread against the west wall of the family sitting room. The beautiful landscape of the Brook's estate showed through the windows and acted as the backdrop for the ceremony.

Pleased with the outcome of the inside decorations, Cynthia moved through the breezeway that was lined with black wrought iron lanterns that held glass globes decorated in gold and white bows, and led to the balcony that was being draped in red and white roses by the florist. Two of her associates were busy directing the action on the veranda which could easily hold a hundred people, with five others inside the five hundred seat white tent that was placed by the pond on the estate. Next to the guest tent was the food tent where Rosaline was busy setting up the tables with heating trays. Cynthia looked at her watch, it was a little past eight. She was scheduled to meet with the waiters at eight-thirty to instruct them on protocol for serving the very distinguished guests. So far she was very pleased with the layout and was sure Ashley would be happy. But more importantly she believed the guests: celebrities, high-ranking government officials, millionaires and a prince, would be impressed. As an executive, she had to make contacts to keep her business flowing in a positive direction. A word in the right circles could be the key to being mediocre or a part of the A-list.

Cynthia encountered Gwen as she turned to reenter the house. The smile on her face signified satisfaction with the layout. "Cynthia, you have turned our home into a wedding delight. I love my home, but would have never been able to accomplish this," Gwen smiled as she hugged Cynthia. "James and Ashley are going to love this. It's simple and elegant."

"You had the backdrop to make any wedding dream come true, before I started with the decorating. Your home is lovely."

"Thank you." Gwen replied as she turned in the direction of someone calling her name. "I'm on the balcony," she called out.

"Mrs. Brooks, the Harrison family has arrived," Charles announced.

"Thank you, Charles. Would you show Martha to the balcony and make sure everyone else is comfortable."

Martha joined Cynthia and Gwen. After exchanging pleasantries, Cynthia went into the food tent and met with the waiters. Gwen convinced Martha to walk with her to the garden that led to the walking trail. "I thought I had a beautiful garden, but this is amazing," Martha smiled as they walked.

"Thank you. I can't take credit for it. We have several gardeners that Avery stays on top of to keep the grounds looking like this. I must say, it is breathtaking first thing in the morning," Gwen smiled proudly. "Let's take a seat," Gwen said pointing to the Gazebo. "This will probably be the only quiet moment we get today." She turned towards Martha. "I'm a private person and not at all prone to sharing family secrets with strangers. I've noticed a rift building between you and James. With James and Ashley getting married today, I feel it's necessary to share at least one situation with you. I'm doing this in hopes that it will give you a little more insight into my son's possessiveness of Ashley especially during the pregnancy." She smiled at Martha's "hmm" and facial expression that clearly show her exasperation with James. "You've met my grandson JJ."

"Yes I have. He's a wonderful little boy," Martha replied.

"Yes he is. A little mischievous, but as you know, they all are." Gwen hesitated then continued, "As you know James moved away under unpleasant circumstances. It seems my oldest son Vernon has always felt a bit of jealousy towards James. Even when they were growing up as children, he always wanted whatever James had. It could have been a truck, which Vernon had no interest in, or a football. If James had it Vernon wanted it and once he got it, he would simply discard it. It was his way of letting James know I can take whatever you have. Unfortunately, it did not change, as they got older. James became wiser and learned to deal with Vernon's insecurities. However, Vernon's jealousy elevated to a different level. Vernon went after every girlfriend James brought home. Then James simply stopped bringing them home, until he got married. When he came home with Katherine, it seemed Vernon respected the marriage. At least that's what we all thought, but it wasn't so. It seemed Vernon and Katherine began an affair. It ended abruptly when James came home early from work one day and found the two of them together. If it had not been for Avery I'm sure James would have killed Vernon that day. At the time of the incident, I stood by Vernon. James in turn felt I had betrayed him. The consequence of Vernon and Katherine's actions did not cease on that dreadful day. Shortly after James and Katherine moved to Richmond, she discovered she was pregnant. Until this incident with Carolyn Roth, none of us ever questioned JJ's paternity. However, it seemed Katherine shared the information of JJ's possible paternity with Carolyn. Recently she admitted to me that JJ may indeed be Vernon's child."

"Therefore, Ashley may be carrying James first child," Martha summarized.

"Yes." Gwen replied with a relaxing exhale.

Martha smiled understanding Gwen's dilemma. "Gwen, why is Vernon insecure about James?"

Gwen looked away then turned back. "Vernon is not Avery's son. I was pregnant when Avery asked me to marry him. He raised Vernon as his own and never differentiated between the children. However, Vernon resented James, from the day we brought him home from the hospital. I think Vernon felt we loved him less once we brought the baby home.

When the incident happened, with Vernon and James, I wasn't choosing between my two children. I was assisting the one that needed me the most, which was Vernon. James has always been a strong, self-assured person. He had to be with all Vernon took him through," she smirked. "I knew of the two, James would survive and move on. I'm not sure Vernon would have if I had turned my back on him."

Martha smiled, "That explains a lot." She covered Gwen's hands with hers. "It's hard to stand between your children, when things go wrong in their relationships. All we can do is continue to love them and be there when they need us the most. From what Ashley has told me, you have done that." Martha laughed, "And you are doing it now by sharing this information. For a while I thought I was truly going to have to kill James to get time with my daughter. Now I understand. He is just as protective of Ashley as JD is of Tracy. It let's me know just how much he loves her."

"We all have come to love Ashley. Lord knows she has brought this family together and that's something I never thought would happen. We owe her so much."

James and Ashley remained quiet as they listened to the conversation between the two women. When the mothers first approached, they both quietly dressed and waited for them to leave. However, fifteen minutes later the two were still there not allowing James and Ashley to leave the morning retreat, behind the trees. Therefore, they waited and listened a while longer. A few minutes later, when they no longer heard talking, James took Ashley's hand to help her off the ground. "I think we better go now."

Ashley smiled at James as she cupped his face with her hands. "Now you know the reasons for your mother's actions." She kissed him gently on his lips and then took his hand. When he started to walk back to the path Ashley yanked back. "I'm not going out there until my mother is good and gone," she exclaimed.

James chuckled, "We are getting married in five hours. I can't believe you are still afraid of what your mother might say."

"Yes I am and I am not going out there until they leave," she pouted. "If you had any sense you would be scared too."

He shook his head, "I'm not afraid of your mother." The look on her face clearly indicated she was serious about not leaving the spot. He pulled her to him, kissed her throat and continued to work his way down. When he reached her navel he could feel her resolve leaving. Cradling his arms around her legs, he picked her up over his shoulders and ran out of the secure area. He came to an abrupt stop when he found their mothers standing at the entrance to where they were.

Martha stood with her arms folded across her chest and Gwen stood with her hands on her hips. "James Avery Brooks what are you doing with Ashley.

"Mother I," James wasn't able to finish his statement before Martha cut in.

"Ashley Renee Harrison, You get down off that man's shoulders right now. Have you lost your mind, with your behind up in the air like that?"

James quickly put Ashley on the ground. "I thought you weren't scared," Ashley whispered to him. James scowled at her.

"Mrs. Harrison, we needed some time alone this morning, so Ashley and I decided to take a run together," James explained.

"That was at seven. It's nine now, what have you been doing for the last two hours?" Gwen smirked.

"And why do you have that look, like you just got caught with your hands in the cookie jar?" Martha asked.

James and Ashley looked at each other, thinking, *because we did*, and then back at their mothers who were both standing there with knowing looks on their faces. "Don't bother to conjure something up Ashley. Both of you go to the house and keep your hands off each other until the wedding," She ordered.

They turned and began walking towards the house, not touching each other. Martha and Gwen looked at each other and burst into laughter. James and Ashley stopped and turned to see the women having a good laugh at their expense.

As the couple reached the balcony of the house, they found themselves greeted by members of the wedding party. Calvin and his wife Jackie, Douglas with Karen Holt, Brian, Nick, Vernon and James friend from college, Prince LaVere greeted them on the steps leading up to the veranda.

Standing off to another corner of the veranda was Katherine who was watching as James Jr. climbed onto the back of his eighteen-year-old R&B star cousin, Taylor who was home from touring to sing at the wedding. Constance, Taylor's mother pulled James Jr. off her daughter's back and sat him on the ground. Then she proceeded to scowl at Taylor for allowing the child to jump on her. She could not allow any injuries, with the end of the summer tour coming up. Taylor complied with her mother's request, but as soon as she went into the house, Taylor picked James Jr. up into a chair and allowed him to climb onto her back for a piggyback ride, she had promised.

James smiled and wondered when Constance was going to realize Taylor is no longer the little girl she was when her music career started. She was now a beautiful young woman with a mind of her own. As Taylor walked down the steps towards him, James Jr. encircled his father's neck, causing all three of them to fall onto the steps below. James turned and tackled both of them. Seeing the wrestling match in progress, Nicolas jumped in, followed by Nicki. Ashley started to join the group on the ground but Martha grabbed her, "Don't you dare," and gave her the mother look that let you know not to cross over into the dark side.

Vernon looked at Ashley, "I'll take care of it for you." He reached down and one by one picked the bodies off James. After picking off Nick and Nicki, Vernon reached for his daughter, Taylor, who was still helping James Jr. pin his father. Vernon grabbed her by the waist and held her like a football. When he reached for James Jr. James held on, "I got this one." He stood and pulled James Jr. to his waist holding him like a football with legs kicking while he giggled. The two brothers looked at each other. For the first time in their life, they were not at odds with each other. They both smiled. Avery and Gwen, who were standing in the doorway, watching gave a silent prayer, thanking the Lord for allowing them to see this day.

Ashley smiled, looking around at the crowd that had gathered in her honor. She noticed that Karen was sitting at one of the tables looking off into the distance. She walked over and took a seat beside her. "Hello Karen." She joked, "If you just happen to smell something a little unpleasant it's me and I apologize. I went running with James this morning and haven't had a chance to make it upstairs to the shower."

Karen looked at Ashley as if she was about to cry. She moved her lips but nothing came out. She hung her head then looked back at Ashley. "I am sorry I did not find out about David earlier."

Ashley took Karen's hand in hers. "I'm sorry I didn't find out about him earlier than I did too. But you know what?" she said in a very perky tone "This is my wedding day and I refuse to have anyone in the vicinity sad and that includes you." She smiled. "I realize you and I don't really know each other. However, you are a friend of James' and that's good enough for me. So today, and I know this will be hard—but there will be no thoughts of David. Now, how about a glass of champagne?"

Karen frowned, "You can't have champagne?"

Ashley waved her hand at Karen, "Oh alright, well that means you are going to have to have enough for the both of us." They walked over to the bar near Katherine, who was also standing off to herself. As they approached, Katherine nodded at Ashley. Ashley responded with a civil nod, and then she thought. This woman was no threat to her. "Katherine, we are about to have a glass of champagne. Would you care to join us?" Katherine smiled at Ashley and joined her at the bar. Ashley introduced Karen and Katherine just as Tracy, Cynthia and Rosaline spotted her.

"There you are," Tracy smiled as she walked over to Ashley. The two hugged as if they had not just seen each other the night before at her bridal party. "I know I did not hear you right. You're drinking champagne?"

"No silly. I need something stronger than champagne," Ashley laughed. "Tracy this is Katherine Stallworth-Brooks. Katherine, my friends, Tracy, Cynthia and Rosaline."

"It's a pleasure to meet you," Tracy smiled and then turned to Karen. "Hello Karen. It's good to see you."

"Hello Tracy," Karen replied and then tried to step away, but Ashley held on to her.

"That's all very sweet," Cynthia chimed in, "however, we have to steal Ashley away. If you ladies would excuse us, we have to get the bride prepped."

"She still has a few minutes before we have to start Cynthia," Rosaline stated, "besides a glass of champagne is not a bad idea."

Cynthia put her hands on her hips and pulled Ashley's ponytail up, "Do you see this? This woman has coarse hair that I have to make look good. That alone is going to take me two hours. If you and prego," referring to Tracy, "want to stay and have drinks, fine, but Ashley is coming with me. Let's go." Cynthia demanded as she grabbed Ashley's arm to pull her away without looking back. She turned quickly and bumped into the very firm chest of a man. The collision caused her to fall backwards hitting Ashley. Ashley fell into Rosaline, who in turn fell on Katherine. JD stepped in and pulled Tracy out of harm's way. All four women looked up at the man that seemed to have caused the chain reaction. The other guests laughed hysterically at the incident that sent women and glasses flying into the air. Brian helped Rosaline,

Calvin helped Katherine, and Douglas helped Karen. James ran over to Ashley to make sure she was okay. Cynthia remained on the ground until a hand reached out to her. She hesitated for a moment, trying to remember the last time she saw someone that looked so regal. She took his hand and he pulled her to her feet. "Are you alright?" the man asked.

"I'll be just fine as long as you keep that lethal weapon of a chest away from me," Cynthia replied as she wiped her clothes off.

James interceded, "Cynthia this is my friend Prince LaVere. I would appreciate it if you would not insult him today. I understand it is difficult for you to control your mouth, so tomorrow you may resume your normal behavior."

The friends that knew Cynthia well laughed. Others, who were not sure if James was serious or not remained silent, stunned at his words. Katherine spoke up first, "Hello LaVere." She kissed his cheek. "It's wonderful to see you again."

LaVere took her hand and kissed it. "Katherine you taste like champagne and it's good to see you again also." He turned his attention back to the beauty he had just picked off the ground. "I apologize for my clumsiness. However, you were at fault as well. Your beauty distracted me."

Cynthia was about to scold the man until she heard the last words. She cleared her throat "Well, we all could stand to be a little more careful I suppose. Unfortunately, for you I can't control my beauty. I've tried and it just won't work." The group of friends all groaned. She turned to the group and glowered at them. This caused most of men to stand straight and the women to laugh, "I'm glad you all remember who is in charge here. Now, let's go Ashley."

Ashley moved forward as ordered after kissing James on the cheek. "I'll see you at the altar."

Cynthia frowned at him, "I might tie her up in the basement until tomorrow when I can speak freely."

James raised his eyebrow. "And I might have you captured, covered in a potato sack bag and placed in the bowels of a ship sailing to Anchorage." James smiled as Tracy and Rosaline joined Cynthia and Ashley.

An hour later, the women were in James and Ashley's suite enjoying the girl talk. It was a joy for Ashley to have all of her friends around. Her cousin Alexis, who she grew up with was there as a bridesmaid—Cynthia and Rosaline who she went to high school and college with—Monica, who was the CEO of their company whom she depended upon at the office—Nicki, her soon to be sister-in-law and new shopping friend was there. Last, but certainly not the least of all was Tracy, who was her rock on all fronts. If it had not been for Tracy, she would have never made it this far with James.

Tracy showed her what true love looked like, made her open up to James, kept her sane during all the hell David had put her through and kept her secrets even when she knew it was wrong to do so. Now she was about to marry the man her mother told her to wait for and it was worth every heartbreak and disappointment she had ever experienced. James was the man that would protect, love and cherish her-that she was certain of.

Ashley stepped into the bedroom of the suite, where Tracy was putting out her accessories. She walked over to her very pregnant friend and hugged her from behind. "I love you Tracy. And no matter what we will always have our friendship. The sister-in-law thing is just icing on the cake."

Tracy looked at her friend's reflection in the mirror. "We have come a long way and you are headed for a wonderful journey." They both sat on the edge of the bed, "We have to remember we are married to two men that are very possessive and very ambitious. They are going to be a handful."

"We can handle them. They just have to recognize who will be wearing the pants in the family," Ashley laughed and Tracy joined in.

"Okay, we have to let the others in the room now. Cynthia is chewing at the bits to get you dressed and ready."

Ashley stood in her robe and swung open the bedroom door, "Ladies, let the games begin." The women, who were all dressed in lavender and crème gowns jumped up and cheered. They all piled into the room and began preparing the bride.

About twenty minutes later Ashley stood before the mirror in the bedroom in an exquisite cream wedding dress. The bodice tied at the back of the neck, forming a v-shape at the breast, exposing the top half of her back and lace ties at the bottom of the back. It fit smoothly down her hips with a tasteful split in the back. Rather than using a veil, Ashley had small roses pinned into her hair that was in a French roll with one strand that hung from her temple and fell just below her shoulder.

"Ashley," her Mother whispered softly from the doorway. "You are still a beautiful baby," she smiled with tears in her eyes. "Your father is smiling down from heaven today."

"Okay," Tracy sniffled, "everybody out. Let's give Ashley and her Mom time together."

As soon as the door closed behind them, Ashley hugged her mother. "I waited Mom. I waited just like you told me to. I waited until I found a man just like daddy," she cried.

Martha hugged her daughter, "Yes you did, baby, yes you did. James is a good man, and he loves you dearly. You have had the best examples to follow on how a marriage should be. Take what you have witnessed into your new life and you will be just fine."

James stood at the entrance of the balcony to the guest suite of the house. He leaned against the doorway watching the activities in his honor. Here he was, thirty-six years old getting married and happy about it. James Jr. came and stood next to his father. They were a sight standing there together, James Jr. marking the stance of his father in his matching tuxedo. James looked down at his son, who at age eight reached his waist. "You look good son. Are you meeting a girl or something today?"

"No daddy," he smiled up giggling, "You are. Don't you remember?"

"That's right, I forgot," James pretended, "I'm supposed to meet. Oh I forgot her name."

"Ashley daddy, Ashley," James Jr. told him.

James smiled and took his son's hand. "Thank you for reminding me. Will you be sure to do that if I forget at the altar?"

"I'll be there daddy," he said as they walked hand in hand back into the house. "I won't let you forget."

"Don't you two look handsome," Katherine said as she walked into the room.

"Mommy," James Jr. jumped into her arms. "Daddy forgot Ashley's name."

Katherine looked at James who was smiling in a way she had not seen before. Then she looked at her son. "I am sure your daddy will never forget that name." She put James Jr. down, "Why don't you go find Uncle Nick while I talk to daddy."

"Okay," he said and ran from the room.

Katherine looked at James and held her arms out, "May I?" James smiled and stepped into her embrace. They hugged and then stepped apart. "Please accept my apology in any part I had in hurting you. I wish you and Ashley all the happiness you deserve."

"Thank you Katherine. One day I pray you will experience this also."

Nick walked in the room, "Is everything okay in here?" he asked suspiciously.

Katherine looked at Nick, then back to James. "James and I have decided to reconcile. We need you to break the news to Ashley."

Nick looked at the two and neither smiled or gave the slightest hint that the statement was false and for a moment, Nick's brows came together in a questioning way.

Finally, James relieved Nick by saying. "When hell freezes over," and laughed with Katherine joining in. It seemed Nick did not see the humor and stood there with a frown on his face. Katherine walked over, kissed Nick's cheek, and walked out of the room. "It's a lot of that going on you know," he said as James walked past him.

James looked back, "What's that?"

"Hell freezing over," Nick replied.

The men gathered in Avery's study, which was located at the back of the foyer. James, JD, Brian, Douglas, Calvin, Nick, Vernon and Avery decided a drink was in order to toast the pending ceremony. Pastor Smith, who was the Harrison's pastor, was there to officiate the ceremony offered a word of caution to the men then joined them in the toast.

JD held his glass high. "Please, allow me." Each man joined the circle and raised their glasses. "James it is an honor to have you join our family. I'm glad you can afford Ashley and relieve my wallet from her grasp." The group laughed. "Seriously, I'm proudly giving you the jewel of the Harrison family. May she bring you as much joy during the years to come as she brought us growing up. I could not have asked a better man to take her hand in marriage. To James and Ashley."

The men chimed in, "To James and Ashley." Then they all consumed their drink in one swallowed.

"Ahhh," James smiled, "Let's go marry that woman," and walked towards the door.

The Epilogue

Precisely at two o'clock, the pianist and the harpist began playing the prelude to the wedding march. Pastor Smith followed by James and Brian, his best man walked in from the balcony to stand before the guests at the front of the room. The groomsmen, who consisted of Calvin, Douglas, Nick, Prince LaVere, and Vernon, lined the right staircase and the bridesmaids which consisted of Cynthia, Rosaline, Monica, Alexis and Nicki lined the staircase to the left. The tone changed in the music as each couple met at the center walkway where the bridesmaids took the arm offered by each groomsman and marched with heads held high and smiles a mile long. Next, Tracy marched down the aisle, followed by James Jr. and Ashley's little cousin Asia.

Once everyone was settled in their positions Ashley appeared at the top of the center staircase with JD at her side. A hush came over the crowd as they descended the steps. James could not believe he felt tears wail up in his eyes. The vision of Ashley dressed in her form fitting gown took his breath away. He watched as she walked towards him and smiled at the simple knowledge that she was about to become his wife.

JD and Ashley stopped at the entrance of the aisle as the musicians began the bridal march. Ashley looked over the crowd and smiled as she recognized a few newlyweds among the guest. Gavin and Carolyn Roberts were there as was John and Lena Roth. Both couples were married a month earlier. She saw her Uncle Joe and immediately missed her father's presence. Ashley whispered to JD, "I wish Daddy could see me now."

JD looked over at her and she looked up at him. He smiled and for some reason remembered one night when she came into his room and shot him with a water pistol while he was talking on the telephone to some girl. He dropped the telephone and chased her into the family room where their parents were looking at television. Ashley ran behind their dad for protection and both parents broke out into laughter. "You are going to need your big brother to protect you one day," he said to Ashley. Then he turned to JD, "You are supposed to watch over your little sister, she needs you."

Ashley smiled, "You okay?" she asked noticing his distant stare.

"You know I will always be here for you right," JD said as a tear dropped down his cheek.

Ashley stopped midway down the aisle. She wiped the tear from her brother's face and kissed his cheek. "I know," she smiled and began walking towards her new life.

When they reached the arch, James' niece, Taylor Brooks, who was better known to her fans as Tay, stood.

She sung, "The Last Time," by Eric Benet as a tribute from James to Ashley. Afterward Pastor Smith began the ceremony and when he asked who gives this woman to this man; JD proudly replied, "I do," then stepped back and took a seat next to his mother. Ashley turned and looked at the two and smiled. She turned back to James. He took her hand and placed it over his heart. "You are the very heart of me."

Ashley glowed as she returned his smile. James saw the minute her mind became mischievous and wondered what she was about to say. "Well I hope that heart is big enough for four."

James frowned, not understanding what she meant, "You care to explain?" he whispered.

"I saw the doctor yesterday. He informed me, we, Mr. Brooks are having twins."

The two began laughing uncontrollably, until Pastor Smith interceded, "Shall we begin."

They stepped forward as James replied, "I think we better. My family is growing by the minute."

LaVergne, TN USA
17 March 2011
220546LV00002BA/41/P